THE WAYS OF EVIL MEN

THE WAYS
OF EVIL MEN

Leighton Gage

Published by
Soho Press, Inc.
853 Broadway
New York, NY 10003

Library of Congress Cataloging-in-Publication Data

Gage, Leighton.
The ways of evil men / Leighton Gage.
p. cm
ISBN 978-1-61695-272-3
eISBN 978-1-61695-273-0
1. Silva, Mario (Fictitious character)—Fiction. 2. Police—Brazil—Fiction.
3. Ava-Canoeiro Indians—Fiction. 4. Indigenous peoples—Crimes
against—Fiction. 5. Brazil—Fiction. I. Title.
PS3607.A3575W39 2014
813'.6—dc23   2013019793

Printed in the United States of America

10 9 8 7 6 5 4 3 2 1

This one is for my grandchildren
Jonathan, Fraukje, Fardou, Anner,
Victoria–and any more to come.

Enter not into the path of the wicked, and go not in the way of evil men.   *—Proverbs 4:14*

Key Characters

Alex Sanches—A Federal Police agent in Belem.

Alexandra Santos—The housekeeper of Jade Calmon, FUNAI agent in Azevedo.

Amanda Neto—The wife of Osvaldo Neto.

Amati—An Indian of the Awana tribe.

Arnaldo Nunes—An agent of Brazil's Federal Police and Silva's partner.

Atuba—Raoni's grandfather.

Barbosa, Estevan—The head of the Federal Police's field office in Belem.

Ana, "Crazy"—A prostitute.

Bonetti, Cesar—A wealthy landowner.

Borges, Fernando—The head of the local police in Azevedo.

Castori, Father Carlo—Parish priest in Azevedo, formerly a missionary.

Cunha, Paulo—Azevedo's wealthiest businessman.

Frade, José—A wealthy landowner.

Fred Vaz—A fishing guide.

Fromes, Davi—The former IBAMA agent in Azevedo, now retired.

Gilda Caropreso—An assistant medical examiner and Hector's fiancée.

Gonçalves, Haraldo, aka "Babyface"—An agent of Brazil's Federal Police.

Hector Costa—Gonçalves's boss, in charge of the São Paulo field office.

Jade Calmon—A FUNAI agent working in Azevedo

Kassab, Renato—Azevedo's only lawyer.

Lana Nogueira—The niece of Nelson Sampaio, a friend of Jade and Maura.

Leon Prado—Jade's boss in Brasilia.

Lisboa, Roberto—A wealthy landowner.

Maria Bonetti—The wife of Cesar Bonetti.

Maura Mandel—A journalist and Jade Calmon's best friend.

Mauricio Carvalho—Maura's editor and boss in São Paulo.

Max Gallo—A young pilot whose father owns an air charter service in Azevedo.

Nataniel Eder—The Belem bureau chief of Maura's newspaper.

Nonato, Raul—The IBAMA agent in Azevedo.

Osvaldo Neto—Husband of Amanda and owner of Azevedo's Grand Hotel.

Otto Cosmos—A truck driver.

Pandolfo, Toni—Lisboa's foreman and a dangerous gunman.

Patricia Toledo—The wife of Hugo Toledo, mayor of Azevedo.

Pinto, Doctor Antonio—A doctor and Azevedo's part-time medical examiner.

Raoni—An Indian boy of eight, member of the Awana tribe. Amati's son.

Rita Cunha—The wife of Paulo Cunha, Azevedo's leading businessman.

Sampaio, Nelson—The Director of Brazil's Federal Police. Silva's boss.

Silva, Mario—A Chief Inspector of the Brazilian Federal Police.

Sonia Frade—Wife of José Frade.

Tinga—Raoni's best friend.

Toledo, Hugo—A wealthy landowner and the mayor of Azevedo.

Torres, Omar—A wealthy landowner.

Welinton Mendes—A prospector.

Yara—Raoni's grandmother.

Chapter One

SUNRISE IS A BRIEF affair in the rainforests of Pará. No more than a hundred heartbeats divide night from day, and it is within those hundred heartbeats that a hunter must seize his chance. Before the count begins, he is unable to detect his prey. By the time it ends, his prey will surely have detected him.

The boy timed it perfectly. The dart flew true. A big male *muriqui* leaned to one side and tumbled out of the tree. The others screamed in alarm. The boughs began to heave, as if struck by a strong wind, and before Raoni could lower his blowgun, the remaining members of the monkey tribe were gone.

THE WOOLY spider monkey, golden in color and almost a third of Raoni's weight, was a heavy load for a little boy, but he was a hunter now. Right and duty dictated that he carry it.

Amati helped his son hoist the creature onto his narrow shoulders. To make sure it didn't fall, he made what he called a hunter's necklace, binding its long arms to its almost equally-long legs by a length of vine.

The hunt had taken them far. The sun was already approaching its zenith when they waded through the cold water of the stream, stepped onto the well-worn path that led from the fishing-place to the heart of their village, and heard the sound that chilled their hearts: the squabbling of King Vultures, those great and ugly birds, half the size of a man, that feed exclusively on carrion.

* * *

When Raoni's father was a boy, the tribe had numbered more than a hundred, but that was before a white man's disease had reduced them by half. In the years that followed, one girl after another had been born. Girls, however, didn't stay. They married and moved on. It was the way of the Awana, the way of all the tribes. If the spirits saw fit to give them boys, the tribe grew; if girls were their lot, the tribe shrank. And if it shrank too much, it died.

The Awana were doomed, they all knew it, but for the end to have come so suddenly was a horrible and unexpected blow.

Yara was lying in front of their hut, little Tota wrapped in her arms, while vultures pecked out their eyes.

Yara's husband, Raoni's grandfather, Atuba, had fallen across the fire, felled in his tracks as if by a poison dart. His midriff was charred and blackened. The smell of his flesh permeated the air.

The tribe's *pajé* lay face-down below a post from which a joint of roast meat was suspended. The tools of his rituals were spread about him: a rattle, a string of beads, some herbs—clear signs he'd been making magic.

But his magic had failed.

The father and his son went from corpse to corpse, kneeling by each. Signs of life, there were none.

They came to the body of Raoni's closest friend, Tinga. The little boy's favorite possession, his bow, was tightly clutched in his hand—as if he couldn't bear to abandon it, as if he planned to bring it with him into the afterworld.

Raoni was overcome with fury. He picked up a stone and flung it at one of the vultures. Then another. And another. But the birds were swift and wary. He didn't hit a single one, nor could he dissuade them. They simply jumped aside and settled, greedily, upon another corpse.

The anger passed as quickly as it had come, replaced by a sense of loss and an emptiness that weakened his legs to the point where he could no longer stand. When they collapsed under him, he threw himself full-length upon the pounded red earth and cried.

Chapter Two

JADE CALMON PARKED HER jeep, uncapped her canteen, and took a mouthful of water. It tasted metallic and was far too warm, but she swallowed it anyway. One did not drink for pleasure in the rainforest. One drank for survival. Constant hydration was a necessity.

The perspiration drenching Jade's skin had washed away a good deal of her insect repellent. She dried her face and forearms and smeared on more of the oily and foul-smelling fluid. Then she returned the little flask to the pocket of her bush shirt, hung the wet towel over the seat to dry, and retrieved her knapsack. Inside were her PLB and GPS, both cushioned to protect them from the jogs and jolts of the journey.

The PLB, or personal locator beacon, was a transmitter that sent out a signal that could be picked up by satellites and aircraft, and homed-in upon by search teams.

"You call us before you go into the jungle," her boss had told her when he'd given it to her. "Then you call again when you come out. It's like making a flight plan. If you get into trouble, push the button. Then sit tight and wait to be rescued."

Sit tight? In the middle of the biggest rainforest in the world? Easy to say. Not so easy to do.

She glanced back at the road.

How ironic, she thought. The damned loggers who scarred the land with their bulldozers actually did the tribespeople some good. Without that road, she would have had to cut her way through sixty-two kilometers of dense undergrowth to reach this spot. Even though the rains had turned much of it to mud and even though new vegetation was quickly erasing the scars of the white men's predations, she could still cover the entire distance from Azevedo to this, the end point, in a little less than two hours.

And, because of that, and that alone, she was able to look in on the tribe twice a month instead of six times a year.

She clipped the PLB to the belt of her khaki shorts, switched on the GPS, and punched in the coordinates of the village. Then she hoisted her knapsack to her shoulders and set off.

SOMEONE OR something stepped on a twig. It broke with a loud *snap*.

A tapir or a man, Amati thought. *Nothing else could have done it*. He grabbed his bow.

"Stay close," he said to his son.

The arrow he chose was tipped with poison. If it was a tapir, he'd kill it for the meat. If a white man . . . well, let it not be a white man. Not after what those monsters had done.

But the figure that emerged from the forest was neither tapir nor man. It was a woman, one he knew, but white just the same. And she was coming toward him with a smile on her face.

A smile!

Consumed with a towering anger, Amati lowered the bow. Why should he waste poison on a creature such as this? Poison was precious, time-consuming to extract. He'd kill her with his knife.

PERPLEXED, JADE came to a stop. She'd been expecting to find dozens of people. Instead, there were only two: Amati and Raoni, and both were staring at her in the strangest sort of way.

It was true that Amati had always been a bit distant, and Raoni a bit shy, but now their body language and grim faces were making an entirely different impression. Hatred.

If she could have spoken to them she might have been able to defuse it, but speaking was a problem. Raoni's grandmother, Yara, was the only person in the entire village with whom Jade could actually converse.

Yara hadn't been born of the tribe. Her native language was a dialect of Tupi, a tongue Jade already spoke, but the language of the Awana was unique. Since the tribe was small and recently contacted, no one else in Jade's organization had ever attempted to master it. Not before Jade. Not until now.

She'd been learning with Yara's help. The two women had been working together on a Tupi/Awana dictionary, one that Jade intended to turn into a Portuguese/Awana dictionary as soon as she completed it. But the work was in the early stages, and Jade's entire vocabulary, at the moment, numbered less than two hundred words.

She remembered advice she'd once received from an expert on the tribes: "When words fail, offer a present. It's the Indian way."

The gifts she'd brought, a little concave mirror about nine centimeters across, the strings of beads, and a little aluminum pot, were all in her backpack. But this was no time to go looking for them.

Get closer, she thought. *Smile. Give the child your knife.*

So she did just that, walked toward them, smiled through her fear, and started unbuckling her belt. The muscles in Amati's arms and legs went taut. She freed the leather scabbard suspended next to her PLB, taking care not to put a hand to the hilt.

The Indian had no such compunction. Slitting his eyes, he bared the steel of his weapon.

She stopped in front of the boy, knelt down and made the offer. Solemnly, he accepted it. In her peripheral vision she could see Amati's hand lowering his knife. She turned her head and looked up at him, still smiling. He didn't return the smile, but he was no longer scowling. He waited for her to speak.

But of course, she couldn't. Silently, she cursed Carlo Castori. Castori was the parish priest back in Azevedo. Once a missionary, he claimed to have lived among the Awana for more than a year. He'd told her he'd attained fluency in their language, but denied ever having made a dictionary—a claim she found difficult to believe. Who tries to learn a language without making a dictionary?

But, true or not, the man had never been of any help to her, and she'd given up trying to extract anything useful from him. Sign language had become her only option—and she was getting rather good at it. She began by pointing around her and simulating a mystified expression, as if to say, *What happened?*

Amati grabbed her wrist. His grip was strong, and it frightened her. She gave a little whimper and stood her ground. Exasperated, he released her, pointed, and took her wrist again, this time more gently. She realized then that he was trying to lead her somewhere, and she went.

With Raoni trailing behind, they passed through the heart of the village, exited the other side, and arrived in a glade occupied by mound after mound of loosely-packed soil. At the head of one of the mounds, the trunk of a sacred Kam´ywá tree had been embedded into the red earth. *Kua-rups*, the Indians called them. They personified the spirits of the dead.

Jade's mouth opened in surprise. Then she closed it and began to count. The mounds totaled thirty-nine, and they were divided into three neat rows of thirteen each. At last count, there had been forty-one members of the tribe. Two, the man and the boy, were standing next to her.

"All Awana," he said. And then, in case she failed to understand, added the word "Dead."

"How?"

"Men kill."

More words exploded from his mouth, angry words, but Jade was unable to understand a single one. While he spoke, she tried to piece together what might have happened. There hadn't been a war among the tribes in this part of Pará in living memory. It could have been disease, of course, but what kind of disease could have killed so many so quickly? And, if disease had been the cause, how was it possible that neither the man nor the boy were showing signs of sickness?

A horrible suspicion came over her.

"Rainforest men?" she asked.

"No rainforest men," he said shaking his head emphatically. "White men." He stabbed a finger into her breastbone and repeated it. "White men."

"When?"

He pointed to the sun and held up seven fingers. A week ago. If he and his son had been doing the burying themselves, they must have been digging graves and cutting *kuarups* ever since.

"You come," she said. "I help. We talk. Hurt bad men."

"Come where?" he asked. "Talk how? Hurt how?"

"Come," she said and then pointed to her chest and made a pillow with her hands as if she was going to sleep. She hoped he understood what she was trying to tell him. She wanted to take him to the place where she slept, to her home, to the little city of Azevedo. She pointed at him, then back at herself. "Talk. Father Carlo Castori help."

He gave a contemptuous snort, said something she couldn't understand, and made a sign as if he were drinking. *Yes, he knows who I'm talking about. Castori is a drunk.* She made a beckoning gesture. He seemed to think it over.

At last he nodded. Then he said, "How long?" She pointed to the sun and held up one finger. Again, he nodded. "I come. Not Raoni. Your place bad for Raoni."

She couldn't argue. Considering the contempt in which the townsfolk held the people of the rainforest Azevedo *was* a bad place for him.

But how will he cope if we leave him for twenty-four hours on his own?

She concluded he'd cope well. Indian boys grew up fast.

"Good," she said. "You come. Boy stay."

Chapter Three

JADE WAS SURE THAT Amati had never seen a jeep, much less ridden in one, but he hopped in and took a seat as if he'd been doing it every day of his life. He didn't run his hands over the dashboard or try the knobs on the door as she expected he might. He simply sat there, seldom uncrossing his arms throughout their entire journey.

As she drove, she tried to press him for more details of what had happened. Initially, he responded to her questions, but when it became clear that she understood almost nothing of what he was trying to tell her, he fell into silence.

They arrived in the hottest part of the day, that time between noon and four when the sun seared the treeless streets. Between those hours, the temperatures were almost intolerable for animals and humans alike and Azevedo was prone to take on the look of a ghost town.

It would have deeply offended the sensibilities of the townsfolk to have a near-naked man circulating in their midst, so Jade made Paulo Cunha's clothing store her first stop. Cunha stocked only the sizes he was likely to sell, and most of the men in Azevedo ran to fat, so all of the shorts were too wide around the waist. Jade had to buy a belt to secure the smallest pair she could find. As for shirts, the Indian's shoulders and arms were well developed from drawing his bow. She needed something broad across the shoulders. To get it, she had to settle for something much too large by the time it reached his hips. But now, at least, his bare flesh was modestly covered.

The other customers in Cunha's shop avoided them. One, a woman of about Jade's age, even scurried backward upon rounding a corner and seeing them coming toward her.

The shrew at the register, a sour-faced individual of about sixty, skewered Jade with a look that went beyond mere disapproval. "You should know better than to bring a savage in here," she said, pointing at Amati with her sharp chin. "If Senhor Cunha was here—"

"Ah, but he isn't, is he?" Jade said, sweetly. She laid a hand on Amati's shoulder. "Where can he change?"

The woman slammed the drawer of the register shut. "Anywhere you please," she said, "as long as it isn't in here."

FATHER CARLO Castori lived in a tiny house adjoining the church. It had whitewashed walls, blue shutters, and a red tile roof.

"Ah," he said, looking none too pleased to see Jade on his doorstep. "Our esteemed representative of the FUNAI. To what do I owe the pleasure?"

His speech was slurred, but he wasn't too drunk to identify his visitor. The FUNAI, the *Fundação Nacional do Índio*, was the federal government's National Indian Foundation—Jade's employer.

"I'm so glad you're at home, Father. I need your help."

He stared at her out of bleary eyes, then looked at Amati. "I know him," he said.

"And he knows you. He's an Awana. His name is Amati."

The Indian said something in his own language. Castori snapped a reply. Jade didn't understand a word, and she didn't have to. It was clear the two men detested each other.

"Can we come in?"

For a moment, Jade thought the priest might refuse, but curiosity must have gotten the better of him. He stepped aside.

In the kitchen, on a table surrounded by four chairs, were an ashtray, half full, a glass, half empty, a Bible, and a bottle. He motioned for them to sit, took a seat himself, pushed the Bible aside and picked up the bottle. "Drink?" he asked, waving it in Jade's direction.

She shook her head. The bottle was clear glass and the content as transparent as water—a sure sign that the cane spirit hadn't been aged. It took a strong stomach to ingest the stuff. She thought he might offer her something else: coffee, water, a soft drink perhaps. But he didn't. Nor did he extend the offer of refreshment to Amati.

"Help with what?" he asked, topping up his glass.

"Translation."

"Why?"

"There's been a disaster."

"Really?" The priest raised the glass to his lips, gulped rather than sipped. "What kind of a disaster?"

She told him.

He stroked his chin, drained the remainder of his glass, reached for the bottle and refilled it. Fumes from the strong cane spirit wafted across the table.

"All of them dead, eh?" he said. "Imagine that." His lack of outrage infuriated Jade. She would have liked to stand up right then and leave, but she knew no one else who could speak the language. She needed him, couldn't run the risk of offending him, but also couldn't trust herself to speak. So she sat there, waiting him out, while he took another sip, then, finally, began speaking in the Awana tongue.

She'd hoped he'd translate the Indian's responses one by one, but he didn't. He simply engaged Amati in conversation as if she wasn't there. It seemed to her that quite a long time had passed before he switched back to Portuguese and began summarizing the story: "He and his son went out hunting. They left the village before dawn, shot a monkey and returned in the afternoon. When they got back, everyone was dead. Everyone. Their whole tribe."

Jade looked at Amati in sympathy. The Indian didn't appear to notice. His eyes were fixed on Castori, who treated himself to more cachaça before he continued:

"Corpses were all over the village. They hadn't been dead long. Most were still warm."

She couldn't contain herself. "Does he know what killed them?"

"Poisoned, he said, by a piece of meat."

"An entire tribe? From a single piece of meat? How is that possible?"

He must have taken her response as criticism—either of his translation or his credulity—because his response was sharp, an explosion of instant anger. "Your question, *Senhorita* Calmon, betrays your gross ignorance of Indians in general and the Awana in particular."

She tried to placate him. "I make no claim to be an expert, Father."

"Then I suggest you look upon this as a splendid opportunity to learn something from someone who is. The Awana share food." He paused to belch, washed the taste out of his mouth with more cachaça, and went on in a milder tone of voice. "The meat derived from every hunt is regarded as common property. If the food is a gift from another tribe, they turn the sharing into a ritual. Everybody is supposed to eat a portion, however small, even if they're not hungry. It's meant to honor the giver."

It took an effort, but Jade moved closer, striving for more intimacy. "Wouldn't they have noticed that the first people to consume the meat were getting sick? And when they did, wouldn't the rest stop eating? Or not eat at all?"

"That depends, does it not, on whether the poison was quick acting? It isn't considered polite to begin until everyone has been served, so they all would have taken their first bites at about the same time. Only the babies, the ones too young for meat, would have been exceptions, but there weren't any babies, were there?"

Jade shook her head. "No, no babies."

"No, there wouldn't have been, would there? A dying tribe, the Awana. Now, let me see, what else did he say? Ah, yes. He buried the bodies and he and his son performed their pagan rituals. They were at it for a number of days before you arrived. Then you came along and promised him justice. And for that reason and that reason alone, he agreed to come here and tell his story."

"What else?"

"That's it."

"That's it? After all that talking?"

"Of course not, but that's the gist of it. He related everything in minute detail, but you don't need to hear any of that."

"I'm sorry, Father, but I think I do. Please, try to remember."

The priest drained his glass, poured another. "Why?"

"It's my job."

"Very well. I'll try, but I'm warning you, some of it is pretty disgusting. They're like that, the Indians. Disgusting. It comes from being too close to the ugly side of nature."

"Nevertheless—"

"He talked about the flies on his wife's face. They were crawling in and out of her . . ."

Castori pointed to his nose.

"Nostrils."

"Yes, nostrils. There was one man who'd fallen across a fire and roasted his belly. And there were vultures tearing at the bodies, opening them up with their beaks, going first for their eyes. You see? You really didn't want to hear any of that, did you?"

"No," Jade said. "But I must. Go on."

"He said the dead people hadn't discharged any vomit or excrement. He said it wasn't that kind of poison. Ridiculous! How could he possibly know what kind of poison it was?"

"They use various kinds of poisons for hunting, some in the rivers to stun fish."

He blinked at her, getting irritated again. "Thank you, Senhorita Calmon. That's a stunning revelation."

"I'm sorry, Father. You knew that."

The priest put down his glass with a *thump*. If the tumbler had been of more delicate stuff, he might well have broken it. "Of course I did! I know everything there is to know about the Awana. I've probably forgotten more than you'll ever learn."

Jade refused to react to his show of temper. "I'm sure that's true," she said. But then couldn't refrain from adding, "particularly considering the fact that there are now only two left. Can you remember anything else?"

"He talked about how the young girls will never again dance at the ceremony for the dead because there are no young girls anymore. And he says he must get back to his village and help his son to put up the *kuarups*. You know what a *kuarup* is?"

"Yes," Jade said. "I know. They'd only erected one when I found them, and they hadn't painted it yet."

"He said it took them a long time to bury everyone and cut the wood."

"Please ask him why he thinks white men did it."

"I already did. He gave me two reasons."

"And they are?"

"The only one I'm inclined to believe was his description of the meat. It wasn't a tapir, he's sure of that, but he couldn't identify it. It might have been a pig. They're not familiar with pigs."

"And the other reason?"

"It's preposterous."

"I'd like to hear it anyway."

"He said that only white men would be evil enough to poison an entire people."

Chapter Four

By the time they left the priest's home, the hottest part of the day had passed and people were appearing on the streets. Without exception, they stared at the Indian and, without exception, the stares were hostile.

Jade decided to get Amati out of sight until she needed him. But where could she bring him?

Her home? No. There'd be shrieks of protest from her housekeeper if she showed up accompanied by a "dirty savage". Jade had explained more than once that Indians commonly bathed twice a day, and that most were cleaner than many white men, but Alexandra Santos didn't believe it. To her, all Indians were dirty, and that was that. She remembered, then, a comment once made by a sales clerk at Cunha's Pharmacy. The woman had remarked that Osvaldo Neto's mother was an Indian. She'd said it disparagingly, as if it was something to be ashamed of, as if Osvaldo were a lesser creature because of it. Jade had disliked the remark at the time, but she was grateful for it now. If it was true, Osvaldo might not share the bigotry that pervaded the town. He might agree to give Amati a room at the Grand.

She parked behind the building and circled around to the front door. Osvaldo was alone in the bar, loading cans of beer into the refrigerator.

"Happy to help," he said when she'd finished explaining the situation. "But we'll have to sneak him in. You know how folks in this town are. Most of them wouldn't like the idea of him staying here. Where is he now?"

"Out back, sitting in my jeep."

"Perfect. You notice the door back there?"

"What door?"

"There's only one. Go there and wait."

Two minutes later, she heard the key turn in the lock. Osvaldo stuck out his head, looked left and right to make sure no one was watching, and ushered them inside.

"This way," he said. "There's a stairway that goes to the second floor."

On the way up, they met one of the chambermaids coming down. When she caught sight of the Indian, she stopped dead. "Is *that* an Indian, Senhor Osvaldo?"

"Yes, Rita, that's an Indian. He'll be staying in two-one-one."

Her mouth set in a firm line. "And you expect me to clean it?"

"I'll do it myself," he said. "Or Amanda will. Get back to work."

She sniffed and continued on her way.

"Bitch," Jade muttered.

"She is," Osvaldo agreed. "But she's reliable, and in this town reliable is hard to get."

Room 211 was at the end of the corridor.

"Not the cheapest one I've got," Osvaldo said, opening the door. "But that's because of this." He opened another door to reveal a small bathroom. "Most of the other rooms have to share the facilities. If someone went into one of the toilets or showers and found him there, they'd be sure to kick up a fuss."

"And this way, he won't have to leave the room. Good idea. I'll try to explain that to him."

Before Osvaldo could reply, the Indian pointed to the toilet bowl and said a few words, probably asking what it was for.

Osvaldo answered him in the same language.

"Wait," Jade said. "You speak Awana?"

"Sure do."

"If I'd known that I would have come here first."

"Come here for what?"

"To get a translation. I've been trying to learn their language, but I still have a long way to go."

"So you went to Castori?"

"I did. Does he know you speak Awana?"

Osvaldo grinned. "He does, but he doesn't spread it around. He likes the idea of being the sole expert."

"Why does he dislike the Awana so? And, given that he does, why did he bother to learn their language?"

"He learned so he could make converts, but he was never able to convert a single one. He blames them for that, but the truth of the matter is he's a drunk."

"What's being a drunk got to do with it?"

"Indians don't respect drunks, and they don't take on new ideas from people they don't respect. I could have told him that, saved him a lot of trouble, but he never asked."

"And you never offered?"

Osvaldo shook his head. "No way. Castori's an asshole. So, tell me, what's going on?"

Jade told him.

"Jesus," Osvaldo said when she was done. "I can see why you'd want to get him off the street."

"You think he's in danger?"

The hotelkeeper gave an emphatic nod. "You bet I do. Think about it. After thirty-nine murders, what's one more?"

"So you think it might be a land grab?"

"I do. People around here have been bitching about that reservation for years, and the only way to do away with it was to do away with the people who lived there. Everybody knew that, but nobody ever had the guts to go that far. Now, somebody has and there's just him." Osvaldo hooked a thumb at Amati.

"And his son," Jade added.

"Right."

"So what you're saying is—"

"That if the killers get a crack at them, their lives won't be worth a *centavo*."

"Who are they, Osvaldo? Who do you think might have done this thing?"

Osvaldo scratched an ear. "One of the big ranchers, probably, or maybe someone who's already stealing from the Indians and doesn't want your agency or the IBAMA to find out about it."

The IBAMA, the *Instituto Brasileiro do Meio Ambiente*, was the country's environmental protection agency.

"You're thinking illegal logging?"

"I am."

"I don't think so. We put a stop to that."

"You only think you did."

"Could you be a bit more specific?"

"As long as it doesn't go any farther than this room."

"Agreed."

Despite the fact that they were within closed doors, Osvaldo leaned close and lowered his voice. "You know Paulo Cunha?"

"Sure. He owns all those shops."

"*And* a lumber business. You know Raul Nonato?"

"The IBAMA guy?"

"The IBAMA guy. *He* owns two cars and the biggest god-damned TV set anybody in this town has ever seen. Had it shipped special all the way from Belem. *Filho da puta* has begun touting it as the town's biggest tourist attraction."

"You think Cunha is taking wood from the reservation

and Nonato is issuing him phony certificates of provenance to enable him to do it?"

"You have another explanation for owning two cars and a monster television set on the salary he's supposed to be earning?"

"So you suspect the guilty party is Cunha?"

Outside, a truck with a faulty muffler was approaching the hotel. Osvaldo raised his voice so she could hear him over the racket.

"Yeah, " he said. "Maybe Cunha. But it could just as well be another one of the Big Six—or maybe more than one, acting together."

"Big Six?"

The noise from the truck was fading. He went back to speaking softly again. "You never heard that term?"

"No."

Osvaldo motioned for her to take a seat on the bed and sank down into the room's only chair. The Indian walked to the window, pulled the curtain aside and looked out. There wasn't much to see, just the wall of the adjoining building, but he kept staring at it as their words flowed over him.

"The Big Six is what people call Cunha and the five major *fazendeiros* in the region," Osvaldo said. "If you take the next twenty landowners and add what they've got all together, it doesn't come close to the amount of land just one of those guys has."

"If they've got so damned much already, why don't they leave the Indian land alone? Why do they need more?"

"They don't *need* it, they *want* it. And they want it because they're all greedy bastards. But I didn't tell you that. I've got to live in this town."

"Fortunately, I don't. Not forever, anyway."

"So you're willing to take them on?"

"I sure as hell am."

The room was small, and his chair wasn't more than a meter from the bed. He was able to reach out and touch her arm. "Good for you," he said. "What do you plan to do?"

"I'm going to speak to Borges."

Osvaldo looked disappointed. "Good luck," he said and leaned back in his chair.

"Who else is there?"

"That," Osvaldo said, "I couldn't tell you. But there's one thing I *can* tell you."

"What's that?"

"You're going to get zero help from Borges."

Chapter Five

DELEGADO FERNANDO BORGES, THE man who headed Azevedo's five-man Civil Police Force, looked more like everyone's favorite uncle than he did a cop. He was friendly, had a ready laugh, and was considered to be good company, even by the drunks who regularly populated his jail. He was also considered—not only by the drunks, but by everyone else in Azevedo—to be as lazy as sin.

He listened to Jade's story in silence, then said, "Thirty-nine, eh?"

"Yes, *Delegado*. Thirty-nine."

Borges made a scratching noise, running the nails of one hand through the stubble on his chin. "That's terrible," he said, "just terrible. But you don't really have any proof, do you?"

"I saw the graves."

"Ah." He held up a finger. "But did you see the bodies?"

"No," she admitted. "But they're there. I'm sure of it."

"Even if they are," he said, "it could have been disease that killed them, maybe even a simple cold. Those Indians die like flies whenever they're exposed to white men's diseases."

He made it sound like catching a disease was some kind of conspiracy on the Indians' part. "I need you to help me prove that the bodies are there, and that it wasn't disease that killed them," she said, striving to keep her voice level.

"And how could I possibly help you to do that?"

She took a calming breath. "By sending Doctor Pinto to examine the bodies."

Doctor Antonio Pinto was the town's part-time medical examiner. Azevedo wasn't big enough to need the services of one full-time.

"Hmm," Borges said. "Who's going to pay for it? The FUNAI?"

She shook her head. "I haven't got the budget, and it's not my responsibility. It's yours."

Borges waved a negating finger. "No it isn't, Senhorita Calmon. It's not my responsibility at all. That's an Indian reservation. Reservations are federal land. They're outside of my jurisdiction."

"Come on, Delegado. What does jurisdiction matter? You're the closest legal authority. We're talking about thirty-nine people here. Human beings, just like you and I."

"Jurisdiction *always* matters, Senhorita Calmon. My brief is narrowly circumscribed. And, as to them being like you and I, I'm going to have to disagree with you. Indians aren't *at all* like you and I. We've civilized. They're savages."

"Do you really believe that?"

"I surely do."

"So you're not going to help?"

Borges looked pained. "I really wish you wouldn't put it that way. You can come to me with a murder that has taken place in this town, and I'll do everything I can to help. But it's unfair of you to expect me to get involved in anything that happens outside the city limits."

"And that's your final word on the matter?"

"I'm sorry. But it is." It wasn't as if Osvaldo hadn't warned her. Borges was giving her exactly what he'd predicted: zero help. Jade gritted her teeth, held her temper in check and left to try the mayor.

HUGO TOLEDO didn't just head up the municipal government; he was also a cattle rancher, one of the Big Six. The property that had made him rich had all been Indian land less than forty years before, so Jade didn't expect much help from him either. But she had to try.

He posed the same questions as Borges. What did he, as mayor, have to do with something that had occurred on a federal reservation? And if Doctor Pinto were to autopsy the bodies, who'd pay for it?

She gave him the same answers she'd given the delegado and got the same response. This time, though, Jade *did* lose her temper and ended the interview by storming out of his office.

Two men had already spoken to her about Doctor Pinto. She decided that her next step should be to talk to him personally.

"A thousand Reais each, my dear," he said when she asked how much he'd charge to autopsy the bodies. "The lab tests, of course, would be extra."

"That's a lot of money, Doctor Pinto."

He looked at her over his spectacles. "A doctor, like everyone else, has to earn his bread," he said. "In a case like this, Senhorita Calmon, you wouldn't be paying me just for the time I'd spend working on the bodies, you'd be paying me for my years of expertise. And there's another aspect you have to consider: if I made an exception for you, I'd be setting a precedent. The news would get around. Soon other people would be appealing to the better side of my nature. You know just as well as I do how small this town is. Before long, I'd be besieged with people asking me to donate my services. And then where would I be? It's a question of survival, you see. Still, I don't want to be intractable about this. How about if I meet you halfway, give you a volume discount? Shall we say two thousand for four?"

"I don't—"

"And I hope you don't think I'll be going with you when you dig them up."

"Your testimony, Doctor, would be fundamental at a trial. It's essential you be present while the exhumations are taking place."

"And spend a night in some Indian's hut?" The doctor shook his head. "Who knows what kind of vermin infest such places?"

"We could bring a tent."

"Me? Sleep in a tent? At my age? No, Senhorita Calmon, I'm seventy-one years old and I'm no boy scout. If you want my collaboration, you'll have to bring the bodies to me."

"It's not that far, Doctor Pinto, and there's quite a service-able road for much of the way. You wouldn't have to sleep at the site. We could go back and forth in a single day."

"Could we?"

"Yes. I've done it often."

He stroked his chin. "How long would it take to get there?"

"Only a two-hour drive."

"And the walk?"

"An easy forty-five minutes."

"Forty-five minutes? Through the rainforest? With the heat, and the insects?" He shook his head. "No, my dear, I think not."

"Just one day, Doctor. That's all I'm asking. I could bring a crew. They could exhume all the bodies at once. Then you could go from one to the other."

He shook his head. "Nothing good comes from being too hasty, young lady. And besides, even if I was willing, which I'm not, would you really want to spend that much money on a few Indians?"

"Yes," Jade said, evenly, "I would. But I haven't got it."

Doctor Pinto held up his two hands, palms upward, in a

gesture of helplessness. "Then may I offer you a cup of tea before you go?"

Jade refused his tea, went home, and called her boss, Leon Prado, in Brasilia.

"None of those people have any intention of helping you—ever," Leon said when she'd finished explaining. "All *they* care about is clearing the land for development, and the odds are that the police chief and the doctor are in on the deal. I'd bet my ass they've got a stake in the business, wouldn't be surprised if they had a hand in poisoning those people."

Leon was passionate about what he did and quick to leap to conclusions.

"I wouldn't go that far, Leon, but they're indifferent to say the least. So what do we do now? Call in the federals?"

She heard a sound, identified it as Leon slapping a palm on his desk. It was a common gesture of his. "Exactly!" he said. "Do you know Estevan Barbosa? The Federal Police guy in Belem?"

"No."

"His field office is responsible for the region. He's the guy to turn to."

"That's absurd. Do you know how far we are from Belem?"

"Not exactly."

"More than seven hundred kilometers."

"It's a long haul, I agree. But we don't have any other option. It's Barbosa or nobody. Give him a call."

"THOSE ARE serious charges you're making," Estevan Barbosa said after Jade had finished explaining. "If we're to have any hope of getting them to stick, we're going to need proof that the Indians were actually murdered and that white men were responsible for it."

Jade wanted to scream, but somehow managed not to. "That," she said, "is exactly why I need your help."

A pause. Static on the line. Finally Barbosa said, "And you shall have it. Except—"

"What?"

"My plate is overloaded at the moment. It's likely to be a couple of weeks before I can get to you."

"Weeks? Did you just say a couple of *weeks?*"

"Yes. Sorry. Best I can do."

"Delegado, we've got thirty-nine bodies rotting in the rainforest. At least *some* have to be autopsied *now*, before they decompose."

"Yes, yes, you've got a point. Well, I can help you with that. All you have to do is to get the bodies to me. Dig three or four up, zip them into body bags, and send them to Belem. We'll do the autopsies here."

"With all due respect, Delegado, I think *you* should come *here*—and bring a medical examiner with you."

Another pause. More static. Just when Jade was beginning to think she had lost the connection, he started to speak again. "Senhora Calmon—"

"Senhorita," she corrected him.

"Senhorita Calmon, you have to understand that this is the only federal police field office in the entire state. Do you have any idea how big it is? The state, I mean, not the field office."

"It's—"

"It's more than one point two million square kilometers, that's what it is. The largest in the republic after Amazonas. We've got eight million people living here and a high murder rate. I'm understaffed. Like it or not, priorities get determined for political reasons, and the lives of Indians are at the bottom of every politician's agenda. Even garbage collection ranks higher."

"We're talking about thirty-nine—"

He interrupted her. "Senhorita Calmon, either you're not listening, or you simply don't want to understand what I'm saying to you. Thirty-nine or a hundred and thirty-nine, it doesn't matter. The principle still applies. White trumps red. I'm really sorry, but that's the way it is. Look, here's what I'm willing to do: let me get a few things squared away here, think about the situation, and call you back in a few days."

"Frankly, Delegado—"

"Please don't misunderstand me. It's not that I'm unwilling to come. Quite the contrary. The fishing is great around there, and the local police chief is a friend of mine. The bodies are all in the ground already, right? They'll keep. As long as we don't get any heavy rain, that is."

MANY WOULD have given up at that point and let the whole situation slide, but Jade Calmon wasn't a quitter. If the authorities weren't willing to act on their own initiative, she'd try to pressure them. She placed a call to her friend, Maura Mandel, in São Paulo.

"How about writing a big, scandalous article in that newspaper of yours?" Jade said. "Maybe it will embarrass someone into doing something."

"If it *was* my newspaper, I'd do it," Maura said. "But I have an ogre for an editor, and he only comes out of his cave to trample my story ideas."

"Why would he want to trample something like this?"

"Money. It's a long way from here to there, and he'd be unlikely to approve a trip to your neck of the woods on hearsay."

Jade snorted. "So what? Get your father to pay for it. He can afford it."

"He can, and he would, and I could even take time off to

do it, but the ogre would still demand proof of wrongdoing before he'd let me spill any ink on it."

"Proof? *Et tu*, Maura? Haven't you been listening? The only way to get proof is to exhume bodies, but if we can't talk the powers-that-be into doing it, it's not going to happen."

"Don't despair, *minha filha*. You remember Lana Nogueira?"

"Of course I remember Lana Nogueira. Worst damned volleyball player who ever lived. If it hadn't been for her we would have won—"

"Don't get me started. You have any idea what she's doing these days?"

"Not a clue."

"She's a lawyer for *Direitos Já*."

"What's that?"

"A civil rights group based in Brasilia. When she hears about this, she's going to be outraged."

"And?"

"And guess who her uncle is."

Chapter Six

AN EC725 SUPER COUGAR was landing on the roof. Chief Inspector Mario Silva took a sip of coffee and waited for the roar to subside.

"Pará is Barbosa's turf, right?" he asked when it did.

The State of Pará was Brazil's modern-day equivalent of the old American Wild West. Life was cheap; violence, rife; ignorance and poverty, endemic. Silva, urban to his fingertips, shuddered at the thought of spending time anywhere in Brazil's far north, but he especially despised Pará. Some other states, like Amazonas and Acre, were as bad. Nowhere was worse. Except, perhaps, Maranhão.

Nelson Sampaio started fumbling with his Mount Blanc, always a bad sign.

Up above, the engine of the big helicopter kept turning over. The pilot had no intention of lingering on the pad.

"Right?" Silva insisted.

"Barbosa is too busy to handle it."

"*Busy?* Barbosa?"

"Don't use that tone of voice with me, Chief Inspector."

Using Silva's title was a warning shot. When cornered, the Director of Brazil's Federal Police turned pugnacious. "I concede that Barbosa is . . . ah . . . not as industrious as I might like, but you know his political connections as well as I do. If he says he's too busy to attend to it . . ." He didn't finish his sentence, and he didn't have to. The meaning was clear.

"So you're going to force me to attend to it instead, is that it?"

"That's exactly it, and let me remind you that I give the orders around here, not you."

The helicopter started revving up for takeoff. When the Director had commandeered the top floor of Brasilia's new Federal Police building for his office, he'd overlooked the noise he was going to have to put up with from the roof. Another man would have moved by now. Not Sampaio. He wasn't one to admit he'd been wrong.

"And lest you think that the FUNAI agent in question is simply an excitable female," he said, raising his voice so Silva could hear him over the racket of the engine, "let me assure you she's a serious young woman."

"And how do we know that?"

"Because she's an old school friend of my niece."

So that's it, Silva thought. *That's what this is all about.*

But he didn't say it.

"Now, ordinarily," Sampaio went on, "I'd take anything Lana says with a grain of salt. Save the whales, feed the children, adopt an animal, every week it's something new, but in this case . . ."

Silva put down his cup. "In this case?"

"Her mother is backing her up."

"Because?"

"Because she knows that FUNAI agent personally. The woman used to frequent their home when they lived in São Paulo."

"And?"

"And my sister is convinced that she's anything but an alarmist. Which means she isn't. So stop being obdurate, and start taking notes."

"Obdurate?"

"Obdurate. There's a two A.M. flight to Belem. I expect

you and that sidekick of yours to be on it, so you'd better get cracking."

BACK IN his office, Silva opened his atlas and tried to find Azevedo. It wasn't listed. Then he tried looking it up on the Internet. He couldn't find it there either. He picked up the telephone and called the number Sampaio had given him.

"We're about seven hundred and fifty kilometers westnorthwest of Belem," Jade Calmon told him.

She sounded every bit the levelheaded young woman Sampaio told him she was. By the time he hung up, he was convinced they were truly dealing with a case of genocide.

"THAT FUCKING Barbosa," Arnaldo said when Silva finished briefing him. "If his cousin wasn't a federal senator, the lazy bastard would have had his ass fired long ago. Does he ever do any work at all?"

"None of which I'm aware," Silva said.

"If it turns out to be disease that killed those people, can we turn around and come back home?"

"We can," Silva said. "But it wasn't."

"How many victims are we talking about here?"

"Thirty-nine."

"Whoa! Did you just say thirty-nine?"

"I did. Maybe you'd like to go home and pack a bag. We're catching a two A.M. flight to Belem."

"Two A.M.? Jesus."

"Sorry. Boss's orders."

"Who are we going to use for a pathologist?"

"I asked him if he'd lend us Rodrigues."

Arnaldo looked shocked. "You didn't!"

"I did."

"I hate working with fucking Rodrigues."

"Don't we all? But when it comes to poisons—"

"She's the best. Yeah, I know." He grimaced. "But to spend time in the middle of the jungle with that woman—"

Silva cut him off. "She's not coming. Sampaio says she's too busy, suggested we use the local guy, said he'd budget for it."

Arnaldo raised an eyebrow. "Sampaio? Shell out money? He must really love that niece of his."

"I think it's more a question of fearing his sister."

"If we rely on a local doctor in a little town in the middle of nowhere it's gonna be hit or miss. And probably more miss than hit."

"Which is why we're going to bring Gilda. I talked him into paying her as a consultant."

Arnaldo managed to look relieved and anxious at the same time. "You think Paulo will collaborate? Give her some time off?"

Gilda Caropreso was an assistant medical examiner in São Paulo, Brazil's largest city. Her boss, Doctor Paulo Couto, was a childhood friend of Silva's.

"He will if I beg him," Silva said. "And I'm going to beg him."

Arnaldo's anxiety vanished. "Good. Great. Who else?"

"Hector. That's why I thought of Gilda. If she goes, he'll complain less."

Hector Costa headed the São Paulo field office. He was Gilda's fiancé—and Silva's nephew.

"You were ever devious," Arnaldo said.

"And have not changed an iota since my youth."

"Anyone else?"

"Babyface."

Haraldo "Babyface" Gonçalves, looked to be in his early twenties, but was, in actuality, well into his thirties. Younger women often fell for him, while the more mature ones tended to want to coddle him. For both reasons, he was regarded as the federal police's "soft" expert on interrogating members of the fair sex.

"Not Mara?"

"No, not Mara. Not on this one."

Mara Carta was Hector's intelligence chief. She was the one they called in when the interrogation had to be hard. Women knew they couldn't charm her. They couldn't charm Gonçalves either, but few figured that out in time to do them any good.

"Anything else you want me to do?"

"Call that lazy swine, Barbosa. Tell him we'll be dropping in."

"Why? All he's going to do is gloat."

"True. But it'll only be a short detour, and maybe he can tell us a thing or two about Azevedo."

AFTER ARNALDO left, Silva called his wife.

"Two o'clock in the morning?" Irene asked. "You're leaving at two o'clock in the morning?"

"The flight is at two. I'll have to leave the house around midnight."

"But you'll be back by Sunday?"

It was the question he'd been dreading. "I'm afraid I won't," he said.

She responded with silence.

"I'm sorry," he said.

More silence.

"Truly," he said. "It can't be helped. I have to go."

She didn't reply to that either.

After a while, he said, "Let me talk to Maria Lourdes."

Sunday, four days away, was their son's birthday. Leukemia

had killed little Mario at the age of eight. Had he lived, he would have been turning twenty-nine. It would be the first time in twenty-one years that Silva wouldn't be there to hold Irene's hand.

And he knew the consequences.

Irene had seldom touched alcohol in the first nine years of their marriage, but she'd turned to it for solace in the aftermath of their son's death.

In the beginning, it had been no more than a cocktail or two before dinner. Now it was half a liter of vodka every night. And, if he wasn't there on Sunday, it would probably be closer to a liter. She'd drink herself into oblivion, undoubtedly starting shortly after getting up in the morning. He'd have to call her well before lunchtime if he expected any coherent words out of her.

Maria Lourdes, Irene's constant companion since the day Silva arrived from work to find his wife dead drunk and unconscious on the kitchen floor, came on the line.

"*Senhor?*"

He told her about the trip.

"But you'll be back on Sunday?"

"I'm afraid not. Look, Maria Lourdes, I know it's your day off—"

"Don't worry, Senhor. You can count on me. I won't leave her alone. Not for a moment. Shall we pack you a bag?"

Chapter Seven

OMAR TORRES ONCE REMARKED that he preferred the Grand to the rainforest because there were "no snakes to bite you in the ass when you drop your pants at the Grand." That was true, as far as it went, but he had another reason as well—a far more important one: Omar Torres slept with other men's wives, and *that*, in the State of Pará, was a dangerous thing to do.

Some of the men he cuckolded hadn't had sexual relations with their spouses in years, but that didn't diminish Omar's risk. If the husbands in question were to discover what he was up to, they'd be obliged to kill him. It was as simple as that: a question of honor.

And, although the rainforest in the vicinity of the town was the usual place for dalliance, it wasn't the impenetrable tangle of vegetation occasional visitors thought it to be. There were paths. There were hunters. There were people out there at all hours of the day and night getting their asses bitten. The risk of someone stumbling across a copulating couple in the jungle was small, but it was real, and it was a risk that Omar, given his supercharged libido and the high frequency of his trysts, assessed as being too great.

Enter the Grand, Azevedo's epicenter of discretion. Opening onto an alley in the rear of the hotel was a stairway that led to the rooms on the second floor. The alley was unlit. Omar left a flashlight in the glove compartment of his jeep to help him get the key into the lock, and the key was his own, issued to him so he never had to be seen asking for one at the front desk. A room set aside for his exclusive use, and the fact that Osvaldo let him pay by the month completed the arrangement.

But Omar wasn't the only one who loved the Grand. Many of the town's other leading citizens did as well. The Grand stocked imported beverages, even a few wines. The Grand served decent, if simple, food. The cleanliness of the toilets was, by Azevedo standards, remarkable and often commented upon. A *faxineira* was always on hand to wipe away the near (and sometimes not-so-near) misses around the urinals, and vomit seldom stayed on the floors for more than ten minutes.

Osvaldo's establishment, the good citizens of Azevedo were fond of assuring each other, had *class*. The classy activity on Mondays and Fridays was bingo. The classy activity on Tuesdays and Thursdays was the playing of cards. In the bar, the game was *buraco* and the drink was cachaça. In a private room, maintained for the use of the town's notables, the game was poker and the drink, Scotch whiskey. Women were welcome in the bar, but they were never invited to the private room.

On the evening of Jade's return to town, the notables numbered seven, and they were seated around a circular table. Omar Torres and the priest, Father Castori, had been drunk when they arrived. The mayor, Hugo Toledo, the *fazendeiros* José Frade, Cesar Bonetti, and Roberto Lisboa were drinking steadily, intent upon achieving the same state of grace. Lisboa's foreman, the *pistoleiro*, Toni Pandolfo, wasn't drinking at all. He seldom did. And that, in the opinion of most of the townsfolk, was a good thing, because he was dangerous enough when he was sober.

"That Calmon woman," Torres remarked, chewing an unlit cigar because he knew the others would object if he set a match to it, "is a bitch." Jade had brushed him off more than once. He'd never been able to forgive her for it.

"Not the word I would have used to describe her," Father Castori said. "But I agree with the sentiment." His lengthy recounting of Amati's story had made him hoarse, a condition he was attempting to rectify by drinking twice as fast as usual.

"Bitch is *exactly* the word," Bonetti said, shuffling the cards. He generally got into town only once a week. And when he did, he was anxious to enjoy the time he was spending there. The enjoyment consisted of drinking to excess, gossip and card-playing. He took a deep pull from his glass and added, "Why the fuck couldn't she have left well-enough alone? Huh? Answer me that! Ante up."

"Because she's a goddamned Indian lover, that's why," Frade said, making his contribution to the pile of chips. He was a man with a temper, a fact that the regular bruises on his wife's face and arms served to substantiate.

Bonetti slid the deck in front of him. "Cut," he said.

Frade cut the cards.

"They all are," Pandolfo said. "All those fucking FUNAI people."

"Draw poker," Bonetti said and dealt them each five cards.

Lisboa looked at his cards and tried, unsuccessfully, to suppress a smile. He'd been losing throughout the night. The big winner, despite the alcohol he'd consumed, was Torres. He was a first-rate poker player, which Lisboa was not. Pandolfo, Lisboa's protector, had taken to fixing Azevedo's Greatest Cocksman with threatening stares, but they appeared to be having no effect whatsoever.

He gave it up and opened with a hundred Reais. When the game got to his boss, Lisboa raised with five. The others followed suit.

"Not all the agents are like that," Bonetti said. "Her predecessor was a good deal more reasonable."

"How about you deal the fucking cards?" Pandolfo said.
"Give me three."

Bonetti gave him three cards, but he took his time about
it, demonstrating he was another person Pandolfo couldn't
intimidate.

Toledo, the mayor, had been awaiting his moment. Now,
he chimed in. "The problem isn't just the FUNAI," he began.
"It's that cabal of bleeding-heart liberals in Brasilia. Get them
out of there and their so-called 'Indian land' will disappear
just like that." He snapped his fingers. "See if it doesn't.
Three cards."

A murmur of agreement went around the table, a murmur
in which Lisboa didn't participate. Bonetti gave Toledo his
three cards.

"One," Lisboa snapped, without the slightest trace of deference in his voice. Lisboa fancied himself an artist, and was
normally a timid man, which was why he always had Pandolfo around to back him up. But when he got drunk, as he
was now, all bets were off. He could be downright aggressive.

"One," Torres said, unmoved. He grinned, showing the
white, even teeth that so many women found attractive. It
was a dead giveaway of the confidence he had in his hand,
but Lisboa was too tipsy to notice it.

Pandolfo, the *pistoleiro*, and Toledo, the mayor, passed.
The others took three each. Lisboa bet another five hundred
Reais. Torres followed suit. Everyone else dropped out.

"Well, damn!" Lisboa said. "I finally get a good hand and
everybody drops out." And then, to Torres, "I raise you a
thousand."

"You can't raise yourself," Torres said. "What have you
got?"

"A pair of tens."

"Three of a kind," Torres said, showing three fours. He raked in the pot.

"*Merda*," Lisboa said.

"So, Padre," Bonetti said to Castori. "What's your opinion? Was that savage telling the truth?"

"I have no reason to doubt that all the other members of his tribe are dead," Castori said. "As to their having been poisoned . . . well, who knows?"

He looked into his empty glass. Toledo took pity on him and pushed the button to summon service.

"Bless you," the priest said. Castori never paid for his own drinks.

"What I've never been able to figure out," Bonetti said, "is why you wasted a year of your life living with those people. What possessed you?"

"Not a year, Cesar," the priest said. "Much more. Thirteen long months and four days. And the answer to your question is that it was God's work. When I went to live among them, my most fervent desire was that I could convert them to the true faith." He was speaking slowly, doing a pretty good job of keeping the slur out of his speech, a *tour de force* for anyone who'd drunk as much as he had. "But they rejected my teaching, made me the butt of their jokes. If I could have saved a single soul, I would have been content, but God chose to deny me that. He chose to make me suffer as Job suffered. And now he has chosen to root out the Awana like—"

Lisboa, impatient as well as drunk, cut him short. "Are we here to play cards or talk about fucking Indians?"

Torres ignored him. "You think it was God?" Another flash of his perfect teeth. "The way I figure it, God got a little help."

"Maybe you should keep your voice down," Frade grumbled.

He was a big man, bigger than everyone there, and he liked a fight.

But Torres was having a great night—and he was too drunk to care. "Why?" he said. "Nobody in this room gives a good goddamn about what happened to a few Indians. How about everybody ante up?"

Everyone did.

"Osvaldo cares," Bonetti said. He belched. "His mother was one."

"Osvaldo isn't here."

The door opened.

"Speak of the devil," the priest said.

"You gentleman rang for service?" Osvaldo said.

"Same thing again," the mayor said, not missing a beat.

"Not for me," Lisboa said. "I gotta concentrate."

"A double," Torres said.

Pandolfo took it as more provocation directed at his boss and glared at him.

"I wonder what she did with the Indian," Bonetti said when Osvaldo was gone.

"She who?" Torres said.

"Jade, of course." He passed the cards to Pandolfo, who began to shuffle them.

"Probably staying at her place," Frade said.

"An Indian? In her own home? I doubt it,"

"Why?"

"Her housekeeper," Bonetti said, "is Alexandra Santos. A sensible woman. She'd never stand for it."

The deck went to Bonetti, who cut. "Same game again," Pandolfo said.

He dealt. Toledo passed. Lisboa opened with a hundred. The others went along. Everyone took three cards, except for Torres who took one, and Frade who dropped out. Again,

Toledo passed. Lisboa bet five hundred. Torres raised him a thousand.

"You're bluffing," Lisboa said.

"You think so? You're gonna have to pay to find out."

"You're right there," the mayor said. He wasn't talking about the cards. He was responding to Bonetti's comment about Jade's housekeeper. "I know the woman well. She'd have a fit. I'm out."

"I'll see your thousand and raise you two thousand," Lisboa said.

Torres kept him waiting, toying with his cards as if he hadn't made up his mind about what to do.

"And besides," Bonetti said, "Jade lives all by herself. Taking some savage under her roof is something I don't think that even an Indian lover like her would be crazy enough to do. He'd have his dick in her five minutes after the door was closed."

"See your two thousand and raise you another two thousand," Torres said.

Everybody looked at him, then at Lisboa.

"Too rich for my blood," the priest said. "I'm out."

So was everyone else, except for Lisboa. "Call, you *filho da puta*," he said and started counting out the chips.

Pandolfo looked at him in alarm. "Boss, maybe you shouldn't—"

"Shut up, Toni, I know what I'm doing." Lisboa threw his chips on the pile.

"I doubt it," Torres said.

Pandolfo sprung to his feet.

Lisboa, seated next to him, grabbed his belt and pulled him back into his chair. "Don't you dare fuck this up." He tossed a full house on the table. "Read those, you prick!" He reached forward to rake in the pot.

"Not so fast," Torres said and showed four queens.

Lisboa gaped. Pandolfo fumed. Torres laughed and pulled the pile of chips toward him.

The mayor cleared his throat and went on as if nothing had happened. "I think you're right, Cesar," he said. "Jade is unlikely to have given the savage shelter in her own home."

"Here, maybe?" Frade said.

"Here?" Bonetti echoed. "In a room some white man may wind up sleeping in? Using the same goddamned toilet? You think Osvaldo would do that?"

"His mother was an Indian, wasn't she?" Frade said. "Next time he comes back here, I'm going to ask him."

"And you think he'd tell you?" Torres said. "Not likely."

"You got that right," Bonetti said. "If he's got him squirreled away somewhere, there's no way he'd come clean about it."

"Rita would," Torres said. "She'd know, and she'd tell. She doesn't like Indians any more than the rest of us do."

"Who's Rita?" Pandolfo asked.

"One of the chambermaids. I fucked her once."

"So has half the town," Toledo said, shuffling the cards. "Let's move along, shall we? There's a more important issue to discuss than what happened to the damned Indian."

"Hold it until I get back," José Frade said. "I gotta piss." He got up and left the room.

Toledo offered the cards to Pandolfo to cut and turned to the priest. "Tell me, Father—" He stopped talking when the door opened. It was Osvaldo, coming in to serve the round.

"Anything else?" he asked when he was done.

"Not for me," the mayor said.

The others shook their heads. Osvaldo left. Frade returned and resumed his seat. A little smile of satisfaction was crinkling his lips. While he was away something had happened to please him, but he said not a word about it.

"Same game again," Toledo said. "Ante up." He turned

back to the priest and continued where he'd left off. "How old did she say the boy was?"

"Eight or thereabouts."

"Okay, gentleman, here's what I'm thinking. Even those bleeding hearts in Brasilia are going to have to agree that a piece of land the size of that reservation is too big for one savage and his eight-year-old kid. At the moment, the whole tribe consists of only those two. And without women, they can't reproduce, right?"

"Wrong," Castori said. "The Indians steal their wives from other tribes. It's their way, nature's solution to inbreeding. As soon as that child is into puberty, he'll be sniffing around the females of the other tribes."

"There *are* no other tribes." Frade said.

"So he finds some slut from around here," Bonetti said, "some old whore who's ready to give up the business. Or he goes to another reservation and brings one back. Or he lives there for the next forty years with his old man and maybe another twenty all by himself."

"All possibilities," Toledo said. "Unless—"

"How about we play cards?" Lisboa said.

Toledo ignored him. "Unless," he repeated, "something bad happened to both."

"Shhh!" Frade said. "Keep it down."

Toledo dropped his voice a notch. When he did, even Lisboa leaned forward to listen. "Mind you, I'm not saying that one of us should take the initiative to do it."

"Oh, no, not you," Bonetti said. "We all know how fond of Indians you are."

"But you have a point," Torres said.

"I certainly do," Toledo said. "If those two were to . . . disappear, we could petition the federal government to give up the whole of that reservation for development."

"Why can't we petition for a piece of it right now?" Lisboa said. "It's already far too big for just two savages."

"Bravo!" Torres said. "I want a piece."

"All of us do," Frade said. "All except for the padre here."

Castori sniffed. "I see no reason why the Church should be excluded."

Pandolfo opened his mouth to put in a bid of his own, but Toledo forestalled him.

"You've got a point, Roberto. A piece is better than none. So we might as well get started. We'll find some equitable way to split it up, but first we have to pry it loose. Tomorrow morning, first thing, I'll have a chat with Renato Kassab; get him to check for precedents."

"That shyster's going to want a piece of it, too," Frade grumbled.

"What if he does?" Toledo said. "Let's not be greedy. There's plenty for all. But I've just come into possession of some additional information, and it presents a complication."

"What kind of information?"

"Just before I came over here tonight, I got a call from our friend, Delegado Borges."

"You got a call? I thought the goddamned tower was down again."

"It's back up," Bonetti said. "Been up for hours. What did he want?"

"Our keeper of the peace got a call from a fishing buddy of his, a fellow by the name of Estevan Barbosa. Ring any bells?"

"He's a federal cop," Frade said. "Lives in Belem, comes here every now and then to fish. So?"

"It seems our friend Jade called him."

Bonetti narrowed his eyes. "Called him? About the fucking Indians?"

Toledo nodded. "Exactly."

"Bitch! What did he tell her?"

"That he was too busy to look into it."

Bonetti smiled. "Good," he said.

"That part of it, yes, but what happened next wasn't good at all. He doesn't know how she did it, but she managed to get his boss to send some guy from Brasilia, a Chief Inspector by the name of Silva. He arrives in Belem tomorrow morning."

Bonetti flushed an angry red. "Somebody should teach that woman to keep her mouth shut," he said.

"Who?" Torres asked. "You?"

"Maybe me," Pandolfo said, "if you guys want to chip in and make it worth my while. A piece of that Indian land, maybe?"

They all ignored him.

"According to what Barbosa told Borges," Toledo said, "this Silva is persistent. If he gets his teeth into something, he never lets go."

"Bad news," Frade said.

"It gets worse. Apparently, he can't be bought, and—"

"That, I gotta see," Torres said. "A cop who can't be bought."

"*And* he's bringing his own medical examiner."

"What?" Bonetti said. "Why? Pinto not good enough for him?"

"Apparently not."

"I need another drink," Lisboa said. He reached over to push the button.

"Guilty conscience?" Torres asked.

"You shut up, Torres. You just shut up. How do we know it wasn't you? You've got as much to gain as the rest of us."

"You'd love to pin this one on me, wouldn't you Lisboa? With all the notes of yours I'm holding. Take me out of the picture, and you might just be able to keep that *fazenda* of yours."

The door opened. Osvaldo came in with a tray. "How's that for quick service?" he said. "This time I had it ready." No one responded. His smile faded as his gaze scanned the table. "What's with you guys?" he asked. "Somebody just fart?"

"Put down the tray and give us some privacy," Toledo snapped.

Osvaldo did as he was bidden.

"So what are we going to do about this Silva guy?" Bonetti asked when he was gone.

"*I'm* not going to do anything," Torres said, reaching for his drink. "*I've* got nothing to hide."

"Nor I," the priest said.

"Who does or doesn't isn't the point," Toledo said. "Finger-pointing is counterproductive. Those people are dead, and nothing is going to bring them back. Whoever killed them is immaterial."

"Immaterial?" Castori said uncertainly.

"Yes, Father. Entirely immaterial. But no one at this table can deny that their deaths bring us benefits. So here's my suggestion: from here on in, we present a united front, stick together."

"In other words, stonewall the fucking cop," Frade said.

Toledo smiled. "José, I couldn't have put it better myself."

THE GAME went on for another hour. Omar Torres, richer by almost nine thousand Reais, most of it out of Lisboa's pocket, and about as drunk as he ever got, was the last to leave the bar. He managed to negotiate his way without incident from the table to the door, but on the porch he tripped, and would have gone down if he hadn't struck his head on a post supporting the roof. The pain took a while to impact upon his fuddled brain. He grasped the wooden pillar with both hands and stood there, blinking, waiting for it to pass. When it did, he realized that he had an overwhelming necessity to urinate.

He would have unzipped then and there had not two women emerged from the hotel, taken up a position two meters behind him, and started talking about the eight o'clock *telenovela*. He could feel their eyes boring into his back. *The alley*, he thought.

He stumbled down the three steps into the street, turned left, and made for the passageway between the hotel and Cunha's pharmacy.

It was a moonless night with a cover of haze concealing the stars. A street lamp some twenty meters away shed only dim illumination on the hotel's façade. The passageway was completely dark.

With his arm extended, and trailing his left hand along the wall as a guide, he rounded the corner and kept walking until he'd almost reached the back of the building. There he stopped, opened his pants, and in blessed relief, began to empty his bladder.

He was still at it when he heard a footstep behind him.

Chapter Eight

"THAT SAVAGE YOU BROUGHT into town?"

It was more of an accusation than a question.

Jade, who had heard just about enough from Alexandra on the subject of Indians, buried her nose in her coffee cup and strove to keep her voice level. "Yes?"

"He killed a man last night."

Jade put her cup aside and looked at her housekeeper in astonishment. "*What?*"

"Killed him in cold blood."

"Who? Who did he kill?"

"Omar Torres. Your bloodthirsty Indian slaughtered him with a machete. And Senhor Torres was such a nice man."

Nice? Jade thought. *Omar Torres was anything but nice. Omar Torres was a pig.*

But she didn't say it.

Instead she said, "Why do they think Amati did it?"

"Is that the savage's name? Amati?"

"It's his name, yes. Stop calling him a savage. I asked you a question: why do they think he did it?"

"They don't *think*," Alexandra said with satisfaction. "They *know*. The two of them were in that alley between the pharmacy and the Grand. Senhor Torres was dead, and the Indian was next to him, covered in blood and holding a machete."

"Next to Torres's body? How—"

"He was dead drunk. He slaughtered poor Senhor Torres, and then he passed out."

"Who found them?"

"Tomas Piva."

"Who's Tomas Piva?"

"That *mulato* with a limp, the one without his two front teeth." Alexandra tapped her incisors with a forefinger by way of illustration. Jade remembered him now. Piva collected garbage for the town.

"He told you himself?"

The housekeeper shook her head. "His mother told me."

"When did you speak to her?"

"This morning in the *padaria*, when I went to buy bread."

"Where's Amati now? Did she say?"

"She did. He's right where he deserves to be. In jail."

JADE CALLED and got Borges on the phone. The delegado was offhand about both the event and the arrest: "Omar Torres was playing with fire for a long time. Truth to tell, I would have taken a bet that someone would have killed him some day. I just never expected it to be an Indian."

"And you're sure it was?"

"Oh, I'm sure all right. Your pal was lying right next to him with the machete that killed Omar still in his hand. And he was so goddamned drunk that he hasn't woken up from that time to this. Not when we cuffed him, not even when we carried him over here and tossed him into a cold shower."

"He didn't do it. He *couldn't* have done it."

"I'm sorry to have to tell you he did."

"I don't believe it."

"No? Then come over here and have a look at him yourself. He's still out. And he smells like a distillery."

"That Indian doesn't drink, Delegado."

"Looks like last night he made an exception."

"I don't believe it. He doesn't drink, I tell you, and he despises people who do. There is no way he would have consumed cachaça of his own volition. Someone must have forced it down his throat."

"Oh come on, Senhorita Calmon. I mean, how likely is that?"

"Where is he now?"

"In a cell about ten meters from where I'm sitting. We dragged him out of the shower, put him there, and called Doctor Pinto to come over and have a look. He just left."

"What did he say?"

"To let him sleep it off."

"So you still haven't heard his side of the story?"

She heard him chuckle. "His side of the story? The savage gets found in an alley, holding a *facão*, covered in blood, next to a dead man, whose throat had been slashed, and you think there's a *his side of the story?*"

"What I think, Delegado, is that there might be some extenuating circumstances."

"Like what? Self-defense?"

"Maybe."

"No way." He sighed. "Look, Senhorita Calmon, it was like this: Osvaldo's place was packed last night. A dozen people saw Omar go out the door. The ones I spoke to are all willing to swear he was so drunk he could hardly put one foot in front of the other."

"And the Indian? Did anyone see him?"

"Not until they found him next to the body."

"Torres had the reputation of being quite a lady's man, didn't he?"

"What's that got to do with it?"

"Who's to say it wasn't some jealous husband who killed him?"

"And then went and got the Indian, filled him with cachaça, covered him in blood and left him unconscious next to Omar's body?"

"It's possible, isn't it?"

"Anything's possible. It just isn't probable."

"Was Torres armed?"

"No, he wasn't. And nobody in this town has ever seen him pick a fight with anybody, drunk or sober. So forget any claims of self-defense. This was aggression, pure and simple. And, besides, it looks like Torres was struck from behind."

"What was he doing in the alley?"

"His fly was open, his pecker was out and he was facing the wall. He must have been taking a piss, smelled like it anyway. What else do you want to know?"

"When can I see him?"

"Omar? Anytime you like. He's on a slab down at the doc's."

"I'm talking about Amati, Delegado."

"Amati? That the savage?"

"That's his name, yes, and he's not a savage."

"In my book, anybody who takes a machete to another man's neck is a savage."

"I agree with you. But in this case, I doubt that the savage was Amati."

"Far as I know, he's the only Indian in town."

"I ask you again, when can I see him?"

"The doc says he expects him to wake up in four or five hours."

"One o'clock this afternoon then?"

"One o'clock should do it. See you then."

Chapter Nine

SILVA, BLEARY-EYED FROM AN almost sleepless night, scanned the crowd in the arrival hall at Val de Cans Airport. Barbosa was nowhere in sight.

"Typical," Arnaldo muttered.

Before Silva could reply someone tapped him on the shoulder. "Chief Inspector Silva?"

The tapper looked to be in his late twenties, was wearing a cheap suit, and had eyes that said *cop*.

"Yes, I'm Silva. This is Agent Nunes. Who are you?"

"I'm Sanches," he said. "Agent at the Belem field office."

They shook hands.

"Where's Barbosa?" Arnaldo asked.

"Delegado Barbosa told me to tell you he was too busy to get away."

Arnaldo lifted an eyebrow. "Told you to tell us, huh?"

"No one but a suspicious man would take it that way," Sanches said.

"What way?" Arnaldo asked, innocently.

"The way you just took it."

"Okay," Arnaldo said. "You got me. I'm suspicious."

Sanches grinned. "I figured you might be. I looked at you, and I said to myself, 'Alex, that guy, Nunes, is one suspicious human being. He might even suspect that the delegado is sitting with his feet on his desk watching the game between Botafogo and Fluminense.' Mind you, I'm not saying he is, simply that a guy like you might suspect it."

"Knowing that the game to which you refer is being aired

58   *Leighton Gage*

as we speak," Arnaldo said, "I might well suspect exactly that."

"Nor am I saying," Sanches went on, "that he instructed me to take you to the office the long way around, thereby assuring that the aforementioned game ends before you get there."

"Agent Nunes and I are well acquainted with Delegado Barbosa," Silva said. "We know how dedicated he is to his work."

"*Exactly* how dedicated," Arnaldo said.

"I've only known him for about eighteen months," Sanches said.

"But it seems like longer, right?"

"Agent Nunes, you took the words right out of my mouth."

"Delegado Barbosa often has that effect on people. Where's the car?" Silva asked.

"This way. Do you gentlemen have luggage?"

"One bag each," Silva said.

ESTEVAN BARBOSA had missed his calling. He was one of the worst cops Silva had ever known, but, had he chosen to be a thespian, he would have been in a class by himself.

They arrived to find his secretary painting her nails, a false note in his *mise-en-scène*, but the rest was masterful.

Files were everywhere: on the desk, the credenza, the windowsill, even the floor. Barbosa's jacket had been tossed haphazardly over the back of his chair and his necktie was askew. The sleeves of his shirt were rolled back to reveal his hairy forearms. A lick of hair hung over his left eye, and a telephone was glued to his left ear. He was the very image of a man struggling with an overwhelming workload.

And he delivered his first line with perfect timing. "I've got a situation here," he said. "I'll have to call you back." He slammed the telephone into its cradle, nodded to his visitors, and snapped orders to his secretary. "Take the files off those chairs. Hold my calls. Get some coffee."

Silva noted, with some pleasure, that Barbosa hadn't been taking care of himself. He'd put on at least twenty kilos since the last time the Chief Inspector had seen him.

Arnaldo helped with the files, the secretary left to get the coffee, and Barbosa got right down to business, as any busy man would.

"We got a call from that Calmon woman."

Silva frowned. "When?"

"About an hour ago," Barbosa said. "Your cell phone went to voice mail, so she called here to make sure you got the message."

"Which was?"

"That Indian? The one she wants you to talk to?"

"Yes?"

"He killed a man."

Arnaldo, clearing away the last of the files to create sitting space, looked up at Silva. Silva kept his eyes fixed on Barbosa.

"*What?* When was this?"

"Last night. Slaughtered him with a machete." Then, to Arnaldo, "Thanks."

Silva sank into one of the chairs Arnaldo had cleared. "Who was the victim?"

Barbosa shrugged. "Some rich landowner. I didn't catch the name."

"Why?"

"Nobody knows for sure, but they think it must be revenge for what happened to his tribe."

"What makes them so sure the Indian did it?"

"They found him dead drunk with a bloody machete in his hand, right next to the corpse."

"Give Arnaldo the FUNAI woman's number," Silva said. "He'll call while we talk."

Barbosa sifted through the disordered paperwork on his desk, located a scrap with Jade's number, and handed it to Arnaldo. Arnaldo took his cell phone out of his pocket and stepped out of the office.

When he was gone and they were alone, Silva said, "So you're too busy to go to Azevedo, eh?"

Barbosa smiled. "You have no idea."

"Actually, I think I do."

The door opened and his secretary came in. There were three cups of coffee and three glasses of water on her tray. "Agent Nunes is outside making a call," Barbosa said, pointing to the door. "Take him his."

She nodded, put down two coffees, two waters, and left.

The interruption gave Silva time to get a rein on his temper. "Tell me about Azevedo," he said.

Barbosa took an appreciative sip of his coffee. "The fishing is great."

"I'm not into fishing." Silva tried his own coffee. It didn't surprise him to discover how good it was. Barbosa made a habit of treating himself well.

"You don't know what you're missing," Barbosa said. "I love it, and I'm willing to put up with a little discomfort in order to do it. Work is something else. When I'm working, I set a lot of store by my creature comforts. If I had to go to Azevedo to work, I'd dread it. But when I go there to fish, I see it with different eyes."

Silva wondered if he was being provocative or just insensitive and concluded it was the former, but he wasn't about to give Barbosa the satisfaction of showing his irritation. "What else can you tell me about the place?"

"Named, I'm told, after Enrique Azevedo, who came up from Rio Grande do Sul and settled there."

"Population?"

Barbosa scratched his chin. "Two thousand? Three? It's growing pretty fast, but it's still a fucking hole in the ground. Smack in the middle of the rainforest. Television and Internet only via satellite. Lots of poor people. A few rich ones, *fazendeiros* mostly, except for one businessman who's got a finger in everything and owns half the town. Half a dozen bars, a couple of whores, one of everything else."

"What do you call everything else?"

"One doctor, one lawyer, one delegado, one hotel. Like that."

"Tell me about the delegado."

"Friendly. A good fisherman. Big family."

"Professionally, I mean."

"I never worked with him. But I told him you're coming, and he said he'll do anything he can to help."

Silva drained his cup, took in some coffee grounds that had been lurking at the bottom. He reached for the water, spooled it around in his mouth to get the grains out of his teeth.

Barbosa watched him doing it. "I should have warned you about that," he said. "She boils the coffee in the water and then strains through a cloth, but the cloth has a loose weave, and—"

Silva cut him short. "What's his name?"

"Borges."

"Why didn't he help?"

"The alleged crime took place on the reservation. Not his jurisdiction."

"How about the mayor? Who is he?"

"His name is Hugo Toledo."

"What do you know about him?"

Barbosa rubbed his lips with a forefinger, thought about it

before he spoke. "Son of one of the earliest settlers, has one of the larger *fazendas*. His daddy was the mayor before him. Let me see what else." He scratched his head. "Oh, yeah, he hates Indians. Hell, they all do. Like I said, the town's growing fast, but they all think it would grow faster without that reservation."

"So if that last Indian were to be out of the way—"

"Toledo sure as hell wouldn't be shedding any tears about it. But poison a whole tribe? Nah! I don't think he'd go that far. Matter of fact, I don't think any of them would. You want my opinion?"

"What is it?"

"You're wasting your time. Either disease killed those people or another tribe did."

"That's not what the survivor says."

"The survivor is a murderer. Why shouldn't he be a liar as well?"

"I don't exclude the possibility. Who else pulls weight in the town?"

"Paulo Cunha."

"Who's he?"

"The businessman I mentioned. He's got a *fazenda* as well, but it isn't one of the biggest."

"Who owns the biggest?"

"I couldn't tell you. Borges will be able to fill you in."

"Okay. Who else might we have to deal with?"

Barbosa pursed his lips, unpursed them when the answer came to him. "The town doctor, a crotchety old bastard, name of Pinto. You're not going to find it easy to get along with him."

"I don't have to. We're bringing our own."

"Rodrigues?"

"No. Someone else."

"Wise move. Rodrigues is a pain in the ass."

If Silva had shown any sign of agreement, Barbosa, being Barbosa, would undoubtedly play the comment right back to Doctor Rodrigues—and cite Silva as the source. The Chief Inspector already had enough problems with the woman, and judged it better, therefore, not to react to the remark at all.

"Who else?" he said.

"A lawyer by the name of Kassab, Renato Kassab. I only met him once, but he struck me as a real shyster. Then there's the guy who owns the hotel—"

Barbosa stopped talking when the door opened. Arnaldo came in. "No luck," he said. "It keeps going to voicemail."

"Could be the cell phone tower is down," Barbosa said. "It happened the last time I was there. It's the highest thing in town, and it rains a lot, so it's constantly getting hit by lightning."

"No generator?" Arnaldo asked.

"Are you kidding? This is Azevedo we're talking about. The town has outgrown its electrical net. The power is off at least a quarter of the time, and in the rainy season, it's closer to half."

"This isn't the rainy season, is it?"

"No. You're lucky. Doesn't mean it doesn't rain a lot though. It just rains *more* during the rainy season."

"So," Arnaldo said, "I don't suppose we can count on the air-conditioning either?"

"Nope," Barbosa said, blandly. "And when it comes to air-conditioners, there's an additional problem."

"Which is?"

"Fluctuations in the voltage. They get fried."

Arnaldo took a deep breath. "What other delights await us?"

"Flies. Billions and billions. Beetles, too—as big as bars of soap, but they don't bite like the flies do. They're just scary.

And you don't want to go wandering around in the rainforest. It's full of snakes."

All of Barbosa's bad news was being delivered with a broad grin, but when he saw the way Arnaldo was looking at him, he tried to suppress it.

"Accommodation?" Silva said, to defuse the situation.

"Like I said, there's only one hotel. It's called the Grand, but it's anything but."

"Simple?"

"Let's put it this way, if one of those tourist publications was handing out stars, it wouldn't get any."

"I can't wait," Arnaldo said.

Barbosa couldn't resist a final dig. "You would if you knew what you were getting into."

"How do we get there?" Silva said.

"You could rent a jeep. The road's unpaved, so you don't want any vehicle that isn't four-wheel drive."

"How far is it?"

"About seven hundred and fifty kilometers, and there isn't much along the way, except for two gas stations. One's about two hundred kilometers out, another about six hundred. No hotels. If you can't make it in one go, which you probably can't, you'll have to sleep in your jeep."

"How long is it likely to take?"

"If you're lucky, between eighteen and twenty hours. But if you get heavy rainfall along the way, all bets are off. The road turns to mud, fifty centimeters deep in some places, and you can't move in either direction. You just have to sit and wait until it firms up."

"So we fly?"

"That would be my advice. But there are no scheduled flights. You'll have to charter a plane. You figure Sampaio is going to pop for that? He's not exactly famous for sharing the wealth."

"If he refuses," Arnaldo said, "we'll squeal to his sister."

"His sister?"

"Never mind," Silva said. "Just Arnaldo's little joke."

Barbosa looked at his watch. "As much as I'm enjoying this visit," he said, "you'd better leave right now if you want to have any hope of getting there today. The runway doesn't have lights. You can't land after dark."

"This is getting better and better," Arnaldo said.

"You think *getting* there is bad?" Barbosa said. "Believe me, what's waiting for you is worse."

Chapter Ten

"T‍HIRTEEN THOUSAND FOUR HUNDRED Reais," the woman at the air charter company said.

"*Thirteen thousand four hundred?*" Silva echoed, incensed. "That's crazy."

"Out and back, fuel and tax, thirteen four," she rattled off, stone-faced. "That's the price."

"That aircraft shouldn't cost more than fifteen hundred an hour."

"It never did until the other charter company went bust, and we became the sole option. That's when my boss raised his prices."

"Your boss is a thief."

"I hear that a lot."

"We can't afford thirteen four. No way."

"I hear that a lot, too."

"And yet it's a matter of life and death. We have to get there before dark."

"Is that a fact?" She looked like she'd heard that one a lot as well.

"It is. Look." He showed her his warrant card.

"Oh," she said. "Cops."

"That's right. *Federal* cops."

She lowered her voice, looked around to make sure no one was listening. "It's just the two of you, right?"

Silva nodded.

"Well, I didn't tell you this, but our other three-forty is fueling for a flight to the same place and with only one other passenger. The three-forties accommodate five. Maybe you could team up and split the cost."

"Bless you," Silva said. "Where is he?"

THE OTHER passenger wasn't a he, it was a she.

"You dropped from heaven," the young woman said. "I was just sitting here trying to figure out how I was going to explain to my editor how I managed to spend thirteen thousand four hundred Reais to charter a plane that should have cost half that."

"So you're a journalist?"

She nodded. "*Folha de Manha*, São Paulo. And you're Mario Silva, right?"

"How did you know?"

"I read my own newspaper. Your picture is in it all the time. Your boss's, too. Now there's a publicity whore if ever there was one. He can't get enough of the limelight, that guy."

"No comment," Arnaldo said.

She turned to him. "And you're Arnaldo Nunes."

"And you're well-informed."

"Actually," she said, extending a hand, "I'm Maura Mandel." She shook hands with Silva as well. "Don't you just love Belem? If I'd known what these people were going to charge, I would have hired a plane in some big town further south, skipped this hellhole entirely, and had them fly me directly to Azevedo."

"We've got three more people coming up tomorrow from São Paulo," Silva said, "and that's what I'm going to tell them to do."

"Maybe," she said, "we can do the same deal on the flight back. Hire a flight down there, and have them come to pick us up. I could drop you off in Brasilia on the way. It's not much of a detour."

"No," Silva said, "it's not. Do you mind if I ask you a question?"

"Fire away."

"It's got to be more than a coincidence that a journalist from one of the country's major newspapers just happens to be going to a little town in Pará on the same day we do. Do you, by any chance, know a young lady by the name of Lana Nogueira?"

"I do."

"And you're aware that she's the niece of my boss, with whom you also seem to have a certain degree of familiarity."

"Yes."

"May I therefore assume that you not only know why Arnaldo and I are on our way to Azevedo, but that you're going there to report on it?"

"People have told me that you're good at what you do, Chief Inspector. I'm beginning to see why they say that."

"Don't try flattering me, Senhorita Mandel. It doesn't work."

"I'm sorry you thought it was flattery. It wasn't."

"Then I apologize. Do you also know Jade Calmon?"

"She's my best friend. She and I and Lana all went to school together. Sacred Heart, in São Paulo."

"What inspired Jade to call you?"

Maura told him.

"I regret," he said when she was done, "that the three of you had to go to such lengths to get the justice system working on this. As an officer of the law, it embarrasses me."

"I don't regret it at all. If we hadn't done what we did, and I mean this most sincerely, we wouldn't have had you working on the case. We would have been stuck with the fellow who runs your field office here in Belem, and he wouldn't have done shit."

"Very eloquently put," Arnaldo said.

"It comes from hanging around in newsrooms. We all talk like that."

"Delegado Barbosa's reputation precedes him, I see," Silva said, "even among the ladies and gentlemen of the press."

"There are no ladies and gentlemen of the press. We're all vulgarians. But yes, his reputation precedes him. Follows him, too, and hangs over his head. I checked up on him after he gave Jade the runaround. If it wasn't for his political connections, I'm told, he would have been out on his ass a long time ago."

"No comment," Silva said.

"But there are those," Arnaldo said, "who might say you've been told correctly."

She grinned. "I see you have some experience of journalists."

Chapter Eleven

DESPITE HER SPIRITED DEFENSE of Amati to Borges, Jade harbored doubts. The Indian was capable of violence. She'd witnessed that the previous day, had almost been a victim of it herself. But if he was guilty, what spark could have set him off? And why would he have chosen Torres as a victim? And how likely was it that he'd consumed alcohol?

Osvaldo might be able to help her answer those questions. She grabbed her purse and made for his hotel, where she found him seated in the bar, almost as if he'd been waiting for her to arrive.

"You heard?" she said.

He nodded. "I think maybe you could use some coffee."

"I could."

The bar was otherwise empty. Amanda was nowhere in sight. He got up from the table and returned with two cups.

"He didn't do it," he said, resuming his seat.

"What makes you so sure?"

"I slung a hammock for him not fifteen minutes after you left. He fell into it like a dead man, was asleep before I left the room."

"So how likely is it that he would have crawled out of it in the middle of the night, gotten drunk, found a machete, and killed Omar Torres?"

"As unlikely as anything could be."

"So someone rendered him unconscious and carried him?"

"That would be my guess."

"How could they have done that without being seen?"

"The back stairway, the one we used when we brought him in."

He took a hearty swig from his cup. Jade picked up her own. It was too hot, and she set it down again.

"What time did Omar leave?" she asked.

"Around midnight."

"Drunk?"

"Any drunker and he would have fallen flat on his face. I remember thinking, some day he's going to kill somebody with that jeep of his."

"Who was with him before he left?"

Osvaldo closed his eyes and rubbed his forehead, as if he was trying to see the scene in his mind. After a moment, he said, "Five, no, make that six guys. They were all sitting around a table playing poker."

"Who were they?"

He started counting them off on his fingers. The mayor, the priest, three *fazendeiros*—"

He'd extended three fingers at once. She put her hand on his. "Which three?"

"Bonetti, Frade, and Lisboa."

"And the sixth man? Who was he?"

"That foreman of Lisboa's, Pandolfo."

"I don't think I know him," she said.

"You don't want to. He's an animal, a *pistoleiro*. Lisboa uses him to keep his laborers in line. He carries a gun, but mostly he uses his fists and his boots."

"Did Torres fight with anybody about anything?"

"No more than usual. Lisboa can't play cards for shit, but he keeps doing it. Torres had a gift. He could play well even when he was drunk. He's taken a lot of money off of Lisboa down through the years, and he can't help crowing about it."

Jade picked up her coffee again. Still too hot. "And that would have made Lisboa angry, right?"

"Not just Lisboa, but that bulldog of his as well. And there's something else that would have pissed them off about Torres, if they knew about it. But I'm not sure they did."

"Which is?"

"I don't like to gossip."

She set down the cup, still untasted. "That's crap, Osvaldo. You *love* to gossip. And you wouldn't have started unless you intended to finish. So let's hear it."

"You know that waterfall on the Jagunami?"

"The one with the pool? The one where people go to swim?"

"Yeah, but mostly on the weekends. During the week, the place is almost always deserted."

"And?"

"And a couple of months ago, on a weekday morning, Torres came into town to buy something or other. His way home goes right by that waterfall. He decided to stop by for a swim. So he parked his jeep, walked through the brush to the falls, and what did he see?"

"What?"

"Pandolfo buggering his boss, right there on the rocks."

"So the two of them are homosexuals?"

"Or bisexuals, or maybe Lisboa just pays Pandolfo to do it. God knows, but I do know one thing."

"Which is?"

"That Torres told the story to everyone who was willing to listen. And those he told must have told others."

"So the whole town would have had a good laugh about it."

"Especially about Pandolfo, him always playing the *cabra macho* and all."

"You think that if they'd found out—"

"They might have killed Torres? Maybe. But there were other people in this town that might have had it out for him."

"Like whom?"

"Torres was a real ladies' man. And most of those ladies are married."

"In a town like this, that's probably dangerous."

"It is."

"You know any names? Of some of the women, I mean."

Osvaldo didn't like the question, she could see that. He pursed his lips, put both palms on the table and pushed back his chair to increase the distance between them.

"Jade, I . . . Look, I'd like to help, I would, but this is my stock in trade. I rent rooms to those people. They have a right to my discretion."

"This is a man's life we're talking about here."

"You got a point. And it's a bum rap. It's clear as cheap cachaça that Borges arrested the wrong man."

"So out with it. In a situation like this, you *can't* keep quiet."

Osvaldo sighed, scratched the side of his nose, leaned forward again.

"Okay," he said. "Okay, I'll tell you, but you didn't get it from me."

"Understood. I promise."

"The wives of three of those guys at the table."

"*Three?*"

"Like I said, Omar was a real ladies' man."

"Which three?"

"The mayor, Bonetti, and Frade."

Again, Jade picked up her cup. It had cooled. She took a sip. "So, from what you're telling me, the only man sitting at that table who didn't have a reason to kill Omar Torres—"

"Was the priest," Osvaldo said.

Chapter Twelve

OSVALDO SERVED HER A light lunch, and Jade tried to do justice to it, but wound up leaving most of it on her plate. Just before one, they left the Grand and walked around the corner to the *delegacia*. A crowd had gathered in front of the little brick building, many of them women.

Someone spotted Jade and said, "It's that FUNAI woman."

Someone else said, "She's here to get that murderer out of there."

Norma Prado, a cashier from Paulo Cunha's supermarket, ran up to Jade and spit in her face.

"Indian lover!" she said.

Another woman kicked Osvaldo in the shin. "Shame!" she said.

"Ouch, Ofelia," he said. "That hurt."

"It was supposed to. Shame on you, helping this, this . . . FUNAI woman"—she made FUNAI sound like an epithet—"to defend some dirty Indian. You make your living in this town. Don't you think you should be on our side?"

Jade recognized her. Ofelia Prado was a close friend of her housekeeper, Alexandra Santos.

"Don't you think the Indian has a right to be heard?" she asked.

"He's got a right to a noose," someone in the crowd said.

Jade thought the voice sounded like Alexandra's. She looked around, but didn't see her.

"Why don't you just go home to São Paulo, or wherever else you came from?" Norma the Spitter said.

"Norma's right," another woman shouted, "the bitch is an Indian lover!"

"Indian lover! Indian lover! Indian lover!" Soon the whole crowd was chanting it.

Jade and Osvaldo, the voices ringing in their ears, jostled their way to the front door. They found it blocked by one of Borges' men carrying a shotgun.

"We're expected," Jade said.

"Yeah," he said. "I know." He didn't sound any more welcoming than the people in the crowd, but he stepped aside.

They found Borges and Father Castori drinking coffee in the delegado's office. Jade found a paper handkerchief in her purse and, spotting a mirror on the wall, went to clean off the woman's saliva.

"What are *you* doing here?" the priest asked the hotelkeeper.

"I brought him along to translate," Jade said.

The priest glared at her reflection in the mirror. "*I'm* here for that," he snapped. And then, to Osvaldo, "I always suspected your sympathies were on the side of the Indians. Now, I'm sure of it. Leave. Your services won't be required"

"I want him here," Jade said, "or I wouldn't have brought him.

Castori opened his mouth and turned to the delegado for support.

But he didn't get it. "She's the FUNAI agent," Borges said. "Sorry, Father, but it's her call. This is a political hot potato, and I intend to play it by the book."

The delegado stood up, snagged a ring of keys from a hook on the wall, and led the way to a door in the far wall. Jade, Osvaldo and the priest trailed along behind them.

"We tried to pump some coffee into him," Borges said over his shoulder. "But he made a face and spit it out."

He opened the door and entered a corridor with two cells

on either side. Amati was in the last one on the left. His eyes lit up when he saw Jade and Osvaldo.

"Looks like hell, doesn't he?" Borges said. "He must have the mother of all hangovers."

Amati did, indeed, look like hell. His eyes were bloodshot, a discolored lump was on his left temple, and the clothing Jade had given him was covered with stains.

"Torres's blood," Borges said. "Let's start by asking him what he had against Omar."

Jade was about to object to the nature of the question, but the priest, in his haste to regain the role of translator, spoke first, eliciting an indignant reply from the Indian.

"He says he didn't have anything against Omar Torres," Osvaldo stepped in before the priest could render Amati's words into Portuguese. "He doesn't even know who Omar Torres is."

"Liar!" the priest said.

Jade turned on him. "Your opinion, Father, isn't germane to this interview."

"And what's *your* opinion, Senhorita Calmon? Do you think this murdering savage is innocent?"

"How about both of you cool down?" Borges said. "You," he pointed at Osvaldo. "Ask him where he got the cachaça."

Osvaldo put forward the question and translated the reply.

"He wants to know what cachaça is."

"Oh, *please*," the priest said.

"You disagree with that translation, Father?" Borges said.

"No," Castori said, "but—"

"Then please let him do what he came here for. Go on, Osvaldo, tell him what cachaça is."

When the answer came back, the priest opened his mouth to object.

Borges put a hand on his arm. "One more interruption, Father, and I'll have to ask you to wait outside."

"I told him it's a drink that makes people crazy," Osvaldo said. "He said we should ask Father Calmon because he knows all about the stuff. Then he said his head hurts. And he wants to know why you have him locked up."

"Tell him."

Osvaldo did. Amati's eyebrows went up in surprise. He shook his head in denial.

"He says he didn't kill anyone."

The priest scoffed.

Borges shot him a cautionary look before posing his next question. "If he had nothing against Torres, and he didn't kill him, what was he doing in that alley?"

Amati's response was a long one. He ended it by touching the lump on his temple, a gesture that caused him to wince.

"He said he's a light sleeper," Osvaldo translated. "When someone came into his room, it woke him up. He turned his head toward the door, but he couldn't see much because the corridor was dark. My corridors usually are, by the way, because the lights work on timers—saves me a bundle on electricity."

"You don't have to editorialize," Borges said. "Just translate."

"Okay. So a light went on, shining right into his eyes. It blinded him. Sounds to me, from what he said next, that it was a flashlight, one of those big ones. He thought I was the one who was holding it because Jade wouldn't visit him in the middle of the night, and no one else knew he was there. He called out my name and asked what I wanted. He didn't get an answer. The light came closer. He asked again. Still no answer, but the light kept moving. It came right up to his hammock and then something hit him hard, right there." Osvaldo pointed to the lump. "And that's it. That's all he remembers. Next thing he knew, he was waking up here. And he wants to know if we can give him something to take away his headache."

"And we're supposed to believe that?" the priest asked.

Osvaldo turned on him. "You claim to know everything there is to know about the Awana, Father. But let me tell you something: if you think he's lying, it proves you don't know shit."

"How *dare* you talk to me that way!"

"The Awana don't lie! Truth is programmed into their genes."

"And there's Indian blood in yours, so of course you'd defend him even though it's obvious—"

"What's obvious, you damned fool, is that somebody knocked him out, forced alcohol down his throat, and set him up to take the fall for—"

"Shut up," Borges said. "Both of you. Okay, Senhorita Calmon, now you've heard his side of the story. Kind of a tall one, if you ask me."

"I don't recall asking you, Delegado."

"No need to get snippy. All I'm after here is justice. Any more questions?"

"Not at the moment, but there's something else we have to discuss and before we do—" She looked at the priest. "I'd like him to leave."

"I'm not going anywhere," the priest said.

"Sorry, Father," Borges said, "but she's within her rights. So you're going to have to."

The priest sniffed at Borges, narrowed his eyes at Jade and left without uttering another word. Seconds later, they heard the front door slam.

Borges smiled. "A little advice for both of you: don't attend communion in this town ever again. If you do, it's likely you'll find something nasty slipped into your wafer."

"I never attend his church anyway," she said.

"And I never will again," Osvaldo said.

"Okay, Senhorita Calmon, out with it. What did you want to say?"

"You have no jurisdiction over the Awana. As a representative of the FUNAI, I'm making an official request that you release this man into my custody."

Borges's eyes rounded in surprise. "Are you kidding? Did you see that crowd outside?"

"How could we miss them?"

"You see how pissed off they are about this?"

"They were quite vocal about it."

"One of the women," Osvaldo said, "spit in her face. Another one kicked me in the shin."

"Which is why," Jade said, "we want to get Amati out of here and take him to a place of safety."

"A place of safety? Around here? There's no place safer than my jail."

"I intend to bring him to the airport and fly him to Belem. He can be incarcerated there until we sort this out."

"No way," Borges said, shaking his head.

"You're refusing?"

"I am."

"Why?"

"The murder took place here in Azevedo, which means I'm in charge. And until a court tells me otherwise, he's *my* suspect, and he's going to stay in *my* jail. You have every right to get a lawyer and try to get him moved. Meanwhile, I intend to do my duty."

"You're making a mistake, Delegado. Can't you see that his life—"

"*Moreover*," Borges said, stressing the word as he rode roughshod over her objection. "Even if I was willing to turn him loose, which I'm not, there is no way you'd ever get him out of here. They're around in back as well."

There was a door with a glass pane at the end of the corridor. Osvaldo frowned, went there, and looked through it. "He's right. Not as many, but just as mad."

Jade bit her lip. "All right," she said. "But it's your job to keep this man safe until I—"

"You don't have to tell me my job, Senhorita Calmon, but if those people out there storm this jail, I'm not going to start shooting my fellow citizens in an attempt to stop them."

"So you're not prepared to lift a finger to help him?"

"A finger, yes. A firearm, no."

"And if they break in and attempt to take him?"

"I won't wound anyone, much less kill anyone. It's a question of the greatest good for the greatest number. Those people out there are acting out of a sense of justice. They're good people, most of them. They believe in an eye for an eye, and since there's no death penalty in this country—"

"They want to kill him."

"That's my guess. And it's also my guess that they wouldn't be averse to killing *me* if I tried to stop them."

Chapter Thirteen

"So what now?" Osvaldo asked, studying the angry crowd through the front window of the *delegacia*. It had become larger—and Father Castori had joined it.

"I want you to call Federal Police headquarters in Belem," Jade said. "Try to get in touch with a Chief Inspector Silva."

"Not that guy Barbosa?"

"No. Silva."

"Okay. Who's he? And what do you want me to tell him?"

"He's a man they're sending to investigate the genocide."

"From Belem?"

"From Brasilia. I've only spoken to him by telephone, but he made a good impression. I left him a message earlier this morning, but that was before we talked to Amati and before this crowd gathered. I want you to update him on what's happening, tell him to get here just as quickly as he can."

"What if I don't manage to talk to him?"

"Talk to Barbosa. Ask him to pass the message along."

"All right. What are you going to be doing in the meantime?"

"Talking to Kassab and seeing if there isn't some way we can pry Amati loose from Borges and get him out of town."

They opened the door. The shouting got louder. A few people detached themselves from the group and followed Osvaldo toward his hotel. A much larger party, about a dozen in all, surrounded Jade, kept pace with her on her way to Kassab's office, and heaped abuse upon her every step of the way.

"Indian lover!"

"*Cretina!*"

"Go home, bitch!"

Kassab's receptionist, shocked by their arrival, locked the door as soon as Jade was inside. Then she called her boss.

The lawyer emerged, left both women in his waiting room, and went outside to talk to the demonstrators. Less than a minute later, the crowd was moving back the way they'd come, and the lawyer was ushering Jade into his inner-sanctum.

"What did you say to them?"

"I appealed to their reason. Now, what can I do for you?"

She suspected it was more than that, suspected he'd told them things he was unwilling to tell her, but there was no time to lose.

"I'd like to hire you on behalf of the FUNAI to represent the Indian, Amati. Delegado Borges is—"

Kassab held up a hand. "I'm sorry, Senorita Calmon, I can't help you."

"Can't? Or won't?"

He sighed. "Look. I'd be the first to agree that everyone, even a murdering savage, has a right to a fair trial. But no one in this town would ever forgive me if I were to speak in defense of that Indian."

"Tell me this, Senhor Kassab: how much of what's going on out there"—she pointed in the direction of the *delegacia*—"is about justice and how much is about getting rid of an impediment to having the reservation declassified?"

"In all honesty? It's probably more about the latter, but there's nothing I can do about that."

"Didn't you just say he had a right to a fair trial?"

"I did. And I stand by that statement."

"So what do you suggest I do?"

"Bring in a public defender from Belem. Ask him to—"

"Wait," she said, holding up a hand. "What's that?"

Kassab paused to listen. The tumult on the street grew louder. A shot was fired, then another.

"Unless I miss my guess," he said, scratching his chin, "that's an indication your Indian isn't going to need a lawyer after all."

Chapter Fourteen

THE AIRPORT AT AZEVEDO consisted of a parking lot, a red earth runway, and a one-room shack. The parking lot was empty, the runway was so short that their pilot had to stand on his brakes to stop the landing roll before they plowed into a stand of trees, and the shack was locked.

"Strange," the pilot said, rattling the door. "I wonder what happened to the kid."

"What kid?" Silva said.

"He holds down the office. His old man owns those Cessnas." The pilot pointed out two 172s with identical paint jobs. "The kid has been flying them since he was twelve. They get him more ass than a toilet seat."

"At least there's somebody in this town who knows how to show a girl a good time," Maura said. "What do the other boys do for amusement?"

"Probably stay friends with the kid," Arnaldo said. "So what's your best guess for what's going on? Local festival, maybe?"

The pilot shook his head. "There's only one, and it was last month. Must be something else."

"How far are we from the Grand Hotel?"

"Too far to walk." The pilot started fishing in the leather bag he was carrying. "But somewhere in here . . . ah, here it is." He brandished a business card. "Azevedo's only cab driver." He took out his mobile phone. "Now if their goddamned phone tower isn't down again . . ."

It wasn't. The cab showed up five minutes later. Arnaldo,

the bulkiest of the four, took the seat in front. The others crowded into the back.

"Heard about the lynching?" were the first words the driver said after he'd greeted them.

"What lynching?" Silva asked.

"Where to?"

"The Grand Hotel. What lynching?"

"An Indian killed a white man. They stormed the jail, took him out, and strung him up."

"No kidding?" the pilot said. He sounded interested.

"No kidding. It was one hell of a show."

"Show?" Arnaldo grumbled. "Where do you get off, calling a lynching a show?"

The guy behind the wheel shot him a sour look. "You ever see one?"

"No."

"Then the way I figure it, I'm the expert, not you. It was a show."

"When?" Silva said.

The driver glanced in the rear view mirror. "Just a few hours ago," he said. "You guys going to smoke, or should I turn on the air conditioning?"

"Turn on the air conditioning," Silva said. "Where were the police?"

"The Delegado came out with a shotgun and waved it around a bit."

"But?"

"Well, hell, everybody knew he'd never shoot anybody with it. He fired it in the air a couple of times. Then they took it away from him."

"Anybody else try to stop it?" Arnaldo asked.

"The half-breed who owns the hotel came running up and tried to interfere. Ha! A lot of good that did him."

"And then?"

"They hustled the Indian down the street to the square."

Silva again: "Why the square?"

The driver was into it now, relishing the story he had to tell. He kept one hand on the wheel and started waving the other in the air.

"It's the only place in town that's got tall trees. I don't think the poor bastard knew what they had in mind even then. What would a savage know about hanging? They want to kill somebody, they use a knife, or an arrow, or a blowgun, right? A rope? That's white man's justice."

"Or injustice," Maura said.

"What? What did you say, Senhora?"

"Never mind. Go on."

"He was screaming and shouting, but nobody could understand what he was saying. Then Father Castori—"

"Who's Father Castori?" Maura asked.

"The parish priest. He gave him last rites, but was the savage grateful? Like hell he was! He just stood there, staring him down. Then he said something, and Castori got all red in the face. He shouted at the Indian, and the Indian shouted back, but it was all in Indian lingo, so nobody but the priest, the Indian, and the half-breed understood it. Then Castori switched back to English and started haranguing the crowd."

"To try to get them to stop?"

"No way. He talked about 'an eye for an eye and a tooth for a tooth,' that kind of shit, but it was all the Word of God, and you don't dick around with the Word of God, so folks quieted down and heard him out. It took him about five minutes to run out of steam. Meanwhile, they got the rope around the Indian's neck, and threw the other end over a limb."

Silva was unable to keep the disgust out of his voice. "Did you recognize any of the people who were doing this?"

The driver narrowed his eyes in suspicion. "What are you? A cop or something?"

"Yes, I'm a cop," Silva said. "And so is he." He pointed to Arnaldo. "Answer the question."

The driver, suddenly cautious, backpedaled. "I didn't recognize anybody. They were wearing masks."

"Everybody?"

"Not everybody. Just the ones who strung him up."

"And we're supposed to believe that?" Arnaldo said.

"Believe whatever you want. I got to live in this town. You guys don't."

Maura was busily scribbling notes. "I'm not a cop," she said. "I'm a reporter. What's your name?"

"Chico Lyra," the driver said sullenly.

"Please tell us the rest of the story, Senhor Lyra."

"Ask someone else."

"She's asking you," Arnaldo said, digging the driver in the ribs.

He was at least a head taller than the man behind the wheel. The driver's Adam's apple bobbed up and down before he went on. "They were just fixing to hoist him up when this FUNAI lady comes running down the street and tells them to leave the savage alone, that he didn't do it, that he was innocent. Yeah, right. Damned Indian is found dead drunk in an alley, covered in blood, with a machete in his hand and the man he murdered right next to him, and he's innocent?" He shook his head. "Damned FUNAI people. I swear—"

"This FUNAI woman," Silva said. "Was it Jade Calmon?"

"She's the only one we've got. Thank God."

"Did they hurt her?"

"Of course not. They just held her arms so she couldn't interfere. You think we're savages?"

"No," Silva said drily. "I'm sure you're all perfectly civilized."

"Damn right."

"Tell us the rest."

"What rest? There isn't any rest. They hung him, that's all. He went up like an elevator. There must have been a dozen people dragging on that rope. So there he is, kicking his feet, his tongue out, his face turning blue, pissing into his white man's shorts, and the FUNAI woman has her eyes closed, and is turning her back on it so she won't see what's happening to him, and she's screaming, and the half-breed is shouting, and everybody else is cheering. All of a sudden, the half-breed got loose somehow, and he made a break for the lamppost where they'd tied off the rope. Mind you, I didn't see that part of it myself. There were too many people between me and him, but they told me about it later."

"He didn't make it though, did he?"

"Of course he didn't make it. It was stupid of him even to try."

"Did they hurt him?"

"Nah! Just slapped him around a bit. You want to see where it happened? It's just a short detour, but I'll have to charge you an extra two Reais."

"Is the man they killed still hanging there?"

"The Indian? Nope. They already cut him down."

"Then no," Silva said.

Chapter Fifteen

WHEN THEY ARRIVED AT the Grand Hotel, Silva tried calling Jade. He got no answer. Then he asked to speak to Osvaldo, the hotelkeeper, and discovered he'd taken to his bed with a bottle of cachaça.

"If you expect to get anything coherent out of him," his wife told them, "you'd best wait until tomorrow morning."

As a last resort, and so the evening wouldn't be a total waste, Silva tried Delegado Borges, finally reaching him on his home number. In the background, Silva could hear a couple of kids fighting. And there was a crying baby situated somewhere close to the phone. Silva asked him about the lynching.

"Terrible thing," Borges said, raising his voice to make himself heard. "I tried to stop it, but I didn't want to kill anyone, and I sure as hell didn't want them to kill me, so—"

"So you just let them do it."

The implied criticism stung him. "Hey, you think you could have done any better?"

"Maybe."

"Easy for you to say. You weren't there."

"Did you recognize anyone?"

"No."

"Where's the morgue?"

"You want to see the body?"

"I want to see *both* bodies."

"We don't have a morgue as such. Doctor Pinto's place used to be a butcher shop. It's got a walk-in meat locker. They're in there."

"This Doctor Pinto is your medical examiner, right?"

"Part-time."

"I want him there."

"Okay. I'll set it up for first thing tomorrow morn—"

"Not tomorrow, Delegado. Now."

"Tonight? Hell, Chief Inspector, this is the night Lucilla is going to tell us who the father of her baby is. Can't it wait until morning? It's not like those corpses are going anywhere."

It took Silva a moment to realize that the Lucilla in question was a character in a popular television *novela*. He suggested the delegado record it.

DOCTOR PINTO'S office was less than a five-minute walk from the Grand. The delegado and the doctor arrived simultaneously. The delegado was wearing a T-shirt with something on the shoulder that looked like a baby's vomit—and smelled like it too. The doctor was emanating an odor more agreeable: Scotch whiskey. *And feeling the effects of it,* Silva thought as he watched the medical man fumble with his keys.

Pinto led them down the hall and through a door lined with stainless steel. The cool air inside would have been pleasant after the heat and humidity of the street had it not been tinged with the pervasive smell of decomposing corpses.

The bodies were nude and lying side by side. The Indian's penis was enlarged and protruded from his groin. Doctor Pinto pointed to it.

"It's shrinking now as his blood seeps out. But you should have seen it when they brought him in. Lest you think, however, that he was, in life, as well-endowed as he appears to be at this moment, let me explain that when a human being is hanged—"

"He can get a death erection," Arnaldo said. "Also called angel lust."

THE WAYS OF EVIL MEN

"Errr, yes." The doctor was disappointed to have his grand-standing curtailed.

The Indian's complexion was blue. His tongue, even bluer, was protruding from his mouth. Silva had never seen a corpse that made such a horrible impression on him—and he'd seen a lot of them.

"So it wasn't a long drop?" he said. "He choked to death?"

"He did. And his execution was ghastly, even for me, a medical man."

"You were there?"

"I was indeed."

"You got no call to be looking at the doctor that way," Borges said. "There was nothing he could have done. There was nothing *anybody* could have done. The people who did it were out for blood. If I or the doc had attempted to interfere, they would have strung us up right next to the Indian."

"It's our understanding," Silva said, "that Osvaldo Neto, the hotelkeeper, made just such an attempt."

"And they didn't string *him* up," Arnaldo said.

"Well, no, but—"

Silva cut him off. "Go on, Doctor. What were you about to say?"

"Scientific curiosity is part of my makeup. I'd never seen a hanging before, and when he first appeared over the heads of the crowd I made a point of glancing at my watch. From that moment until he stopped moving, seventeen minutes and twenty-three seconds elapsed. Mind you, I'm not saying he was dead by then, just that he stopped twitching."

Silva pulled a pair of surgical gloves out of his pocket, snapped them on and stepped in for a closer examination of the Indian's body. He'd expected the ligature mark left by the rope and the petechiae under the corpse's eyelids. What he hadn't expected was the bruise on Amati's forehead just below the hairline.

"What can you tell me about this?" he asked, pointing it out.

"Pre-mortem," the doctor said promptly.

"Yes. But by how much?"

"Several hours at least."

"Could it have been inflicted at about the time he's supposed to have killed his victim?"

"Yes."

"That's what I thought."

"He spun us a story," Borges said, "about being in his bed and being knocked out. A half-assed alibi if ever I heard one. And believe me, I've heard a lot of them."

"Hmm," Silva muttered. He transferred his attention to the other corpse. After a minute inspection of the wounds in Torres's neck, he said, "It's my understanding that the Indian was found drunk."

"Dead drunk," Borges said. "We couldn't wake him. Why?"

Silva turned to the doctor. "Did you take fingernail scrapings?"

Doctor Pinto raised his chin. "I didn't deem it necessary."

"I do," Silva said. "Do it. And fingerprint them as well."

"Scraping's a waste of time," Borges said, "unless you guys are willing to pay for the DNA testing. My budget is too small to afford it. And what do you need fingerprints for? We know who they are. And there isn't going to be anything on file for that Indian anyway."

"How about their clothing? And the murder weapon? Where are they?"

"The clothing is over there in those plastic bags," the doctor said.

"And I got the Indian's knife in the trunk of my car," Borges said.

He didn't like having his questions ignored. He sounded peeved. Silva didn't care.

"Go get it," he said.

Chapter Sixteen

MAURA AND THE PILOT were seated in the bar. Maura seemed pleased to see them. The pilot didn't. He stood up as soon as Silva and Arnaldo sat down.

"Gotta get some shut-eye."

"Hold on a second," Silva said.

"What?"

Arnaldo handed him a package. The pilot turned it over in his hands and felt the contents through the plastic bag they'd wrapped it in.

"What's this?" he asked.

"A fellow by the name of Sanches will be waiting for you when you land in Belem. Give it to him."

"We charge extra for deliveries."

"I'll be sure to tell him."

The pilot grunted and left.

"Hitting on you, was he?" Arnaldo said.

"Big time," Maura said.

Amanda, Osvaldo's wife, arrived to take their order.

"Your husband still indisposed?" Silva asked.

"Nice word for it," she said. "And yes."

Both men ordered whiskies.

"I'll nurse this one," the journalist said.

Amanda left to fetch their drinks.

Maura switched to professional mode. "You discover anything by looking at the bodies?"

"Maybe," Silva said.

"Maybe? What's that supposed to mean?"

"It means, Senhorita Mandel, that to tell you anything further at this point would be premature."

Before she could respond, Maura's telephone rang. She retrieved it from her purse. "There's our girl now," she said, glancing at the caller ID.

The conversation was a short one.

"On her way?" Silva asked when she hung up.

"Uh-huh. She'll be here in five minutes."

JADE WAS an athletic type with short blonde hair and deeply tanned skin. Maura, knowing her preferences, ordered her a *caipirinha*. It was waiting for her when she arrived, but she dropped heavily into a chair, left the sweating glass untouched and began to speak with barely contained fury.

She told them about her conversation with her house-keeper, her call to Borges, her visit to the *delegacia*, her frustrating consultation with Kassab, and, finally, about the lynching.

"I couldn't watch. I turned around and faced away. Every-one else, everyone in the crowd, just stood there and drank it in. Even the priest and the doctor. The only person who lifted a finger to stop it was Osvaldo." She looked around. "Where is he, by the way?"

"Drunk," Silva said shortly. "Tell me, Senhorita Calmon, other than what he told you, do you have any hard facts that might substantiate the Indian's innocence?"

"The alcohol. That was pure crap! Amati didn't like the stuff."

"Sure of that, are you?"

"Absolutely sure. Ask Osvaldo, if you don't believe me. He was there. He heard—"

"Please calm down, Senhorita Calmon. I'm not saying I don't believe you."

"There was something else, too."

"Oh? And that was?"

"He had a bruise on his forehead."

"Yes, we saw it."

"Saw it?"

"Arnaldo and I have already made a cursory examination of the bodies."

"Well, do you think he could have inflicted that wound on himself?"

"No. I do not."

"You see? So the story he told us makes sense. Something else, too: Amati had no reason to suspect Omar, no reason to attack him, and when we spoke to him at the *delegacia*, he didn't even know the man was dead."

"He said that, did he?"

"Yes, and I believe him. But there's one reason that trumps all the others."

"Which is?"

"Amati loved his son. And he wasn't stupid. If he murdered a white man and was murdered in turn, it would put the boy's future in jeopardy. He knew that."

"So he'd never do it?"

"Never!"

"How old is the child?"

"Eight."

"Eight," Silva echoed. He kept his face impassive, but it was as if she'd put a knife into his gut and twisted it. Amati's son was the same age as his own son had been when they'd lost him.

"What is the boy's name?" he asked.

"Raoni."

"Where is he?"

"In his village."

"You left an eight-year-old alone in the rainforest?"

"It was Amati's decision to make, not mine."

"You didn't try to argue him out of it?"

"The Awana, Chief Inspector, speak—make that spoke—
a language unique in all the world. I only know a few words
of it."

"How, then, did you get his story, the one you told me on
the telephone?"

"There's a priest here in town, a man by the name of Carlo
Castori. I got him to translate for me."

"Yes," Arnaldo said. "We've heard of him."

"Anything good?"

"No."

"Then you've been well-informed. Castori is a drunk and
a hypocrite. When he lived with the tribe, he professed to
care about them, but he never made a single convert, so now
he hates them. These days, he spends more time ingratiating
himself with the people who pay his bar bills than he does
ministering to the needs of his flock. What his patrons want,
he wants. And today they wanted Amati's blood."

"And what will happen to Raoni?"

"I'm going to send him to an orphanage in Belem. It's a
dreadful place, but there's nothing else I can do."

"Let me think about that one," Silva said.

"Is there some way you might be able to help? Get him
into an institution where he'd get better care?"

"Maybe."

"The Chief Inspector is full of maybes," Maura said.

Silva didn't rise to the taunt. "How does it come about
that a fellow I've heard described as a half-breed, a man
whose mother was an Indian, came to be the owner of this
hotel? Where did he get the money?"

The change of subject seemed to do Jade some good. The

tendons in her neck became less taut. She leaned back in her chair and reached for her drink.

"Osvaldo's mother died when he was born," she said. She took a sip, then another sip, before she continued. "They were poor, but he was an only child, and his father doted on him. The old man scrimped and saved and somehow got the money together to send Osvaldo to school in Belem."

Silva drained the last of his whiskey and held up his glass for a refill.

Amanda saw the gesture and nodded at him from behind the bar.

"Why Belem?" he said.

"In those days, there were no schools here in Azevedo. None at all. Most of the children grew up illiterate, and most of the parents didn't care, because they were illiterate themselves. But Osvaldo's father was different. Like I said, he doted on him."

Amanda arrived with a refill and removed Silva's empty glass. He thanked her with a nod.

"While he was in the capital," Jade continued, nodding at Amanda's retreating back, "he met her. Amanda's folks had left her a small inheritance. They'd owned a hotel them-selves, and she'd worked in the business. Azevedo had no hotel at all, and a little bit of money goes a long way here. They built this place, and they've made a success of it."

"How? I can't believe there are that many visitors."

"There aren't. But a lot of . . . sexual recreation goes on. And, other than in the rainforest, this is the only place to do it. The restaurant, too, is a going concern. And so is this bar. According to Amanda, they're doing well." She turned to Maura. "Where's your luggage?"

"Upstairs."

"Go get it. You're staying with me."

"Jade, I don't think—"

"I need you, Maura. I don't want to be alone right now."

Maura nodded and stood up. When she was gone, Silva leaned closer.

"There's something I'd like to tell you. But if I do, you're going to have to keep it to yourself."

"You mean you don't want me to tell Maura?"

"Or anyone else."

"She's my best friend. She's here on my behalf."

"Nevertheless, if you want to see justice done—"

"Of course I want to see justice done! If it's my discretion that concerns you, why run the risk? Why tell me anything at all?"

"You're going to guide us to the village. I think it's likely you'll witness things there that we'd like to keep to ourselves."

"Why are you so concerned about confidentiality, Chief Inspector?"

"When information leaks out, it warns the guilty. And that makes our work more difficult, because they react by covering their tracks."

"You've already discovered something, haven't you?"

"We have."

"Tell me."

"Not until I have your word."

"You have it. Tell me."

"The slash wounds on the murdered man's neck are closely spaced."

"So what?"

"An intoxicated person wouldn't have had the degree of physical control necessary to strike over and over again in the same place."

"So that means—"

"It means, Senorita Calmon, that your Indian friend was almost certainly innocent."

Chapter Seventeen

"I think I'm gonna be sick." Osvaldo Neto bolted from his chair and headed for the toilet.

"There goes his breakfast," Arnaldo said, studying the hotelkeeper's retreating back. "He must have really tied one on."

"Did I ever tell you," Silva began, "that my father was stationed in Italy during World War Two?"

"You did. Brazilian Expeditionary Force. What's that got to do with Osvaldo?"

Silva took a sip of his coffee. He didn't intend to be hurried. "Does the name Emmet Till mean anything to you?"

"Black kid in America, murdered for talking to a white woman? That one?"

"That one."

"I saw the movie. So what?"

"His father, Louis, was an American soldier."

Arnaldo expelled a sigh that lowered the oxygen level in the Grand's restaurant. "Mario, where are you going with this?"

"Pisa, nineteen forty-five. Louis Till raped and killed an Italian woman. They hanged him for it. My father witnessed the execution and was sick for a week. Watching a hanging, he told me, could do that to a man."

"You think that might be Osvaldo's problem? The hanging and not the cachaça?"

"I wouldn't be surprised."

"So talk to him about something else."

"I'm about to do just that."

Arnaldo put a finger to his lips. "Here he comes."

Osvaldo resumed his seat. He'd brought a paper towel and was using it to blot his mouth. "I didn't quite make it. I suggest you guys avoid the toilet for a while. If you need the facilities, use the ones upstairs. What else do you want to know?"

"Let's talk about the townsfolk," Silva said, "those of them who would most profit if the Indians were out of the way."

Osvaldo leaned forward and lowered his voice. "If Torres wasn't already dead, he would have been one. Now that he is, it leaves five."

"Who are they?"

Osvaldo glanced over his shoulder to make sure they were still alone in the restaurant, then started counting off the Big Five on his fingers.

"Hugo Toledo. He's the mayor. Hugo's old man, Hugo Senior, and Enrique Azevedo, the founder of the town, were friends and partners. Azevedo never married. When he died, Hugo's father bought up his land and then croaked before he had any other kids. Two years later, his wife died, too, and Junior inherited the lot. His Honor can deliver three thousand votes in any election. And that, I'm told, has bought him a piece of the governor and also a piece of a federal *deputado*."

"Only a piece?" Arnaldo asked.

Osvaldo smiled. "What do you expect for three thousand votes? Even *deputados* are worth more than that."

Silva took out his notebook, jotted down Toledo's name, and kept his pen poised over the paper. "Who else?"

Osvaldo extended another finger. "Roberto Lisboa. Lisboa fancies himself a painter. Not houses. Canvases."

"Is he any good?"

Osvaldo lifted his shoulders. "I couldn't say. But I can tell you this much: he's lousy at poker. He's lost thousands to Torres. Nobody knows exactly how many thousands, but some folks say Torres could have taken over Lisboa's place any time he wanted to."

"Damned good reason for Lisboa to kill him," Arnaldo said.

"And not the only one," Osvaldo said. "Lisboa has a foreman, a guy by the name of Toni Pandolfo."

"And?"

"And Torres was running around town telling people he saw Pandolfo buggering his boss."

"Buggering?"

"Yeah, like sticking his dick—"

"I get the idea. When was this?"

"A couple of months ago, and if that story got back to the loving couple, there's no knowing what Pandolfo might have done. He's a hard case. He broke a man's jaw once, right over there, just because the guy laughed about one of Lisboa's pink shirts."

"Okay. Who else?"

Another finger. "José Frade. An absolute pig, but lots of men like him because he's generous when it comes to buying drinks."

"Why did you call him a pig?"

"He beats his wife and he treats his daughters like shit, tells everybody he wanted sons, and blames Sonia for not giving him any. She's a little thing, shy, skittish, and scared to death of him. Frade proposed to her down south somewhere. Porto Alegre, I think. She was an orphan, not even eighteen and all on her own. She accepted him without knowing anything about this place or what she was getting into. But she's miserable here. Not cut out for this life. If she had money, she would have left him long ago. Probably would have left him anyway if she didn't have her girls to worry about."

"How come you know so much about her personal life?"

"She talks to my wife. Matter of fact, Amanda is about the only person she *does* talk to. Like I said, she's shy."

"Did Frade have anything in particular against Torres?"

Osvaldo squirmed in his seat. "Well . . ."

"It's a murder investigation, Osvaldo. You have to tell us."

"All right. But you didn't get it from me."

"Agreed."

"Sonia was having an affair with Torres."

"You know that for a fact?"

"I do."

"How? She told your wife?"

"No. Even *I* didn't tell my wife."

"So how come you know?"

"Out back, there's a door opening on a staircase leading to the second floor. Torres had a key, one he used to get to a room he rented from me by the month. I was up there, one night, changing a light bulb, when I heard footsteps on the stairs. I figured it was Torres, and I knew he wouldn't appreciate me seeing whoever he had with him, so I hid in a closet. But I was . . . well, you know, curious, so I left the door open a crack. And who do I see but Torres and Sonia going into the room together. He had an arm around her shoulder and a hand on one of her tits. There wasn't any doubt in my mind about what they were about to do."

"It surprised you?"

"It surprised me. But you know what? I don't blame Sonia. I question her taste, but I don't blame her. God knows, she has no joy in her marriage."

"You think Frade knows his wife was cheating on him?"

"Not unless he found out recently. What I just told you, that was a couple of months ago."

"But?"

"But if he did, you've got another suspect right there. In this part of the world, men look down on other men who don't defend their honor."

"And defending his honor would have constituted killing Torres?"

"Yeah, and maybe her, too. You see why I kept my mouth shut? Not for Torres. For her."

"Okay. Next?"

Another finger. "Cesar Bonetti. He's from Paraná, another one of those guys who came north to make his fortune. He keeps saying he'll go home once he has. Can you beat it? Going on twenty years in Pará, and he still calls Paraná home."

"He have anything against Torres?"

"Not as far as I know."

"Okay. Anyone else?"

"Just one more. Paulo Cunha, the guy who owns the pharmacy."

"Pharmacy?"

"You're thinking what I'm thinking, right? Looks like the tribe was poisoned, and a pharmacist would know all about poisons."

"A pharmacist would."

"He's also got some other shops, but it's with wood that he made—you'll excuse the expression—a killing."

"Wood?"

"Hardwood. From the rain forest. Around here, they call it 'green gold' 'cause it's worth so goddamned much. You get it to the docks in Belem, you can sell it for upwards of sixteen hundred American dollars a cubic meter."

"Where does Cunha get it from?"

"He *used* to get it from the other guys we've been talking about."

"No more?"

Osvaldo shook his head. "None left. They've cleared their land."

"So now he gets it from . . ."

"Take a guess."

"The reservation?"

"I can't prove it, but—"

"He'd need licenses from the IBAMA to ship it."

"He would. And the IBAMA guy here in town owns two new cars and a sixty-inch television set."

"What's his name?"

"Raul Nonato."

"I think maybe we'll have a little chat with Senhor Nonato."

"Again, you didn't get it from me." Osvaldo had been balling the paper towel in his hand. Now, he used it to wipe his sweating brow. "Listen, guys, I'm not feeling well at the moment, so if you don't mind, I—"

"Sorry," Silva said. "Just a few more quick questions. We're expecting reinforcements. Have you got room to lodge three more?"

Osvaldo shook his head. "Only two vacancies. It would have been one if that reporter hadn't checked out."

"Two are a couple. Can they share?"

"Sure. Are they from down south?"

"They are."

"So it's beds, not hammocks?"

"You offer a choice?"

"Uh-huh. All hotels do in this part of the world. Lots of white folks have never slept on anything else, so I've got hooks in every room. When do they arrive?"

"This afternoon."

"I'll arrange it. Anything else? Really, guys, I gotta go lie down."

"We'll need cars."

"No, you won't. You'll need jeeps. Once you get outside of town, the roads are shit. A vehicle without four-wheel drive is as good as useless.

"Thanks for the tip. Where's the rental agency?"

"That would be me. There are no real rental vehicles in town, but there are folks who own jeeps and are looking to pick up a few extra Reais. I serve as intermediary. Their vehicles may not look good, but they'll run. Tomorrow morning okay?"

"I was hoping we could go out to the Awana's village this afternoon."

"Forget it. You haven't got time to get there and back before dark. And believe me, you do *not* want to get stuck in the rainforest at night."

"How about we visit some of those *fazendas?*" Arnaldo asked. "Start working our way through the list of people we need to talk to?"

"*Some,*" Osvaldo said, "would be too ambitious. You might get in one, no more than that."

"They're that far apart?"

"They are. The holdings are huge and the roads are bad."

Arnaldo muttered something. The days they were likely to spend in Azevedo were adding up.

"Then we'll leave those visits for later," Silva said. "Just as well. We'll be here when our people arrive. Are you free tomorrow? Could you accompany us to the village?"

"To help communicate with the boy?"

"Yes."

"Sure. Glad to."

"And could you arrange for some men to dig for us?"

"You gonna unearth bodies?"

"Yes."

"Have to be guys with strong stomachs." The word stomach seemed to remind Osvaldo of his own. He ran the hand not holding the towel over his abdomen, and was looking more miserable by the moment, but he soldiered on. "How many do you want?"

"Six should do it."

"Consider it done. Now, if you'll excuse me, I really—"

"Just one more," Arnaldo said. He put a hand on Silva's arm. "You got enough people going out to that village with you. You don't need me and Babyface, right?"

"I suppose not. Why?"

Arnaldo turned back Osvaldo. "How many ways are there to get from here to Belem?"

"By road? Only one. And you don't want to drive it unless you have to."

"I'm not thinking of driving it," Arnaldo said. "I'm thinking of blocking it."

Chapter Eighteen

THE TWO FEDERAL COPS dedicated the remainder of the morning and the better part of the afternoon to interviewing the townsfolk. Arnaldo's conversation with Carol Luz, a cashier in Cunha's supermarket, and Silva's with Renato Kassab were conducted with people from opposite ends of the social spectrum, but the information they gleaned—or rather the lack of it—was strikingly similar.

Arnaldo hadn't been talking to Luz for more than five minutes before she began her attack.

"Are you dense, Agent Nunes, or are you trying to irritate me?"

"Neither one, Senhora. It's a simple question. How can you justify a lynching as self-defense?"

The cashier, a blousy woman with black roots in her blonde hair, blew out a breath he could feel on his face. "Because my children could have been next, that's how!"

"Assuming the Indian did it—killed Torres, I mean—what makes you think he'd go after your kids?"

Another breath. She could have benefitted from an oral disinfectant. "*Assuming he did it?* Are you serious? How much proof do you need? Do you know where they found him? What he had in his hand? He was a crazy, murdering savage. He was running around town with a knife the size of a stallion's dick. Would you have taken a risk like that if it was *your* kids? What kind of a father are you?"

"You don't like Indians, do you?"

"Oho. Well, a question like that shows where *you*

stand, doesn't it? Around here, we've got a name for people like you."

"I don't want to hear it. And I'd appreciate it if you'd stop doing that."

"Doing what?"

"Turning the conversation around. I don't want to talk about me. I'm here to talk about what *you* saw, what *you* heard, what *you* think."

A third exasperated breath. Arnaldo almost raised a hand and waved it in front of his nose, but caught himself before he did.

"What I think?" she said, and then repeated, "What I think? I think you should drop this stupid investigation of yours, go back to wherever you came from, and leave us alone. Whatever you say, those masked men, whoever they were, did this town a favor."

"*Whoever they were*, eh?"

"You heard me. And there's nothing you can say that will ever make me change my mind about that."

"You watched the lynching from the time they hustled him out of the front door of the *delegacia* until the time he was swinging from a tree, and yet you can stand there and tell me you didn't recognize a single one of the perpetrators?"

"I can, and I just did."

"And I still find it hard to believe."

"Too bad. You've got my answer."

"This is a small town, the kind of a place where everybody knows everybody else—"

"It *is* a small town. We *do* know each other. And we stick together." She crossed her forefinger with her middle finger and held them up scant centimeters from his face. "Like that."

"All the time?"

"When it comes to outsiders like you, and that FUNAI woman, yes."

"What do you have against the FUNAI woman?"

She threw up her hands and expelled another one of those pungent breaths of hers. "I've said all I'm going to say."

And it was. He couldn't get another word out of her.

BACK WHEN Silva was a two-pack-a-day man, cigarette smoke never bothered him, and he couldn't understand why nonsmokers objected to it. For a year after he quit, people used to ask him if he minded when they smoked in his company. He'd always told them he didn't.

These days, he did. He wanted, however, to put Renato Kassab at his ease, so he didn't utter a word of protest when the lawyer ignited his second unfiltered *Caballero* in the space of fifteen minutes.

"It's my understanding," he said, rubbing his irritated eyes and hoping that Kassab would notice, "that Jade was here, talking to you, when they broke into Amati's cell."

"Indeed she was," Kassab said, ignoring or oblivious to the eye rubbing. "I heard a gunshot. Later, I discovered it was Delegado Borges, firing his shotgun into the air to dissuade them. Unfortunately, it did little good."

"*No good at all* might be a better way to put it."

"Quite right, Chief Inspector. I stand corrected."

"Before you spoke to Jade, you went outside and talked to the people who'd followed her down the street. Is that correct?"

"It is."

"And you managed to convince them to disperse."

"I did."

"What did you say to them?"

"I don't recall."

"I see."

What Silva saw was that Kassab was lying, but there wasn't a chance in hell he'd admit it. He let it drop. "There seems to be a consensus that the Indian killed Omar Torres," he said.

"Do you doubt it?"

"I do."

"Why?"

"We have forensic evidence to the contrary."

"Do you mind sharing it?"

"It would be a bit premature at the moment. As a lawyer, I'm sure you understand."

"Perfectly. But it's a revelation. We've all been operating under the assumption that the Indian was guilty."

If Silva had been interrogating a criminal, he would have pounced upon the words 'all' and 'operating,' both indicators, in his opinion, of collusion. Instead he said, "What did Jade do when she heard the shot?"

"Took off as if the devil was after her."

"Did you follow her?"

"No."

"Were you close to the murdered man?"

"Torres? I knew him. We weren't close. I thought he was a brute, a womanizer, and a braggart. I won't miss him."

"A brute, a womanizer, and a braggart—and yet the whole town stepped up to avenge him?"

Kassab picked a fragment of tobacco off his tongue with the tips of his thumb and forefinger. "They were acting out of a conditioned response as much as anything else. This is a frontier community. The people of Azevedo have been defending themselves against Indians ever since the town was built."

"So there have been cases, in the past, where the Indians have proven themselves to be a threat?"

"Look at any history book."

"I'm not talking, Senhor Kassab, about incidents out of history books. I'm talking about instances here in Azevedo."

"Well . . . no. Not that I recall."

"But it is true, is it not, that certain townsfolk have had their eye on the Indian's land? They'd like to have the reservation declassified and sold off?"

"Yes. There's a certain . . . conflict of interest between the Indians and the townsfolk. I admit that."

"And where do you stand on that issue?"

"I'm a citizen of this town, Chief Inspector. I make my living here. These people are my friends and my neighbors, my colleagues and my clients. You could hardly expect me to take a position against them. But I don't want you thinking, even for a moment, that I'm a racist or a bigot. I don't believe, as some do, that Indians are dirty or diseased." He waved his forefinger. "That said, it's undeniable that they stand in the way of progress. Look at a map, Chief Inspector. Look at a map."

"I'm afraid I don't follow you."

Kassab ground out his cigarette into an overflowing ashtray, swiveled his chair around and opened the drawer of a credenza. He took out a topographical map protected by a transparent plastic envelope and put it on the table.

"This is the reservation," he said, stabbing a finger at an area hatched in red. "This here"—he ran the same finger along an irregular black line—"is the Jagunami River. It's the border. Private land on this side, and the reservation on the other."

"Except for here," Silva said, putting his own forefinger on the map. "Why is that?"

"Historical precedent," the lawyer said. "That used to be the founder's land, and he built a bridge. Out of consideration for what he'd done in colonizing the region, the government let him keep it, that part of the land *and* the bridge. These days, it all belongs to the mayor. His father doubled the size of his *fazenda* by buying this whole area here"—Kassab circumscribed it with his forefinger—"from Azevedo's heirs."

Silva continued to study the map. "Cunha's piece looks rather small in camparison to the others."

"Cunha is more of a businessman than he is a *fazendeiro*. He owns the pharmacy, the supermarket, and a few other establishments."

"Does the reservation border on any land *not* owned by a citizen of Azevedo? Any public land?"

"Only on the far side."

"Who are the others with property adjoining the reservation?"

"Roberto Lisboa, José Frade, and Cesar Bonetti." Kassab pointed out the properties, one by one. "And this one belonged to Omar Torres."

Silva leaned forward for a closer look. "So, on the side of the town, the sole access to the reservation is through the property of the men you've just mentioned."

"At the moment, yes. If, however, a road were to be cut around this way—" Kassab traced a great circle around Lisboa's *fazenda*, the one situated farthest from the town.

"But that road doesn't exist, does it?" Silva leaned back in his chair.

"No," Kassab said.

"Nor would there be any reason to cut it if the declassification were to occur sometime soon."

"True. And if you're implying our great landowners would benefit from a declassification of the reservation—"

"I am."

"—then you'd be right. But indirectly, it would benefit almost everyone else in this town as well."

"A rising tide floats all ships, eh?"

"I couldn't have put it better myself."

Chapter Nineteen

Silva looked up when he heard an aircraft heading toward the airport. It prompted him to return to the Grand, where Osvaldo greeted them with a thumbs-up. He looked much improved from their conversation earlier in the day.

"I heard it, too," he said. "I expect it's the people you were waiting for."

"I hope so. Seen my colleague?"

"He's in the bar, came in about fifteen minutes ago. He got stonewalled. He isn't happy."

"Neither am I," Silva said.

"If it helps, I can give you a list of people I saw at the lynching."

"It won't. They'll all give me a list of people who'll swear they were somewhere else. We all set up for tomorrow?"

"I got the jeeps, and I recruited six guys to dig. They've got their own tools and their own truck."

"Truck?"

"With four-wheel drive. You're going to need it to bring the bodies back."

"So we are. Good thinking."

"They'll be here at eight."

Silva gave the new arrivals half an hour to freshen up. Then he briefed them and handed out assignments. First, he addressed Gilda Caropreso, their medical examiner and Hector's fiancée. "Gilda?"

"Senhor?"

"Go examine the bodies. Pay particular attention to the wounds in the *fazendeiro*'s neck. We'll talk about them later."

"I'll go get my kit. Where are they?"

"Doctor Pinto's office. Out the door and to the right. It's a short walk."

"This side of the street?"

"This side of the street. And be prepared for what you're going to see. The Indian was suspended."

"Yes," she said. "I gathered that from what our taxi driver told us."

"Same one we had, no doubt. I'm told there's only one in town. Hector?"

"Senhor?"

"Early this morning, I sent prints, nail scrapings, clothing, and what's reputed to be the murder weapon to São Paulo. Call Lefkowitz, and stress that I want a quick turnaround."

Lefkowitz, Hector's top forensic person, was the best in the business. Silva employed his services whenever he could.

"Will do."

"I suppose your pilot has already left?"

"He's been here before—and couldn't wait to get away. Why?"

"There's no air courier service. Any future lab work will have to go by charter."

"It'll cost a bundle. Sampaio will have a fit."

The Director of the Federal Police would not have been pleased to see the expressions the mention of his name elicited.

"Fuck him," Arnaldo said.

"My sentiments exactly," Silva said. He turned to Gonçalves, the third and last of the São Paulo team. "Haraldo?"

"Senhor?"

"You get the plum job, an assignment you're going to like.

A journalist from São Paulo, name of Maura Mandel, is staying with Jade Calmon, the FUNAI agent."

"Attractive?"

"They both are. That's why you're going to like it. The woman at the reception desk will know where Jade lives. I want to get our signals straight for tomorrow morning. Go over there and invite them both to dinner."

"My pleasure."

"Let's go, people. The sooner we get this cleared up, the sooner we'll be out of this hellhole."

"Amen to that," Arnaldo said.

BY THE time they sat down to eat, Gonçalves, the Federal Police's lothario, had already made inroads with Maura and had spirited her away to a table in a far corner of the restaurant. They had their heads together and were conversing in low tones. Jade was left with Gilda and the cops.

"Babyface works fast," Arnaldo said.

"Babyface?" Jade said.

"That's what we call him, but never to his baby face. It gets his nose out of joint."

"Well, I can see why you would. He doesn't look to be more than—"

"Exactly," Arnaldo said.

"How old is he, anyway? Twenty-two? Twenty-three?"

"Well into his thirties."

She looked at Gonçalves with renewed interest.

"Really?"

"Really."

Jade looked perplexed. "What's with the 'working fast' bit? Somewhat of a charmer, is he?"

"You have no idea," Arnaldo said. "Many are the households in which the caring parents of pining young women are careful never to mention any last name beginning with the letter G for fear of eliciting a hysterical outburst."

"They're well matched then."

"A charmer herself, is she?" Silva asked.

"You have no idea. Many are the bars where sad young men spend their nights drinking to forget her. The development of this relationship should be interesting."

"A battle of champions? The seductress seduced?"

"Or vice versa." She looked around to make sure they weren't being heard, lowered her voice, and leaned across the table to Gilda. "On a more serious note, did you . . ."

"Examine the bodies? Yes, I did. Why don't we talk about it tomorrow on the way to the village?"

"Couldn't you at least tell me one thing tonight?"

"All right. If I can. What is it?"

"Do you agree with the Chief Inspector?"

"About the Indian being innocent?"

"Yes."

"I do." She looked at Silva. "You were right to draw my attention to the wounds. They were delivered by someone at least as tall as Torres was, probably taller."

"And the Indian was a shorter man. Good. Anything else?"

"They were laid on, one on top of the other. If the Indian was drunk, as they say he was, they would have been all over the place."

"Yes, I spotted that one."

"The killer was right-handed."

"I spotted that, too. Anything else?"

"The wounds were deep, deep enough in one instance to sever one of the vertebrae. Only a man, or a stronger-than-average woman, could have inflicted them. And the fingernail scrapings, the ones you've sent off for analysis, are unlikely to be of any help."

"Why?"

"The wounds were all on one side of Torres's body, which wouldn't have been the case if he'd been able to turn around. There were none on his hands, or on his forearms, as there would have been if he was facing his assailant and trying to defend himself. I doubt that he saw the person who killed him. If there's anything under those nails, it's unlikely to be from the killer, unless they had an altercation earlier in the evening."

"Good work, Gilda. How about the Indian?"

"That conversation," she said, "I really would prefer to leave for tomorrow."

Chapter Twenty

ARNALDO PICKED UP THE butter dish and sniffed. "Rancid again."

"It's actually a flavoring agent. Because of the heat around here, people got used to the taste of rancid butter, and that's the way they prefer it," Silva said. "And by the way, they get it out of a can."

"I hate Pará."

"Stop bitching and try the fruit."

It was fuzzy and brown and about the size of a mango. Silva cut into his and used his fork to pop white pulp into his mouth. Arnaldo studied him for a reaction.

"Well?"

"Kind of a cross between a banana and a pear. It's not bad."

"Not good either, I'll bet. I'll pass. Heads up. The ladies just came in."

Silva turned to see Amanda and Maura approaching their table. The journalist, in a long sleeve shirt and cargo pants tucked into hiking boots, was dressed for the bush.

"Uh-oh," Arnaldo said. "You didn't tell her last night?"

Silva shook his head. "It would have ruined dinner."

He stood up. "Good morning. Senhorita Mandel, won't you join us for breakfast at least?"

"What do you mean by, *at least?*" Maura asked, suspiciously.

"You won't be accompanying us to the village."

"Oh, yes, I will."

"Oh, no, you won't."

"Why not? Don't you think the public has a right to be informed about what's going on?"

"Not when it might hinder an investigation."

"I'll keep it all off the record, won't write a word until you tell me I can publish it."

"Sorry, the answer is still no."

"I don't think you're sorry at all. And I'm certain your boss wouldn't agree."

Silva bristled. "My *boss*, Senhorita Mandel, is obsessed with seeing his name in the newspapers, which is something that interests me not at all. My obsession is apprehending criminals."

"Is that for publication?"

"No, it is not."

"Then it's my turn to be sorry, Chief Inspector. I don't like playing the game this way, but you leave me no choice. If you don't agree to bring me along, I'm going to call Sampaio and quote you."

"It is I, Senhorita Mandel, who might be said to be quoting you."

"What? What are you talking about?"

"What was the term you used back in Belem? Publicity whore? Yes, that was it. Publicity whore."

"Are you threatening to squeal to him about something I said to you in confidence?"

"Are you?"

TEN MINUTES later, a fuming Maura Mandel, her arms akimbo, stood in the doorway of the Grand Hotel and watched the caravan prepare for departure.

Gilda got into the rear of the lead jeep, next to Hector. Silva sat in front. Jade, after casting an apologetic backward glance at her angry friend, took the wheel. And then they were off.

About five kilometers beyond the outskirts of the town, they branched off onto an unmarked and narrow road and crossed a bridge.

"That's the Jagunami," Jade said, pointing down at the sluggish brown water. "In most places, it's the border of the reservation."

"But not here?" Silva said.

"Not here. Enrique Azevedo, the founder of the town, staked out this land. In deference to him, and what he'd done for the region, the people drawing the reservation's boundaries allowed him to keep it. He built the bridge. His house is over there, among those trees to the east."

Silva squinted against the light. "It looks abandoned," he said.

"It is. Azevedo's heirs sold out to Hugo Toledo, the mayor's father. Toledo had his own house, and it was bigger than that one, so he left Azevedo's to rot."

"So why is this road in such good condition?"

"It was graded, leveled, and extended by a gang of loggers. Until Davi Fromes put a stop to it, they were running heavy trucks into and out of the reservation."

"Who is Davi Fromes?"

"The former IBAMA agent, now retired. He would have as soon shot himself in the foot as kill a tree. Gilda?"

"Yes?"

"I'm going to have to arrange for Amati's burial. There isn't anyone else to do it. Are you finished with . . ."

"Studying his corpse? Yes, I am. You can take him whenever you like."

"I'll make the arrangements for tomorrow then. I think the most appropriate place to lay him to rest would be next to his family and the other members of his tribe. I'm sure it's what he would have liked."

"You wouldn't consider cremation?"

"Cremation? No. The Awana don't cremate. Why?"

"Well . . . you saw the hanging, didn't you?"

"No," Jade said. "When they started hoisting him up, I turned my back. I didn't want to see him die."

Gilda wanted to make sure: "And you never once laid eyes on him after he was dead?"

She shook her head. "I preferred to remember him alive."

"Quite right. And that's the way his son should remember him as well. Not like he is now."

"What if Raoni insists? It's his father, after all."

"Refuse."

"Couldn't you—"

"Do something cosmetic? Make his father look presentable? That's what you're asking?"

Jade nodded.

"No, I can't. Nobody can."

"Why not?"

"He was suspended."

"Can you explain the significance of that without getting into grisly details?"

"No."

"All right then. Explain it anyway."

Gilda looked out at the monotonous wall of vegetation hemming them in, no flowers, no animals, nothing but green. After a while, she said, "You're sure you want to hear it?"

"I don't *want* to hear it. I think it's my duty to hear it. I need to know what I'm dealing with."

"Very well." Gilda leaned back in her seat and switched to didactic mode. "What it comes down to is this: there are three ways to hang someone." She counted them off on her fingers. "The long drop, the short drop, and suspension. The short drop is the traditional method. You stand the victim on a chair, or a cart, put a rope around his neck and remove whatever is under him. For hundreds of years, that was the most common method. Back in the day, hangings were public, and killing someone was a spectacle. It was entertainment. Have you ever been in London?"

"London? As in London, England?"

Gilda nodded.

"Once. Why?"

"Did you see that big Marble Arch near Hyde Park?"

"Yes."

"Not far away was the Tyburn Tree, the public gallows. They hung people there for over two hundred years. A crowd of thirty thousand wasn't uncommon. They put up stands, charged admission. People came from all over the continent to watch. The English were regarded as Europe's greatest hangmen, and to watch them at work was considered an educational experience."

"*Educational?*"

"It was a different time. The values were different. The hangmen were celebrities. But then, as refinement grew, they decided to transfer the executions beyond prison walls."

"A step forward at least."

"Yes, but one that created problems. Hanging people in front of just a few witnesses, it turned out, was harder on the warders and jailers. Without the crowds to cheer them on, they started having psychological problems. They quit by the score. The turnover became too great. Something had to be done. By then, it was the scientific age, so they studied the problem scientifically. The solution they came up with was the long drop. At the time, they viewed it as a great leap forward."

"Why?"

"Because it was considered more humane."

"*Humane?*"

"Not for the victims. For the wardens and jailers."

"So what is it? What's a long drop?"

"You stand the condemned person on a trap door, open it, and let them fall between one and three meters before they're brought up short by a pre-stretched rope. The distance, in each case, is calculated on the basis of tables that take into account body weight, bone structure, and the thickness of the victim's neck. Most of the time, it works. Sometimes, it doesn't. If the drop is too long, it decapitates the victim. If it's too short, it's no different from the short drop. But if it's done right, it snaps at least two cervical vertebrae, which causes instant paralysis, immobilization, and in most cases, unconsciousness. The victim still dies of asphyxia, but with less suffering, and without the . . . physical manifestations that display in the other two systems."

"And suspension?"

"You put a rope around the victim's neck and hoist him up. The English excelled at that, too. In their Royal Navy, they'd execute mutineers by running a rope through a pulley attached to a yardarm. One end went around the victim's neck, and the other was given to sailors who'd haul away. The suspended man kicks, and jerks, and thrashes, and chokes to death. It can take twenty minutes, sometimes even more, to kill him. Meanwhile, he turns blue, the capillaries in his eyes and face burst, his tongue protrudes—"

"And that's the sort of thing you saw when you examined Amati's body?"

"Yes. It's just about the most horrible way to go that there is. You do *not* want that kid to see what they did to his father."

TWO HOURS of potholes, ruts, heat, and flies took them to the end of the road. The space, once sufficient to turn a truck, had been reclaimed by the jungle, so the diggers set to work with axes and machetes to clear away the undergrowth. It took over an hour.

When it was done, and the vehicles had been positioned for the return to Azevedo, Gilda gathered the members of the expedition around her. "You're all aware," she said, "that we might be dealing with a mass poisoning. And if it *was* poison that killed the Awana, that same poison could kill us, so we have to approach the village with extreme caution."

When she said 'kill us,' the diggers started looking at each other. She had the distinct impression they hadn't considered what they were getting themselves into.

"To that end," she continued, "I'd like to say a few words about poisons in general." She had their full attention now. They were hanging on her every word. "The most dangerous are the so-called nerve agents developed by the Germans in the years just prior to the Second World War. Sarin is one you might have heard of. Sarin is absorbed through the skin. Think of it as insecticide for humans. It's estimated to be five hundred times more toxic than cyanide. If you start to get a runny nose, feel any tightness in your chest, have trouble breathing, or experience nausea, come to me immediately."

She held up a syringe with a plastic cap over the needle. "This is atropine. It's an antidote, but it has to be administered quickly. And by quickly, I mean *very* quickly—no more than one minute after sensing the symptoms."

"Jesus," one of the diggers said.

"Now the good news: I doubt very much that we're dealing with a nerve agent. If we were, it almost certainly would have killed Amati, his son, Raoni, and Jade, all of whom were in the village after the disaster."

Another digger, a wiry little man with weathered skin and

a wart next to his right nostril, held up a hand. "So what do you figure it was?"

"I have no idea. I'm no expert. If I had to guess, I'd say it was something they ingested, something without a disagreeable taste or smell. That rules out a lot of options. Strychnine, for example, is very bitter, so it's unlikely to be that. And it would have been fast-acting, because no one had time to take to their beds. Heavy metals, like arsenic, act too slowly to drop people in their tracks, so those, too, we can rule out."

"How about some kind of gas?" Jade said.

"Unlikely," Gilda said. "Gas is tricky to control. It disperses. It can't move upwind. If they'd used gas, there would have been survivors."

"But we shouldn't rule it out? Is that what you're saying?"

"It would be premature to rule anything out, and that brings me to my next point. Gases leave residues; contact poisons can kill for weeks. Don't touch anything in that village with ungloved hands."

She put the syringe into the canvas bag slung across her shoulder, fished out a box of surgical gloves, and held them up for all to see.

"I have plenty. Put on a pair before you enter the village. If one rips, come to me and get a replacement." She put the box back in the bag. "I guess that's all. Any questions?"

Jade and the cops shook their heads. The diggers drew apart from the group and started talking to each other in low voices. The others waited. After a while, the group of men seemed to come to some kind of conclusion. The guy with the wart stepped forward as their spokesman.

"Our price just went up," he said.

Chapter Twenty-One

MAURA WAS FURIOUS. FOR all of about a minute after the caravan left, she considered packing her bag and going home. But then, in her mind's eye, she saw herself marching into the office of Mauricio Carvalho, her editor, and telling him she'd come back without a story. He'd never let her forget it. And he'd go ballistic when she turned in her expenses with nothing to show for them.

No. That option was off the table. She had to stay, and she had to come up with a story. But how could she do that if the damned Federal Police wouldn't collaborate? Racking her brain for a solution, she went to the bar, sat down, and ordered a *café com leche*.

"First time?" Amanda asked, putting a little glass on the bar in front of her.

"Huh?" Maura said, still distracted.

"First trip to Pará, I mean."

"Second," Maura said, focusing on the twin spouts pouring white milk and black coffee.

"And that first time, was it business or pleasure?"

There were no other customers in the bar. Amanda was fishing for a chat. Maura, having nothing better to do, elected to indulge her.

"Business," she said. "Want to join me?"

"Glad to. It's not like I'm overwhelmed at the moment." She fetched another glass.

"My first time," Maura said, as Amanda settled into a high

stool she kept behind the bar, "was when I did a story about Serra Pelada."

Amanda studied her with a critical eye. "You don't look a day over twenty-five."

"Thirty-one."

"No kidding?"

"No kidding."

"Like that young cop. He doesn't look his age either."

"If he doesn't look it, how do you know it?"

"I heard one of the other cops referring to him as Babyface."

"So you asked?"

"Yep. Apparently, they never call him that to his face. He hates it. Anyway, I'm thinking the two of you would be a good match. You could grow old, looking young, together."

Maura smiled. She worried, sometimes, about being in her third decade and still unmarried. A comment like Amanda's was balm for her soul. But work came first, and one never knew when chatting with one of the locals might lead to something. So she pursued it.

"The story wasn't about the mine in its heyday," she said. "It was about what happened to the town after the gold ran out."

It had all been Mauricio's idea, but Maura had won the prize—a "first in category" for ecological reporting. She'd always be grateful to him for that. She proudly displayed the little gold-plated statuette on her bookcase at home (fearing that someone would steal it if she left it in her office) and regarded the distinction as her greatest professional achievement.

Serra Pelada, Bald Mountain, had once been the site of the world's largest open-pit gold mine. From 1979, when a child swimming in a local river had found a six-gram nugget, until 1986, when it closed, an estimated three hundred and sixty tons of the yellow metal had been wrested from the ground—all but forty-four and a half tons of it "extra officially."

Brazilian law requires prospected gold to be sold to the government at slightly under market price and the income to be taxed. Most small-scale operators, anxious to avoid that tax, declare as little of it as possible. Back then, Serra Pelada was composed *exclusively* of small-scale operators, almost one hundred thousand of them, all working tiny claims of just two by three meters, all moving the earth by hand.

The gold rush spawned a town of "stores and whores" where water sold for the equivalent of nine American dollars a liter, thousands of teenage girls sold their bodies for flakes of gold, and as many as eighty murders occurred every month.

The activities in the great pit had been immortalized in the brilliant black and white photographs of Sebastião Salgado, images that had become famous all over the world, but most of what he'd seen and shot was long gone by the time Maura arrived. She found a sleepy little town, where a few prospectors hung on in the hope of a strike. The huge hole, where once the mine had been, had become a lake.

". . . without a fish or any other living creature in it," she summed it up to Amanda, "and the water poisonous as hell."

"Why poisonous?"

"Mercury. The miners used tons of the stuff."

"For what?"

"Purification. If you bring mercury into contact with gold, the mercury draws it in."

"Okay, it draws it in. But then how do you get rid of it?"

"You boil it off."

"Boil it? Like water?"

"Like water, but with one critical difference: it's toxic. It gets into the atmosphere. When it condenses, which it soon does, it gets into the ground and, worst of all, into the rivers. The rivers carry it to the sea. And in the rivers, and in the sea, it gets into the fish. And people eat those fish."

"It should be illegal."

"It already is, and none of the big operators do it anymore, but almost all the small ones do. Some people think a gold strike is a blessing, but I'm here to tell you, Amanda, you can consider yourself lucky there's no gold around here."

"I'm not so sure about that," Amanda said, swirling the remainder of her beverage.

"No?"

"No." She drained her glass, put it on the bar and leaned closer. "Let me tell you a little story."

SILVA FOUND their hike through the rainforest more difficult than he'd expected. There was no real path. The GPS guided them in a straight line, but they often had to detour around towering trees or thick clumps of undergrowth. The heat was oppressive, and the humidity worse, but it was the flies, most of all, that made the journey sheer hell.

The repellent Jade had given them proved to be effective for only as long as it took to sweat it away, and while they were smearing on more, flies settled onto every bit of exposed skin. A slap from a single hand could kill as many as half a dozen at once, but it didn't dissuade the others. They kept coming.

What with the slapping, the cursing, and the birds and monkeys expressing their resentment at being disturbed, the expedition's progress had been anything but silent. They were not surprised, therefore, to find Amati's son waiting for them, bow and arrow at the ready.

He stood in a clearing surrounded by huts, each of a

different size, but similar in construction, rooftops slanting up to a sharp apex, vertical walls fashioned of reeds dried by the sun to a uniform gray.

Raoni scanned each new face as it appeared from the forest. That his father's wasn't among them visibly disappointed him, but when Jade held up a hand and waved, he lowered his weapon.

"Don't dig," Jade instructed the others. "Don't do anything at all until I tell you to."

She walked to one of the huts, dropped to her hands and knees to crawl through the low opening, and beckoned to the boy to follow. After a moment's hesitation, he did.

"She's going to need me," Osvaldo said. And he entered as well. The others kept silent and waited.

After about a minute they heard a sound reminiscent of the cry of some small, wounded animal, not like the little boy's voice at all. But it was.

About five minutes later, Jade left the hut with tears running down her face. "This way," she said and led them to the graves.

Chapter Twenty-Two

"THERE WAS THIS OLD coot who used to prospect around here," Amanda Neto said. "Welinton was his name, Welinton Mendes. He kept finding little pieces of gold, enough to keep him in food and cachaça, but no more than that. Folks laughed when he'd go on and on about finding the mother lode, and go on and on he did, every single time he got drunk, which when he could afford it, was every Saturday night. After a while, some of the men folk started buying him drinks just so they could tell him he was crazy and watch him get riled up."

"Sounds like there isn't a hell of a lot to do around here on Saturday nights," Maura said.

"You've got that right. But most of them were drunk themselves, and drunks find just about anything interesting. Anyway, one night he came in and slapped down a hundred-and-two-gram nugget right here." She stabbed a finger at the bar in front of her.

"How did you know it was a hundred and two grams?"

"He told Osvaldo that if he'd buy it for cash, he'd order drinks for the house. Osvaldo jumped at the deal and sent me to fetch my scale out of the kitchen. I argued with him, said he didn't know a damned thing about gold, couldn't possibly have any idea about how pure it was or even if it was gold at all, but he kept telling me to let him handle it. So I did. In the end, he wound up offering old Welinton three thousand Reais for it. At the time I thought it was a foolish thing to do, but Osvaldo had been drinking himself. There was no talking him out of it."

"And was it? Foolish?"

"On the contrary. The nugget was worth three times that. Welinton knew it, too, but he laughed and said he didn't give a damn. He wanted to celebrate, and there was a lot more gold where that came from."

"Were there many people here that night?"

"The place was packed. And when word got around that the drinks were on Welinton, it turned into the best night we ever had. We went through our whole stock of imported whiskey and our only bottle of French cognac. Every time somebody would order cachaça or a beer, Welinton would tell them to order something better. Our Italian wine, our French champagne, we sold it all, the best of the best, and every drop of it on Welinton's tab. Nobody who was here is ever going to forget it. They all got good and drunk, including my husband."

"And including Welinton?"

"Especially Welinton. Then, around ten, he said he was going to share some of his good fortune with Crazy Ana, and he stumbled out the door."

"Who's Crazy Ana?"

"A whore, and she must be a good one."

Amanda smiled, but Maura, curious, didn't return it. "Why do you say that?"

Amanda waved a hand, palm upward, as if the answer was obvious. "I say it because she manages to make a living at it, which couldn't be easy in a town where so many women are giving it away for free."

Maura nodded. "Ah," she said. "I see."

"But you never heard me say that."

"No. Of course I didn't. So then?"

"So then, the next morning, people started looking for Welinton high and low. All of a sudden he'd become a popular guy, like someone who'd struck it big in the lottery. They'd heard him say there was more gold where that nugget had come from, and they were all hoping he'd repeat his performance of the night before. Not that he could have, mind you. It took us five days to get more of the good stuff shipped to us from Belem. In the interim, all we had to serve was beer and cachaça. As for Welinton, the consensus was that he'd gone back to his strike to fetch more gold."

"How long did it take before he showed up?"

"He never did."

"Disappeared?"

"Without a trace. Nobody has seen him from that day down to this."

"Did he make it as far as Crazy Ana's?"

"He did. People asked her, of course. She swore he left around midnight."

"Is she still in town?"

Amanda nodded. "Still doing business at the same address. You think there's a story in it for you?"

"Maybe. It wouldn't hurt to talk to her, right?"

"Right." Amanda looked at her watch. "And this would be a good time."

"Why?"

"She'll be alone. The women in this town won't associate with her, and the men folk don't like to be seen paying her a visit. They go after dark."

CRAZY ANA was a surprise.

She turned out to be a matronly type, conservatively dressed and running to fat.

When she opened her door and found Maura standing

there, her smile of welcome faded. "I don't do women," she said, her tone far from friendly.

"I'm not here for that." Maura handed her a card. "I'm a journalist. I want to talk to you about Welinton Mendes."

Ana took the card and looked at it. "I charge for my time, Senhora Mandel."

"It's Senhorita. How much?"

"A hundred Reais. In advance. It will buy you an hour."

"I don't think I'll need an hour."

"It's still a hundred Reais."

"All right. A hundred Reais."

Ana stepped aside. Her front door opened into a tiny parlor that smelled of floor wax and, faintly, of lavender. It was cozy and immaculately clean.

"Tea or coffee?" she asked, as any other hostess might have done.

"Coffee."

"I've got some fresh. Make yourself comfortable. I'll be right back."

While she was gone, Maura put two fifty Real notes on the coffee table. When she returned, Ana put the tray on top. A rather elegant way, Maura thought, to get them out of sight.

"Why crazy?" she said. "You don't strike me as crazy in the least."

Ana sat on the couch next to Maura and started to pour the coffee. "Sugar?" she asked.

"Two," Maura said. "And no milk."

Ana handed her a cup before she answered. "Because I *was* crazy. Something bad happened to me."

"But now you're better?"

Ana sipped at her coffee and put down the cup. "Not the way I was before," she said. "But better."

"Want to tell me about it?"

She shrugged. "The whole damned town knows the story. So why not you? My husband worked for Paulo Cunha—"

"Cunha? Didn't I see that name on the supermarket?"

"You did. You can also see it on the pharmacy, the hardware store, and a lumber business. He also owns a lot of buildings. Not this one. I wouldn't live in any building owned by Paulo Cunha. Back then we did, though. My husband managed his ranch, and we lived in a nice little house on the property. Cunha charged us rent, and we had to buy everything we needed in his store, so we never managed to put any money aside."

"So he had your services for free?"

"He did."

"That's terrible."

"No, *querida*, it wasn't terrible at all. Terrible is what came next." She took a sip of her coffee and stared at the wall, remembering. "It was the day before Christmas. Everybody was celebrating. Cunha told my husband to take the truck, go into town and pick up a case of whiskey. I asked if I could go along. Cunha agreed. We decided to take the kids. At Christmas, some people put up colored lights, and we thought the girls would like to see them. And then . . ."

She fell silent. It went on for so long, Maura felt she had to prompt her.

"And then?"

"About halfway there, on a deserted part of the road, another car came around a curve and headed straight at us. He was on our side, and he was speeding. My husband swerved into a tree. He died in the crash. So did my two daughters. They were four and five."

"No!"

Ana nodded.

"And the other driver?"

"Kept going."

"Was he drunk?"

"He was the mayor's brother-in-law, driving one of the mayor's cars. He'd come up from Curitiba for a Christmas visit. He swore, on oath, he hadn't been drunk at the time of the accident, but that the steering and the brakes had given out on him at the same time. He couldn't get out of the way, and he couldn't stop, so he had to keep going."

"Both sets of brakes? The foot brake *and* the hand brake?"

"Pretty thin, isn't it? He went on to say that, when the car lost forward momentum, he was some distance away and the road was deserted. It took him some time to find a telephone. When he did, he called both an ambulance and the mayor. The mayor backed him up. Said he was stone-cold sober, but that they stopped off at his place before they went back to the scene of the accident."

"Where he insisted that his brother-in-law have a few drinks to fortify himself?"

"'Calm him down' was the term he used."

"How about the car?" Maura asked in disbelief. She was still trying to absorb the extent of the tragedy. "Wasn't it ever examined?"

"Oh, it was," Ana said sadly. "But the mayor is the mayor, so the mechanic backed him up."

"The bastard!" Indignation dripped from Maura's voice, but the reaction she got surprised her. Ana laughed, actually laughed.

"You have no idea what it means to be poor in Pará, do you? Or what it means to be rich?"

"No. But I can tell you one thing: it isn't only Pará."

"Yes, it's all over Brazil. I know."

"Not only Brazil. All over the world. There was a young man once, a *wealthy* young man, in the United States. He got drunk and caused an accident that resulted in the death of a young woman. But his brother had been the president, another brother their minister of justice, and he was a senator, so he wound up being sentenced to two months in jail, but the sentence was suspended, so he never spent a day behind bars. He kept getting re-elected, too, year after year, for the next forty years."

"In the United States? That's hard to believe."

"It happened. People forget. What about the man who killed your husband and daughters? What became of him?"

"Nothing. No charges were ever made. He went home a week later. He still comes every year for Christmas, and I see him on the street, but he doesn't recognize me. I . . . I look different now."

"Look, I don't mean to pry, but—"

"I know what you're going to ask, and I'm about to tell you. My parents were dead. I have no brothers or sisters. My husband and his family never got along, and they'd dropped us out of their lives. I had no job and no money. Julio and our girls weren't in their graves for a week when Cunha told me he needed our house for his new manager."

"Cunha threw you out? Just like that?"

She laughed a bitter laugh. "No, *querida*, not *just like that*. There were no honest jobs for single women in this town, and I had no other place to stay, no money, no food. But I was pretty good-looking back then—"

"You're pretty good-looking now."

"It's kind of you to say so, but I know I'm not. I was never a great beauty, and it's only been eight years, but they've been hard years."

"So you turned to . . . entertaining men?"

"Not right away. That came later. Back then, it was just a proposition from Cunha."

"To sleep with him?"

"Not to *sleep* with him. Just to fuck him. He made it clear from the outset that he'd never be spending the night. He has a wife, and she's a real bitch. She would have cut off his balls if she'd found out."

"And in exchange for that—"

"I could stay in the house, and he'd feed me. And he did. For as long as it took him to get tired of me."

"How long was that?"

"Three weeks."

"*Three weeks?*"

She nodded. "I was lousy company. I cried a lot. He didn't like that, said I'd goddamned well better stop, or I'd be history. But I couldn't. So I *was* history."

"And then?"

She shrugged. "I went from man to man until all the ones with money got tired of me, too. I went from wife, to mistress, to everybody's whore in about six months. But by that time, I'd learned to hide my feelings and be a good-time girl, or act like one anyway. In reality, I was dead inside, and in some ways, I still am."

Maura reached out and put a hand on her arm. She liked this woman, felt an urge to comfort her. "You seem fine to me. I mean, after all you went through . . ."

"I've been saving my money. It won't be long before I can make a fresh start somewhere. Maybe I'll even meet a decent man. Other whores have done it. Why not me?"

"Indeed," Maura said. "Why not you?"

"And that's my story. What do you want to know about Welinton?"

"Anything you can remember. What kind of a guy was he?"

"That's a hard question."

"Is it? I thought it was pretty simple."

"Not really. Think about it. What kind of people are any of us? Take you, for example."

"Me?"

"Sure. Some people think of you as interesting, others as boring. Your parents see you one way, the people you work with, another. You follow what I mean?"

"Yes, I suppose I do."

Ana smiled, pleased to have gotten her point across. She paused a moment to let it sink in even further, then continued: "So when I talk to you about Welinton, I can only tell you about *my* Welinton. I'd be willing to bet no one else in this town saw him the way I did. Not even close. Most folks, up until the day he made his strike, thought he was crazy. As far as they were concerned, it was crazy to think there was any gold around here, and crazy for him to spend all his days searching for it. And then he found it. But did they stop thinking he was crazy? No. To them, he was still crazy, but he was crazy in a different way. They thought he'd have to be crazy to throw his wealth away like that, going into a bar and dropping a couple of thousand Reais buying drinks for a bunch of people he hardly knew. There wasn't a single person in this town who could relate to that, although they accepted his charity readily enough."

"And you, Ana? What did you think?"

"I thought he was a man with a dream, a dream that made him happy. Even though he was as poor as anything, and spent most of his days sleeping rough, he was convinced a big strike was in his future. It wasn't a question of *if*; it was a question of *when*. He'd get up every morning thinking, *this may be it, this may be the day*. It wasn't the gold he cared about so much as just *finding* the gold. That was what he was going to measure his success by, not by the wealth it was going to bring him."

"It sounds as if you liked him."

"I did. He was a better man than almost anyone in this town. And I don't say that just because he was nice to me. He was nice to everybody. He had a mule and a dog, and he was nice to them, too. You know what he always said?"

"What?"

"That when he struck it rich, he was going to pay for all of my time, take me somewhere nice."

"He proposed to you?"

"Not in so many words. He was talking about . . . well . . . buying my services. But he'd never married. He was a simple man, and that was the only way he knew how to relate to a woman, so that's what it came down to: a proposal."

"What do you remember of your last night together? What did you talk about?"

"Us. We talked about us. He wanted to take me to Portugal. Imagine that. Portugal."

"Why Portugal?"

"He'd seen a book when he was a kid, a book with photos of castles and things. He could describe every photo, and he hadn't seen that book for forty years, maybe fifty."

"Did he talk about the whereabouts of the strike?"

"Now *that*," she said, "is the first question anybody asks me about Welinton. But think about it, *querida*, if I knew where that gold was, would I still be here in this town turning tricks?"

"No, of course not. But that's not what I meant."

"Then what did you mean?"

"Did he happen to mention if it was on Indian land?"

"He was too cautious for that. Even with me. That night . . ." She hesitated.

"Yes?"

"Well, I could tell that he was just dying to tell me. But

as drunk as he was, he didn't. And I didn't push him. I knew that if he talked, he'd hate himself in the morning. And he was too nice for me to want him to feel that way. But you know, this is all water under the bridge. He must have carried the secret with him to the grave. Otherwise, someone would be exploiting it by now, don't you think?"

"Maybe they are, and we just don't know about it. Maybe they want to keep it secret. You remember what happened in Serra Pelada?"

"All those people flocking there? Everyone trying to get a piece of it?"

"Yes, and then the government coming in and regulating it all and trying to buy the gold officially. You can make a good deal more money if you mine it in secret. Let me ask you this: did Welinton ever tell you what he planned to do next?"

She blinked. "Next?"

"Yes. Did he talk about working the mine on his own?"

"Oh, I see what you mean. No. No, he didn't. As a matter of fact . . ."

"What?"

"He said exactly the opposite."

"Tell me."

"It came just after that conversation I told you about. The one about Portugal. He was pretty lit up, so I decided to have a few drinks myself, and I wound up getting enthusiastic about the idea. I asked him when we could go, told him I wanted to leave right away. And he said he'd like to do that, too, but we couldn't. That it was going to take a little time."

"Did he say why?"

"He did. But, like I said, I was drinking. And I'm not technical anyway. It had something to do with needing some kind of special equipment."

"What kind of equipment?"

"Equipment he didn't have the money to buy."

"A sluice?"

"Not a sluice. Something else. Something with gasoline."

Maura racked her brain, trying to remember the technical details she'd learned when she was researching the Serra Pelada story. "A gasoline-powered dredge?"

"That sounds like it."

"So he found the gold in a river?"

"I told you, he didn't say. And I don't understand that kind of stuff. What I do remember is that he said he needed a partner, somebody with money to invest. But he said it was a guaranteed return, and he could prove it was, and there was so damned much gold that he could afford to give away a fifty percent interest and still have enough left over to make him a millionaire a couple of times over."

"So he intended to approach someone."

"Without a doubt."

The two women looked at each other, thinking the same thing, but Maura said it first: "And the person he talked to," she said, "was the person who killed him."

THE SIX laborers, under Gilda's supervision, began to excavate the bodies. Meanwhile, Silva, Jade, and Hector made a cursory examination of the village, steering clear of only one hut. After that one cry, Raoni had made no further sounds, but they avoided intruding on his grief.

Reinforcing Gilda's suspicion that a nerve agent wasn't involved, they found no sign that any of the villagers had either vomited or lost control of their bowels, but they did find one anomaly: up against a wall of green formed by the encircling forest and on the opposite side of the village from the graves, there was still another mound of freshly dug earth.

Hector called over two men from Gilda's crew and set them to digging.

Fifty centimeters down, their shovels struck something soft. They cleared away the remaining dirt to expose silk-like material attached to evenly spaced nylon cords.

"Get it up here," Silva said to one of the diggers.

The man jumped into the hole. "Some kind of a bundle," he said.

"A dead child?" Jade asked.

"No. Feels like something else."

The object hadn't been buried deep. The digger was able to extract whatever it was without help from his colleague. He manhandled it to ground level and set it next to the hole.

Jade hung back, but Silva and Hector moved in for a closer look. The cords had been wrapped around and around the silk.

"Well, I'll be damned," Silva said, when it registered what he was looking at. "Unroll it. Let's see what's inside."

Chapter Twenty-Three

THE DAY was almost done, the sun setting into a bank of ominous gray clouds, when a Scania R144, with massive logs piled to a height well above that of the cab, rounded a curve and lumbered toward them.

Arnaldo screwed the cap onto what remained of the bottle of mineral water he'd been drinking, tossed it into the back of the jeep and grunted in satisfaction. It was the first truckload of wood they'd spotted in an entire day of waiting. He took out his pistol, walked into the road and held up a peremptory hand.

Instead of slowing down, the driver floored the accelerator.

Arnaldo barely missed being hit. In leaping aside, he stumbled and fell headlong into a pool of mud. Cursing, he got to his feet just in time to see the Scania disappearing around the next bend. By then, it was doing better than fifty kilometers an hour.

Gonçalves started the engine. Arnaldo flopped into his seat with a *squish*, splashing mud onto his companion's pants.

"Ewww," Gonçalves said, "that's more than just dirt. It smells like something died in it."

"Shut up and drive."

"Keep your shirt on. He's got nowhere to go. And besides, we're faster than he is."

The unpaved road had enough potholes and ruts to shake out the fillings in their teeth. At a bone-jarring eighty kilometers an hour, they soon came close enough to read the pithy phrases painted on the truck's rear bumper.

IF SIZE WAS EVERYTHING, ELEPHANTS WOULD OWN THE CIRCUS was in pink. ADAM WAS LUCKY; HE DIDN'T HAVE A MOTHER-IN-LAW OR A TRUCK was in blue (complete with semicolon).

"The guy's a philosopher," Gonçalves said.

"He'll need to be when I catch up with him."

The thoroughfare was narrow, lined on both sides with thick jungle. Every time they tried to pass, the driver swerved to prevent it.

"Watch it," Arnaldo said. "If you come up alongside him, and the bastard cuts his wheel, he could bury us under tons of wood."

"Rather than stating the obvious," Gonçalves said, "a suggestion about what to do would be nice."

"Maybe there's a lay-by somewhere ahead. If you spot one, you could detour into it and get in front of him."

"Oh sure. A lay-by. On a back road in a jungle in Pará. Fat chance."

Arnaldo was gathering sarcasm for a reply when the truck came to a sudden stop. "Thank you, Jesus," he said and leapt out of the jeep.

A pickup truck piled high with sacks of *castanhas de Pará* was stuck in mud and blocking the road. The driver they'd been pursuing, already out of his vehicle, was off and running for the safety of the rainforest. And he might have made it, too, had he not tripped over a root.

"You, my friend," Arnaldo said, putting one foot on the writhing man's back, holstering his pistol, and pulling out his handcuffs, "are under arrest."

"Arrest? You guys are cops?"

"Damned right."

"Well, thank God for that," the driver said.

* * *

THE WRAPPING was a parachute. The silk-like cloth was its canopy, and the ropes were its cords. Enveloped within the folds was a rotting piece of meat.

"Roasted, by the look of it," Silva said. And then, to one of the men: "Wrap it up again and go get a body bag."

"You're bringing it with us?" Jade asked, pinching her nose against the smell.

The flies attracted by the rotting meat, now denied access to it, began to settle on the bystanders. Silva waved a hand to shoo them away and nodded. "Gilda can examine it back in Azevedo."

Jade pointed to the meat. "The only forest animal anywhere near that size is a tapir, and that's no tapir."

"No," Silva said. "Unless I miss my guess, it's a side of pork."

"White man's meat. I doubt the Indians would even have known what it was they were eating."

"And yet they would have eaten it?

"They're always on the lookout for protein. They even eat termites. When that . . . thing . . . came floating down they would have welcomed it as a gift from the gods. They would have made a ritual of sharing it."

"All at the same time?"

"According to Father Castori, yes, and I have no reason to doubt him. Not on that score, anyway."

"That explains a lot," Hector said. He probed at the parachute with his foot. "Which one of those *fazendeiros* owns an airplane?"

"Every damned one of them," Jade said bitterly.

Chapter Twenty-Four

THE PHOTO ON THE truck driver's identity card showed him at the age of fourteen, or maybe fifteen. Arnaldo compared it to the face of the grizzled veteran Gonçalves was securing by an arm. One bore little resemblance to the other.

"See?" the driver said, oblivious to the contrast. "It's me. I wasn't lying."

"Otto Cosmos?" Arnaldo said. "What kind of a name is that?"

The driver bristled. "What do you mean *what kind of name is that?* It's my name, that's all. Don't folks have the right to name their kids any way they want?"

Arnaldo ignored the outburst and continued inspecting the documents he'd found in the driver's wallet. The license had expired the previous February, but the photo on it was more recent. It confirmed that he was, indeed, in the presence of one Otto Cosmos, native and resident of Belem.

"I got nothing to hide," Otto said.

"So why did you run?" Gonçalves said.

"What would you have done?" The driver pointed a belligerent chin at Arnaldo. "I come around a curve in the middle of the fucking rainforest. This gorilla is standing in the middle of the road with a gun in his hand and signaling for me to stop—"

"Who the hell are you calling a gorilla?" Arnaldo said with a growl, but the driver went on, undaunted.

"He's got no uniform. He's not showing a badge. You"—he shot an accusing glance at Gonçalves—"are sitting on your ass in a jeep. The jeep isn't marked. You're not wearing a uniform either. What the fuck did you expect me to do?"

"You thought we were trying to hijack you?"

"Fuck, yes, I thought you were trying to hijack me. You got any idea what that load of green gold over there is worth? Not to mention my truck?"

"Your truck," Arnaldo said, "looks like a worthless piece of crap."

"Which only goes to show," Otto said indignantly, "that you know fuck-all about trucks. My truck is one of the most—"

"Many hijackings around here?" Gonçalves asked, cutting off the flow.

"Well . . ."

"Well what?"

"Maybe not around here, but on the Dutra it happens all the time."

The Via Dutra was the main road connecting Brazil's two largest cities: Rio and São Paulo. Despite its being the most heavily traveled interstate road in the country, truck hijackings were common, sometimes exceeding ten a day, often with fatal consequences for the drivers.

"We're a long way from the Via Dutra," Gonçalves said. "So why would hijacking be on your mind?"

"I got a copy of O *Caminhoneiro* up there in the cab," Otto said. "It's this month's main story."

O *Caminhoneiro*, the truckers' magazine, was devoured by drivers who could read. By law, that should have been all of them, but Brazil's departments of motor vehicles were notoriously corrupt and tens of thousands had obtained their licenses by bribing the inspectors.

Gonçalves delivered Otto's arm into the custody of Arnaldo and climbed up into the cab to retrieve the publication. The cover showed a photo, obviously staged, of two men emptying their pistols into a third. A title, emblazoned across the top, read THIS COULD BE YOU and below that in smaller letters, PAGE 37.

"See?" Otto said. "It's all about how bad it's getting, and it gives advice about what to do if it ever happens to you."

"Which is?" Arnaldo said.

"Which is, among other things, never stop when some asshole stands in the middle of the road and waves a gun at you."

"*Asshole?* Listen, you—"

Gonçalves interrupted before the dispute could escalate. "Are you in possession of documentation that permits you to transport that load of wood?"

"Of course. I'm an honest businessman, I am."

"An honest businessman with an expired license," Arnaldo said.

"Oho, so now you're going to bust my balls about that? Why am I not surprised? Okay, how much?"

"You offer me one *centavo*, you little bastard, and you're going to be in bigger trouble than you are already."

Otto blinked. "So that's not what this is all about?"

"No."

"Not a shakedown?"

Arnaldo shook his head. "Let's see that documentation."

"Take off these handcuffs, and I'll get it."

"Tell me where it is, and *he'll* get it."

"In the glove compartment."

Gonçalves fetched the papers and set about examining them.

"See?" Otto said.

"You know this guy Raul Nonato?" Gonçalves asked, his forefinger tapping one of the pages.

"No. Who's he?"

"The IBAMA guy who signed this permit."

"Why the fuck should I? I don't do the logging. I don't do the fucking paperwork. I just transport the wood."

"How about this guy Cunha, the guy the permit was issued to?"

"Him, I know."

"How?"

"He's my fucking client, that's how. I bring him stuff from Belem for his supermarket. I take his wood back."

"How long have you been doing it?"

Otto thought about it. "Four months. More or less."

"Anybody else transport his wood?"

"Lots of guys. We got an organization. We got a website. We got rules about prices and how to spread the work. Anybody with cargo to ship in this state goes in there, says how much of it there is, and where it's going to, and we work it out."

"So you're an independent contractor?"

"Well, duh! How about you take off these fucking handcuffs?"

"Not yet. First, we're going to search your truck."

"And when you don't find fuck-all?"

"Then we'll think about letting you go."

Chapter Twenty-Five

Back at Jade's place, Maura sat on the back porch, watching the light fade from the sky and reflecting about what she'd learned.

Gold. The old prospector had found it. The odds were that someone had killed him for it. And the strike he'd made was located within the reservation. Why the reservation? Because, if it were anywhere else, it would belong to whoever held title to the land. Maybe the man whose gold it was might have given him a finder's fee, but no more than that. And if that gold was, indeed, somewhere on the reservation, there was another aspect to the business as well, something more disturbing: Welinton's discovery might well have been the motive for rooting out the entire tribe.

So what now? Tell Silva? No. He'd tell her to stay out of it. File a story? Not yet, not without digging deeper. Without more facts, more proof, it was page two stuff, maybe even page three. But beating the federal cops to the truth would transform it into a front-page scoop.

So that's the course she had to follow. She had to keep her investigation confidential until she had all the facts. That would not only please Mauricio, her editor, it would show Silva he'd made a mistake not to trust her in the first place. In some ways, he reminded her of her father, and as was generally the case with her father, she had an avid desire to prove him wrong.

Welinton had talked about a partner, someone with money. Was he likely to know anyone with money who didn't live in the town? No. So how many people had to be considered? The Big Five, surely. How many others? The doctor? The lawyer, Kassab? A group? No, probably not a group. They could, all of them, be considered among Brazil's wealthy—and only a few of Brazil's wealthy understood the concept of sharing. Whoever old Welinton had first taken into his confidence would likely have wanted all the gold for himself.

Crazy Ana thought the prospector might have been speaking of a gasoline-powered dredge. Gasoline-powered dredges were used in water. If she was right, the gold was in a river. And because it was a small-scale operation, they were using mercury to extract it.

Mercury killed fish!

It was full dark by now. Maura got to her feet and strolled over to the Grand. It was early in the evening, and the place was still bereft of customers. Amanda was behind the bar, leafing through an ancient magazine. Once again, she appeared eager for company.

"I understand the fishing around here is pretty good," Maura said, taking a seat.

"The best," Amanda said. "What'll you have?"

"A beer, please. Brahma, if you've got it."

"I've got it."

Amanda wiped off the top of a can, popped it, and set a glass next to it.

"How did it go with Ana?" she asked as Maura poured. "Did you manage to talk to her?"

"I did," Maura said. "Didn't learn anything of note, though. Your husband back yet?"

"Anytime now. He called when they got in range. Nobody likes to get stuck out there in the forest after dark, GPS or no GPS."

"Why? Big animals?"

"No. A lot of nasty small ones. Snakes, especially."

"Yuck! I hate snakes."

"Me, too. I never knew the glories of nature before I moved here from Belem."

"The federal cops are freezing me out of their investigation, but I have to hang on to see what they come up with, which means I've got some time on my hands. I think I might like to try the fishing. Are there any guides?"

"Sure. Want me to find you one?"

"Could you?"

"Glad to. When?"

"If he could drop by tomorrow morning, about eight, it would suit me fine."

"Leave it to me. Look, there they are."

Maura turned to see Hector and Silva entering the bar. Her heart gave a little leap when Gonçalves entered behind them. Amanda's remark of the morning was having repercussions.

"Eight o'clock then?" she asked, lowering her voice. "Can I count on it?"

"It's off-season, shouldn't be a problem. I'll make some calls."

Amanda's husband was the next man through the door. The federal cops waved and headed for the stairs. Osvaldo came over to join the women. His wife came around the bar to greet him.

"I need a shower," he said.

"Who cares?" she said and embraced him anyway.

"Where's Jade?" Maura asked.

"We brought Amati's son back with us. Cute little fellow, name of Raoni. She took him home."

"From what she told me, her housekeeper isn't going to like that," Amanda said.

"Alexandra?" Osvaldo said. "No way! Bigoted bitch!"

"How old is the boy?"

"Eight."

"You discover anything new at the village?" Maura asked.

"Sorry," Osvaldo said. "Can't tell you. Chief Inspector's orders."

"Oh, come *on*," Maura said. "The public has a right to know."

Osvaldo smiled. "He said you'd say that. He also said I shouldn't believe it, that the public *doesn't* have a right to know."

"He's full of—"

"Hey, don't shoot the messenger. I'm just telling you what he said. And there's no use leaning on your friend Jade. He made her promise to keep a lid on it as well."

Two can play at that game, Maura thought.

"I think he might have cause to regret his attitude," she said.

It was too early for dinner. Maura went back to Jade's place and found her seated on the couch, a comforting arm around Raoni. They were watching a cartoon.

Raoni turned his big brown eyes on Maura, but not for long.

"He's really into it, isn't he?" she asked.

"You're the third white woman he's seen," Jade said. "But this is his first cartoon."

"Third?"

Jade made a face, and lifted her chin toward the kitchen, where Alexandra was banging pots and pans.

"Is she always that noisy?" Maura asked.

"It's a protest. For a while, I thought she was going to quit."

"Might not be a bad thing if she did, a woman like that."

"I've been thinking the same thing."

"The boy looks okay though," Maura said. "Better than I expected."

"He cried all the way back."

"I thought Indian boys weren't supposed to cry."

Jade scoffed. "That's nonsense. Where did you hear that?"

"I think I saw it in some movie."

Jade raised an eyebrow. "Movie?"

"About American Indians."

"Ours are different. They cry all the time. He's going to do a lot of it tomorrow."

She shot a quick look at the boy. If he was aware of the fact that they were talking about him, he didn't show it. His eyes remained fixed on the screen.

"Why tomorrow?" Maura said.

"Because tomorrow is the day we're going to bury his father."

Maura, too, looked at Raoni. "Where?" she said.

"In the same spot where the others are."

"Can I go?"

Jade shook her head. "The Chief Inspector nixed it. He says it's still a crime scene."

"I've had about all I can stand of that Chief Inspector." And then, when Jade didn't react, "Could we have a word? Privately?"

"You can talk right here. He won't understand anything you say."

"Maybe not, but . . . could we go into the kitchen?"

"With Alexandra in there? Forget it! Let's go onto the back porch."

"I want you to come clean about what happened today," Maura said when they were seated. "I need to know what you found in that village."

Jade sighed, shook her head and set her mouth in a stubborn line. "I can't tell you."

It took Maura some effort not to lose her temper. "Do I have to remind you, Jade, that I came all the way up here from São Paulo to help you out? That I took time off from the series I was working on? That Silva and his people wouldn't be here if it wasn't for me? If I hadn't put the screws on Lana Nogueira—"

Her friend threw up her hands. "I *knew* you were going to take it like this. Look, Maura, I owe you big time. I don't deny that. And I'm sorry. But he's the cop, not you. He's running the case, not you. He has the experience. We don't. I, for one, intend to trust him—and let him get on with it."

"It's not a question of not trusting him. I'm sure he's a good cop, but—"

"You're not going to wear me down, Maura. I love you, but you're not going to wear me down."

"But *why*? That's what I want to know. Why does he insist on keeping me in the dark?"

"He feels that if any information were to leak out at this stage it might prejudice—"

"Stop right there. Do you think that if you told me something in confidence I'd pass it on? That I'd talk about it to anyone if you told me not to?"

Jade smiled. "He told me you'd say that."

Maura didn't see the humor in it. Her reply was sharp. "What is this guy? A mind reader?"

"He said you'd promise not to tell a soul, but that satisfying your personal curiosity isn't a good enough reason to tell you anything. He said that, in circumstances like these, he wouldn't tell his own wife."

"And you believed that?"

"I did."

"Oh for heaven's sake!"

Jade stood up. "I'm tired of trying to placate you, Maura. I don't think there's anything I can say to you that will make you see it my way."

"There isn't."

"Then I'm going to see to the boy, and I'm going to sleep. Do you want Alexandra to serve you some dinner?"

"No. I'm going back to the Grand."

"Don't drink too much."

"I'm not going to drink too much. I'm going have a crack at getting something out of that cute young cop."

Chapter Twenty-Six

DINNER WAS OVER. FOR privacy's sake, the cops adjourned to Silva's room, but they were a chair short, so when Gilda joined them she and Hector had to sit side by side on the bed.

"So the way I figure it," Arnaldo was saying when she came in, "if our friend Otto is guilty of anything at all—"

"Which both of us doubt," Gonçalves interjected.

"—it's transporting lumber he knew was harvested illegally. Big deal, right? More of a distraction than anything else."

"So you let him go?" Silva asked.

"We did," Arnaldo said.

"He won't be there for hours and hours," Silva said, "so let's do this: call Alex Sanches. It doesn't have to be tonight. Tomorrow morning is good enough. Give him the truck's registration and tell him to stop it on the way to the docks. He's to get a statement from the driver, photograph the wood and copy the paperwork. Then, he's to find out who else has been transporting wood from Azevedo. I'd say it's a sure bet we can nail him, and that IBAMA agent, for illegal logging if nothing else."

"Leave it to me," Arnaldo said.

Silva turned to Gilda. "Your turn, my dear. What have you learned?"

"The meat wrapped in the parachute was from a pig," Gilda said, "and strips had been cut from it after it was roasted. There were pieces of that same meat in the stomachs of the victims. And all died immediately after ingesting it."

"So now we'll need a toxology report," Silva said. He turned to Hector. "Get samples off to Rodrigues as soon as the airport opens in the morning. Tell her to copy Lefkowitz on her findings. Then call him and tell him what's happening."

AT THE same time Silva was conferring with his colleagues, another get-together was taking place at a *fazenda* some thirty kilometers away. The mayor, Hugo Toledo, was meeting with his fellow landowners, José Frade, Cesar Bonetti, and Roberto Lisboa. Also present were Lisboa's foreman, Toni Pandolfo, Paulo Cunha, Doctor Pinto, and Father Castori.

"Why couldn't we do this at the Grand?" José Frade said as he took his seat.

"More confidential this way," Toledo said. "We don't want to be seen getting together while those federal cops are in town."

"You got any idea how long it takes to get from my place to here? I could have been at the Grand in half the time."

"I know exactly how long it takes," the mayor said. "But after you've heard what we've got to say, you're going to agree that this way is best."

"*We?*" Frade said. "Who's we?"

"All in good time, José. Anybody want to refresh their drink before we start?"

Roberto Lisboa did, but the priest got to the bottle first. While Castori was pouring, Frade, still irritated, looked at his watch.

"It's late," he said. "How long is this going to take?"

"Not long," Toledo said.

"So how about you get down to it," Cunha said. "What's it about?"

Toledo rose from his chair and looked at each one in turn before he continued. "I think we've got a chance—a good chance now that those damned Indians are gone—of getting the federal government to abolish the reservation. I've got the men in Brasilia who can make it happen."

There was a generalized murmur of approval.

"But," Toledo said, holding up a finger and waiting for silence before he went on, "now we've got a gang of federal cops sticking their noses into our business. And the longer they stay, the more they stir the pot, the more complicated things are going to get."

"Complicated?" Frade asked. "Define complicated. It's going to take longer? Or it's going to cost more?"

"Both," Toledo said, "so the time has come to take countermeasures to neutralize our unwelcome visitors. I've asked you here tonight to get our stories straight."

"What's *he* doing here?" Bonetti said, cocking a thumb at the priest.

"He's here," Toledo said, "because of what he can bring to the party. And so is Doctor Pinto." He turned to Frade. "And that, José, is what I meant when I referred to *we*. Doctor, how about if you begin?"

The doctor took a sip of his whiskey and sat up straighter in his chair. "The Federal Police," he said, "have gotten it into their heads that the Indian didn't kill Omar Torres."

"The fuck he didn't," Cunha said.

The mayor held up a hand. "Hear him out, Paulo, hear him out. Go on, Doctor."

"The man conducting the investigation, one Chief Inspector Silva, demonstrated suspicion the first time he saw the body. But he refused to share his observations with me or with Delegado Borges, who was also present. Later, he sent some snip of a girl to conduct a more detailed autopsy. I was there when she did it."

"And?" Cunha prompted.

"And she was more forthcoming than the Chief Inspector had been. He'd failed to instruct her to keep me out of the loop."

"She agreed with Silva?" Frade said. "She thought some-one else killed Torres? Not the Indian?"

The doctor nodded. "She did."

"Well, fuck her," Frade exploded. "Who cares about any stupid theory she might have come up with? Or Silva either, for that matter."

"I'm afraid it's more than a theory, José," the doctor said. "They might well have a point."

"What point? The savage was found next to Omar's body. There was blood all over him, and the murder weapon was right next to him. What more proof do you want?"

Toledo walked over and put a friendly hand on Frade's shoulder. "It's not what *I* want, it's what the Chief Inspector wants. Doctor, would you kindly tell José—and the rest of us—how the Chief Inspector came to his conclusion."

The doctor cleared his throat. "The angle at which the blows were struck seems to indicate that they were delivered by a man at least as tall as Omar was. But the Indian was much shorter. Furthermore, the cuts were on top of each other. A drunken man, they believe, wouldn't have had that much control over the knife."

"Maybe it was a drunken woman," Bonetti said.

It was meant as a joke, but the doctor took him seriously. "The wounds were delivered with great force," he said. "It's unlikely a woman could have inflicted them."

"Unlikely," Bonetti said, looking around at the others. "But not impossible, right?"

"Dead right," Lisboa said. "It's all supposition on their part, pure supposition."

"I considered filing a report with different conclusions,"

the doctor said. "It's my right as the town's medical examiner, except . . ."

"Except what?" Frade asked.

"I'm afraid that any objective analysis would come down on her side, not mine. It would be putting my competence into question for no purpose whatsoever."

"So if you were to do it," Cunha said, "you'd want to be well-paid for it."

"And maybe it wouldn't do us a damned bit of good anyway," Bonetti said.

"Right on both counts," Doctor Pinto said. He drained his glass and got up to pour himself more whiskey.

"Before that damned FUNAI woman started pulling strings, we had everything tied up in a neat little package," Frade said. "The Indians were gone. And any investigation into what happened to them was stalled."

"Yes," Toledo agreed. "And even after she managed to get the attention of Federal Police Headquarters, we were blessed by another stroke of luck."

"Which was?" Cunha said.

"Omar's murder."

"Luck? You call that luck?"

Toledo laughed aloud. "Oh, come on, Paulo. No crocodile tears. No one in this room was any great friend of Omar's. Can you honestly say you're sorry he's dead?"

Cunha waved his hand as if swatting at a pesky fly. "Of course not. But I still don't see how you can call it luck."

"Think about it. Who's to say it wasn't Omar, acting alone, who eliminated that tribe?"

"Now, *that* would be convenient," Lisboa said.

"Wouldn't it?"

"And maybe even true," Bonetti said.

"Exactly," Cunha said. "Who's to say it isn't?"

"No one," Toledo said. "And whether he did, or he didn't, doesn't matter a damn. Whoever killed off that damned tribe did us all a favor. And Omar did us another favor, by getting his ass killed, thereby providing us with a perfect scapegoat."

"Who might not even be a scapegoat," Cunha said, "because he might well have done it."

"Precisely. So that's the first story we have to tell. We're going to say that every one of us, at one time or another, heard Torres say he was going to do away with those Indians."

"Good," Cunha said. "But then how would the Indian have found that out? How are we going to prove that?"

Toledo turned to the priest. "Padre, you're on."

Father Castori licked his lips. "If someone who spoke his language were to say that he heard the Indian threaten Omar's life, wouldn't that be enough?"

"Hell, yes," Cunha said. "Are you telling me that you—"

Toledo didn't let him finish. "Father Castori and I," he said, "had a little chat several hours ago. He has recalled that while he was translating the Indian's words for the Calmon woman there were a few things he neglected to impart."

"Like the Indian being convinced that Torres killed his people?"

"Exactly."

"Come on, Hugo, the FUNAI bitch will never buy that, and neither will the federal cops."

"The padre here assures me that Jade doesn't speak enough Awana to contest it. As to the federal cops, so what? They might not believe it, but what can they do? They have no *proof*, and if we stand together they'll never get any."

"Makes sense," Bonetti said, "So what's next?"

"What's next," Toledo said, "is that we brief our wives

about this. You know how women like to talk. They'll get the story around town faster than we can."

"Excellent idea," Cunha said. "Let's do it."

Toledo looked at Lisboa. "Roberto?"

"I'm in," Lisboa said.

"José?"

"Hell, yes. You were right, Hugo. It *was* worthwhile driving out here."

"Then I think, Doctor, that we might be able to make use of your medical expertise after all. I'd like you to write a report that contests that of the young medical examiner from São Paulo."

"I'm willing," the doctor said.

"For the right price, of course," Toledo said.

"Of course. What do you intend to do with it?"

"Muddy the waters. Our position, as the most prominent citizens of this town, will be that Silva and his people are chasing ghosts."

"And that the longer they stay," Cunha said, "the longer it's going to take for the people in Brasilia to get the money you've promised them for getting the reservation declassified."

"Correct. We'll give Silva a week or so before we drop a few words to the right people."

"What kind of words?" Frade wanted to know.

"Words suggesting Silva is pursuing an absurd hypothesis and is obstructing our plans of a mutually-lucrative outcome."

"He must have friends too," Lisboa said cautiously.

"He probably does," Toledo said, "but in Brasilia, money always trumps pure friendship."

The priest cleared his throat. "Speaking of money," he said. "I'd like to discuss my fiscal participation in all of this."

Toledo turned to him with a smile. "And we will, Father. You're a key figure in the whole equation. Now, let's go over our version of events in detail. Only then will we all be able to sing to the Chief Inspector in harmony."

Chapter Twenty-Seven

"HAVE YOU, OR HAS anyone else in your crew, come up with any proof that white men were behind the genocide?" Maura asked.

Rather than meet her eyes, Gonçalves stared at his drink. "I'm sorry, Maura, but—"

"But your Chief Inspector bla, bla, bla. Don't repeat yourself, Haraldo, it's boring."

They were alone in the bar. Most of the lights were out, and the front door was locked. Maura was grilling him, and Gonçalves was feeling uncomfortable.

"Is that why you got me down here?" he said. "Just to interrogate me? Just so you could get a scoop for your scandal sheet?"

She bristled. "It's not a scandal sheet. It's one of the most respected newspapers in the country."

"Whatever," he said and stood up.

"Sit down, Haraldo. You know you want to."

"Do I?"

"Yes, you do." She extended a hand. He took it and sat down again.

"As long as you stop with the questions."

She smiled—and ignored his plea. "You, and by you I mean the Federal Police—"

"Maura, *please*."

"—think the killers were after one of two things: land they could add to their *fazendas*—"

"Enough, Maura! You're—"

"—or hardwoods they could steal, is that right?"

Gonçalves leaned back in his chair, suddenly cagey. "Who said anything about hardwoods?"

"Where were you all day while your buddies were out at the Awana village?"

He avoided her eyes. He was a pretty good liar, but for some strange reason he was having a problem when it came to Maura. "I can't tell you," he said.

"Maybe not," she said. "But you know what? I've got a pretty good idea." And then, before he could get a word in, "You guys come up with any proof that somebody else might have killed that *fazendeiro*? Someone other than the Indian, I mean."

He released her hand. She withdrew it into her lap.

"Stop it, Maura. Stop it right now. I'm not kidding. If you don't lay off with the questions, I'm going to bed."

She was losing him, and she knew it. She decided to take a chance. "How about this? How about we exchange information? How about I tell you something that's going to set your investigation off in an entirely new direction?"

"What makes you think you could?"

"I know some things you don't."

"Now you've got me curious."

"Good." She put her hand back on the table. He didn't take it.

"But I'm still not going to tell you anything."

She curled her fingers. "Damn it, Haraldo—"

"You're cursing at the wrong guy. If you've got something to contribute, and you're only willing to give it up if we clue you in, you should go and negotiate with the Chief Inspector."

"And get him out of bed? You think he'd appreciate that?"

"If you're in possession of any information that would contribute to the solving of this case, he certainly would."

"Now you're sounding like a cop again."

"I *am* a cop."

"In a couple of days' time, you people are going to be sorry you didn't play ball," she said.

"I guess we'll have to take that risk."

He reached for her hand, and she let him take it.

"What's on your schedule for tomorrow?" she asked.

"That's confidential."

"I was asking because I'm following an independent line of inquiry, and I don't want you people stepping on my toes any more than you want me stepping on yours."

Gonçalves squeezed her hand. She didn't squeeze back.

"I thought I might look up that fellow Cunha," she said.

If anyone was involved in stealing hardwood, the most likely candidate was the man who had a business trading in the stuff. She wasn't particularly interested in Cunha any more than the town's other movers and shakers, but by mentioning him, she'd hoped to provoke a response. And she did.

"Not a good idea. Not tomorrow."

"Right. Okay, that's clear enough. How about if I were to talk to the delegado. What's his name?"

"Borges. That would be okay."

"And the town's medical examiner?"

"If you want to waste your time."

"And the mayor?"

"The mayor is one of the big landowners. You might want to leave all of those guys for later in the week."

"*Want*," she said, "is not the operative word. Okay, that's it."

"You're going to bed?" He sounded disappointed.

"I'm not. What I meant was, that's enough business for one night. Let's get down to the more important stuff. Have you got a girlfriend back in São Paulo?"

Chapter Twenty-Eight

"HIS NAME IS FRED Vaz," Amanda said. "He's in the restaurant."

After her late night with Gonçalves and far too little sleep, Maura was back at the Grand. She glanced at her watch. It wasn't yet 7:45 A.M.

"Yeah," Amanda said. "Early. He must need the money. He gets two hundred a day during the busy season."

"And this isn't the busy season?"

"No. It's not."

"Offer him a hundred?"

"I didn't tell you that."

"Thanks," Maura said. "Any of those cops come down for breakfast yet?"

Amanda shook her head. "You're the first."

"Good."

Maura had hopes of finishing her conversation with the fishing guide before Silva or anyone on his team showed up. But that was easier said than done. Before she'd had a chance to ask a single question, even before she'd gotten herself seated, Fred Vaz was off and running. He was, it soon became evident, a man in love with the sound of his own voice.

According to him, the denizens of Azevedo's rivers were the smartest, biggest, hardest-fighting, meanest, hungriest, and tastiest fish in all of Brazil. But you couldn't just expect to stroll over to a riverbank, get into a boat, or drop a lure into the Jagunami and catch them. Not without an experienced guide, you couldn't. No, you needed a man like him. A

man with years and years of experience. A man who'd show
you where all the best places were and—

Maura waved a finger. "I don't want to know about the
best places," she said. "I want to know about the worst."

"Huh?"

"And I'm willing to pay well for your expertise. But you've
got to be honest with me."

"Well . . . sure. Whatever you say."

"Have you noticed any dead fish in the rivers around
here?"

He looked away. "There are . . . always dead fish in the
rivers," he said. "That's what they do. They hatch, they live,
they die."

"I'm talking about something other than the natural life
cycle of fish. But you already knew that, didn't you?"

"I—"

"Of course, I could be barking up the wrong tree."

"Uh . . ."

"Let me give it to you straight, Fred. If you don't know of
a river or stream where fish are dying on a massive scale, I'll
pay you two hundred Reais right now, and we'll call it a day.
The two hundred will more than compensate you for coming
here to talk to me this morning, but two hundred is all you're
going to get."

"But . . . uh . . . if by any chance, I should happen to know
about a place like that? A place with a lot of dead fish?"

"Then I want you to take me there."

"You want to fish in a place that's full of dead fish?"

"I don't want to fish. I want you to guide me there. I want
to see the dead fish. I want to take samples of the water, and
I want you to bring me back here. You do that, even if it only
takes half a day, and I'll pay you an additional five hundred
Reais."

"Five hundred Reais? And I also get the other two hundred?"

"That's what the word *additional* means, Fred. You get the two hundred, and you get the five hundred, and that's seven hundred in total. How about it?"

"Hmm."

"Why are you making that noise?"

"I'm thinking."

"What's to think about? There *is* such a place. I don't know where it is, but from what you've already said, I know it exists. And I know there are other fishing guides. And I know it's the off season, so . . ."

"Don't be hasty, Senhora. I'm not saying I won't do it. Not yet."

"It's Senhorita. And what's with the *not yet?*"

He looked pained. "To show you those dead fish we'd have to go into the Indian reservation. That's where they are."

"So what?"

"I'm not supposed to go in there. Nobody is, not without permission from the FUNAI. If I did, I could lose my license."

"Why would they take away your license? It's not like there are any Indians left."

"It doesn't matter. Rules are rules."

"What if I could get permission?"

"Then there'd be no problem. But you can't."

"Why not?"

"Because the FUNAI agent is a real hard ass."

"That hard ass is my best friend."

"Oh."

"How far inside the reservation?"

"Just a couple of kilometers. The spot is a tributary of the Jagunami."

"And the Jagunami is the border between private land-holdings and the reservation, right?"

"Mostly. Except for the property that used to be owned by Enrique Azevedo."

"What happens there?"

"It straddles the river, and there's a bridge that crosses it. The mayor, Hugo Toledo, owns the land these days, but he lets the hard a— I mean the FUNAI lady use the bridge. Once we're across, all we'd have to do is walk downstream until we get to this little creek the Indians call the Sapoqui. Then we follow that upstream—"

"It's okay, Fred. I don't need any further explanations. You guarantee me dead fish?"

"Oh, yes, Senhorita. Lots and lots of dead fish."

"Then we've got a deal."

"You'll talk to your friend? Get the paperwork?"

"I will."

"Make sure my name is on it, okay. It's Vaz."

"I know that. Can we go today?"

"Certainly, Senhorita. If you like."

"I like. You know where she lives? The hard ass?"

"Believe me, Senhorita, I didn't mean—"

"Just kidding you, Fred. Just kidding. Answer the question."

"Yes, Senhorita, I know."

"Good. I'm staying at her place. Meet me there in an hour."

Fred nodded and left with a smile on his face. When he was gone, Maura took out her cell phone and called the newspaper's regional office in Belem. She asked to speak to Nataniel Eder, the bureau chief, and after the usual pleasantries said, "Nat, I need a favor."

"I didn't think you were calling just to be friendly. What is it?"

"If I sent you some samples of river water could you get them analyzed?"

"Sure. For what?"

"Mercury."

"Oho. Like that, is it?"

"Yeah," she said. "I'm not sure yet, but I think—"

"Say no more," he said. "You get 'em to me, and I'll take care of it."

After she hung up, she went to the front desk, where she found Amanda writing in a ledger.

"How can I get something to Belem in a hurry?" Maura asked.

"That depends on how much of a hurry, how big it is, and how much you're willing to pay."

"Very much of a hurry. No bigger than a shoebox, and whatever I have to."

"There's a kid out at the airport—"

"The one whose old man runs the charter service? The one who reputedly gets more ass than a toilet seat?"

"The very one, and no reputedly about it. He *does* get more ass than a toilet seat. He also delivers stuff. Give the package to me, I'll say it's for Osvaldo, negotiate the best price, and put it on your bill. It's best if I call him ahead of time. When?"

"This afternoon—late."

"If you don't get it to me by dark, it won't go before tomorrow morning."

"Yes, I know. Thanks."

Her next stop was the pharmacy. She bought six sterilized bottles, the kind they kept on hand for the collection of urine samples. Following that, she visited the supermarket, where she purchased self-adhesive labels. Then she went back to Jade's place to change—and to wait for Fred Vaz.

Chapter Twenty-Nine

MAURA FOUND HER FRIEND under the awning on her back porch, finishing breakfast.

"I need your permission," she said, "to enter the reservation. Not to go to the village. Somewhere else."

"Where?"

"It's a secret."

"Then no permission."

"Hard ass."

"What?"

"Just something I heard someone say. Come on, Jade. Don't be a pain. Write me a pass."

"There's no way I'm going to let you go into the reservation on your own. You have no idea how easy it is to get lost."

"I'm not going on my own. I'm going with Fred Vaz."

"The fishing guide?"

"Yes."

"Forget it. White people aren't allowed to fish that reservation. And since when are you interested in fishing anyway?"

"I'm not."

"So what *are* you interested in?"

Maura sank into a chair. "If you swear to keep it to yourself, I'll tell you."

Jade drained her cup of *café com leite*. "Why the secrecy?"

By way of reply, Maura put one of the bottles on the table.

"What's that for?"

"Promise and I'll tell you."

"Okay, I promise."

"Gold?" she said when Maura had finished explaining. "But that's—"

"As good a reason as any for someone to wipe out the Awana. Yes, it is."

"Okay, I'll write you the pass, but we're going to have to tell the Chief Inspector about this."

"And we will, but only after I'm a hundred percent sure I'm right. And only when I'm ready."

"No. I really think—"

"It's a secret. Remember? You promised."

Jade sighed, and might have said more, but just then a sour-faced Alexandra Santos came out of the kitchen carrying a coffee pot.

"More coffee, Senhora?"

Jade shook her head. Maura expected the offer to be extended to her, but it wasn't. The housekeeper went back inside.

"A ray of morning sunshine, that one," Maura said. "Where's Raoni?"

"In my bedroom, watching the same cartoon over and over. I taught him how to use the DVD player."

"When are you leaving?"

Jade looked at her watch. "In twenty minutes."

"Who's going?"

"All of us, Osvaldo, Gilda, the cops."

"The whole gang?"

"It was the Chief Inspector's idea. He thinks Raoni needs the support."

"And he's willing to take time out of his precious investigation to give it to him? Well, there's a surprise."

"It surprised me, too. Apparently, he has a weakness for kids." She stood up. "Let me get a pass and a pen." A minute later, she came back to the table with a form.

"Make sure Vaz's name is on it," Maura said.

"I will. It has to be." Jade wrote out the pass and handed it over. "How did it go last night?"

"I haven't slept with him, if that's what that sly smile of yours is implying."

"And you've already known him for what? Almost twenty-four hours? That's what I call remarkable restraint."

Maura didn't rise to the bait. "The cops are monopolizing all the male suspects," she said. "I thought I might try to learn something from their wives. Who should I talk to first?"

"Patricia Toledo."

"Why her?"

"She'll get her nose out of joint if you approach anyone else."

"Because?"

"She sees herself as the community's leading female citizen. Her husband's father was one of the founders of the town. This place could as well be called Toledo as Azevedo, and Patricia thinks it should be. She got Hugo to propose a name change to the city council, but it got voted down. There are people she still doesn't speak to because of that."

"Animosity loosens tongues. I'll need a list of those people."

Jade looked at her watch again. "I'll make one when I get back. Meanwhile, why don't you start with Patricia and her two best friends?"

"All right. Who are they?"

"Rita Cunha and Maria Bonetti."

"What about Frade's wife?"

"She's not part of the intimate circle."

"Why not?"

"They don't respect her."

"Because?"

"She lets José push her around."

"Physically?"

"Physically. He beats her. None of the other three would stand for that kind of treatment, but Sonia is . . . different. She was an orphan. José married her when she was eighteen, brought her up *his* way, as he likes to put it. She's very meek, and she's completely under his thumb."

"Why doesn't she go to the cops about it?"

"Borges? He wouldn't do a thing. He wants to get on with everybody. And, by everybody, I mean the men."

"How about we tell Silva and his people?"

"What could they do? He'd behave until they've gone and then start up again, harder and worse than before. No, I think the only person who can do something about Sonia is Sonia. She's got to run away, or stand up to him, one or the other."

"You ever tell her that?"

"I did. Once. But maybe she took part of the conversation to José, because now she's afraid of being seen talking to me whenever he's around."

"Then, as far as the big *fazendeiros* are concerned, that only leaves Lisboa. No wife, right?"

"Right. He's gay."

"How about the doctor's wife?"

"She died last year. Some say she might have lived if he hadn't treated her himself. Kassab, the lawyer, just got a divorce, and his wife left town about three months ago. The police chief and his wife have seven kids under the age of ten. He's Fernando; she's Fernanda. How do you like that? Fernando and Fernanda Borges."

"Charming."

"Uh-huh. And it's the only charming thing about her. She's a homebody, dull as ditchwater, and folks hardly ever see her. I guess the kids keep her busy." Jade stood up. "I have to get going."

Maura rose as well. "Have you got a telephone number for Patricia?"

"In my address book, top right-hand drawer of my desk."

"Thanks, Jade, you're—"

From somewhere inside the house, a small voice cried out in alarm.

"Raoni!" Jade said.

They burst into the living room to find Father Castori holding fast to the child's arm. The housekeeper, her arms wide, was blocking his escape toward the back porch.

"What is this?" Jade said. "What do you think you're doing?"

Alexandra spun around. The priest released his grip. Raoni ran to Jade and wrapped his arms around her legs.

"I'm taking the boy, Senhorita Calmon," Castori said.

"Like hell you are," Jade said, putting her hands on Raoni's shoulders. The terrified little boy locked his hands around her waist and buried his head in her stomach.

"A dirty Indian has no place in this house," Alexandra said.

"*I'll* decide who has a place in my house," Jade said. "How *dare* you help him kidnap this child?"

"It's not kidnapping," Alexandra said. "It's the Lord's work."

"Are you defying me?"

"Between the Lord and the Devil, I choose the side of the Lord."

Jade could feel Raoni trembling. It was only the fear of traumatizing him further that helped her to control herself. "So I'm the Devil?" she said. "Is that what you're saying?"

Alexandra crossed her arms above her breasts and didn't deign to reply.

"I've had enough of you," Jade said. "Go pack your things."

The housekeeper dropped her arms and opened her mouth in surprise. "You'd choose a filthy Indian brat over me?"

"I just have. You're fired. Get out."

Alexandra snapped her mouth shut and stalked off toward her bedroom.

"As for you," Jade said to the priest, "the boy's welfare is a FUNAI matter. Leave my home. Now."

The priest raised his chin and tried to look down his long nose at her. He couldn't quite pull it off. She was taller than he was.

"Not without the boy," he said. "There are higher laws at play here than those of the federal government."

"Higher laws? What are you talking about?"

"The laws of God."

"Yes, I thought that was what you're about to say. And in this case, I don't buy it. I'm not violating any of God's laws by taking care of this child."

"You're being blind and obstinate. I'm fluent in his language, Senhorita Calmon. You are not. I intend to convert that little pagan to the One True Faith, and I'll require daily and constant contact to teach him the errors of his ways. He's going to live with me."

Father Castori advanced on Raoni. Which is when Maura, who'd been watching the exchange in stunned silence, ran out of patience. She whipped out an aerosol can and sprayed him in the face. Jade, grasping Raoni by the hand, took off at a run for the Grand.

Chapter Thirty

"*Maced* HIM?" ARNALDO SAID and burst into a hearty laugh. "Your buddy Maura used chemical mace on the priest?"

Jade nodded. She was still nervous and not seeing any humor in it.

"You should talk to Delegado Borges about this," Silva said.

"Delegado Borges won't do a damned thing, Chief Inspector."

"How do you know? Did you ask him?"

"No, but I know him, and he prides himself on being a good Catholic. He's more likely to arrest Maura for assault than he is to take action against Father Castori."

"You're the FUNAI agent. This child is your responsibility. The law is on your side."

She started nodding before he'd finished speaking. "But I know Borges, and he's going to come down on the priest's side, not mine."

"Would you like me to speak to him on your behalf?"

"No, Chief Inspector. What I want is for you to dispatch a man to cover my house and keep Raoni out of Castori's clutches until I can send him to the orphanage in Belem."

"So that's your decision? You're going to send the boy to Belem?"

"It's the last thing I want to do, but allowing the priest to have him would be worse."

"And you wouldn't be willing to raise him yourself?"

"I would, you know. But if I tried, my own people at the

FUNAI would take him away from me. It's strictly against the rules."

Silva studied the boy for another moment, rubbed his chin, and stood up. "Hector."

"Senhor?"

"Where's Gilda?"

Hector looked at the little boy, said, "Getting you-know-who nailed into a coffin. She wants to make damned sure it can't be opened by little fingers."

"Make sure it gets loaded as soon as she finishes. Babyface?"

For once, Gonçalves didn't even flinch at his nickname. "Senhor?"

"Tell Osvaldo we're about to leave. Then call Lefkowitz and inform him we'll be out of range of our telephones until sometime in the afternoon. Tell him to contact us at the end of the day."

The two men nodded and left.

"The rest of you wait here," Silva said. He took out his cell phone and left the restaurant.

Arnaldo looked down at the boy, then up at Jade. "Does he understand anything we say?"

"Nothing. Where did the Chief Inspector go? What's he up to?"

Arnaldo hesitated, scratched the back of his head, seemed to make up his mind. "Let me tell you something about Mario Silva," he said. "He had a son, an only child. The kid died of leukemia when he was the same age as that young man you're holding by the hand. It was a long time ago now, but it changed his life forever. He thinks kids are God's most precious gift. Nothing bothers him more than the abuse of children, either physical or mental. If he'd been there with you, he would have maced that fucking priest himself—and probably beat the crap out of him, too."

"So you're saying . . ."

"I'm saying you don't have to worry about Castori getting his hooks into this kid. I'm saying Mario is out there, right now, solving the problem."

"How?"

"I wouldn't like to say."

"But you know."

"I *think* I know. Let's just wait and see, shall we? He won't be long. Where's your friend Senhorita Mandel?"

"I . . . I don't know exactly."

It was true. Fred Vaz had shown up just as they were leaving, and Maura had gone off with him. But, at the moment, she didn't know her whereabouts *exactly*.

"I have two questions for the boy. Would you kindly put them to him?"

"I'm not sure I can, but I'll try."

Arnaldo's questions were short ones, and Jade was able to ask them in her limited Awana, although she had to use a number of gestures to do it.

Had the boy's father buried the meat? (He had.)

Had they seen, or heard, anything besides birds or insects in the sky at any time before discovering the bodies? (They hadn't.)

By the time Arnaldo had gotten his answers, Silva was back.

"I'm going to open my home to him," he said to Jade.

"You're going to do what?" She glanced at Arnaldo. He gave her a little nod, as if to say, *I told you so.*

"I've just spoken to my housekeeper," Silva went on. "I'm going to charter a plane to bring the two of you to Belem. From there, you'll take a commercial flight to Brasilia. She'll meet you there when you arrive."

Jade shook her head. "Out of the question," she said. "I can't just pick up and leave."

"Why not?"

"I should think that's obvious. I have responsibilities here."

"Do you? It seems to me, Senhorita Calmon, that your responsibility is the welfare of the Awana tribe. And the Awana tribe has been reduced to this one little boy."

"I'm not sure my superiors would see it that way."

"Don't worry about your superiors."

"Easy for you to say, Chief Inspector—"

"Actually, Senhorita Calmon, it is. There are some people in your organization who owe me favors. I'm one hundred percent sure I can secure approval for what I'm proposing."

"But—"

"Think about it. If you send him off to an orphanage, there will be no one he can talk to, no one he can trust. Look at the way he clings to you. You're the most important person in his life right now. The boy has suffered enough."

Jade frowned.

"Plus," Arnaldo cut in, "there's the fact that the only thing his tribe's killers have left undone is . . . him. I don't like putting it that way, but—"

"My housekeeper is a good person," Silva said. "And like me, she once lost a child. Take him to Brasilia. Please. Stay at my home. The two of you will be in excellent hands."

Jade glanced at the wedding band on Silva's finger. "How about your wife? We can't just show up on her doorstep. What's she going to think?"

"My wife has a drinking problem," Silva admitted. "She sleeps late, so we haven't yet spoken. But I assure you she'll make Raoni welcome. We have an extra bedroom. She loves children. She volunteers at an orphanage five days a week, never starts with the alcohol until she gets home. And he'll be in bed, sleeping, before she gets very far along."

"Well—"

"And my housekeeper doesn't drink at all. She'll be there all the time. Believe me, it's our best alternative. Tell me you'll do it."

Jade bit her lip, thought about it, and said, "All right, Chief Inspector. I'll do it. When do you want me to leave?"

"As soon as we get back. We'll go from the village to your home, where you can pack a bag. And then Arnaldo and I will take you to the airport. We won't let you, or him, out of our sight until you leave. Arnaldo?"

"Mario?"

"Call the airport. Reserve a plane to take them to Belem at five o'clock this afternoon. I know the pilot won't be able to get back before dark, but I don't care. Tell them they can bill us for a hotel. Then call Sanches, give him an approximate arrival time, and tell him to meet them at the airport. As soon as he's put them on a flight to Brasilia, he's to call me with the arrival time, so I can get in touch with Irene and Maria Lourdes."

"Consider it done."

Arnaldo went out. Silva turned back to Jade. "Go talk to Osvaldo's wife. Get her to take the boy's measurements. Then, while we're gone, she's to buy him clothing. Shirts, pants, shoes, socks, underwear, anything he needs. Put it on my bill. I'll have more money waiting for you when you get to Brasilia."

"You're going to pay for all of this yourself?"

"I am, and I don't want to hear a word about it. I can't think of anything better to spend my money on. Now, go. We have to bury this young man's father and make sure we're back here before we lose the light."

Chapter Thirty-One

"Damn," Maura said, waving a hand in front of her face.

Fred glanced over his shoulder. "That repellent I gave you not working?"

He seemed oblivious to the flies. Not once had he attempted to shoo them away.

"It's their buzzing," she said. "It's driving me insane."

"You get used to it."

She followed him over the trunk of a fallen tree, extending her arms to balance herself. "You know what, Fred? I don't *want* to get used to it. It's even worse than the stench." The rank odor of rotting fish was on the wind, getting stronger with each step they took.

"Not yet," Fred said, "but wait until we get there."

It took them another three or four minutes to reach the site. And, by the time they did, she had come to agree with him. The smell was worse than the flies.

"Jesus," Maura said, holding her nose.

Wire mesh had been stretched across the river and anchored to posts on either bank. On the downstream side, there were no fish; on the upstream side, hundreds. Some were fighting for breath, their gills working to keep them alive; many were on their backs, their white bellies exposed. Most were covered with the omnipresent flies; others had birds standing on their stomachs, pecking at their insides with greedy beaks. Maura turned away in revulsion.

"You think this is bad?" Fred said. "Look over here." He pushed aside a curtain of leaves. Behind it, was a huge pile of rotting fish. "They have to haul them out now and then," he said. "If not, the water gets backed up and overflows."

"Who's *they?*"

"God knows."

"How long has this been going on?"

"Months."

"You ever see anyone here? Hauling out dead fish?"

He shook his head. "So what do you think?" he said. "That what you came to see?" He sounded as proud as if he'd constructed the whole scene for her benefit.

"It's *exactly* what I came to see," Maura said. "What's this river called?"

"The Sapoqui."

"It flows into the Jagunami, right?"

"Right."

"How much further downstream?"

"Just around the next bend, a couple of hundred meters."

"Why didn't we follow the big river to get here?"

"It curves a lot. I took a shortcut." He pointed at the wire. "You got any idea why somebody would do that?"

"Pretty obvious, isn't it? To prevent dead fish from floating into the Jagunami."

"I still don't get it. The water is going through the wire. Won't it just kill more?"

"It will. But it will be diluted by the water of the larger river, so it will kill more slowly, and the fish won't accumulate."

Maura slid out of her knapsack, opened a flap and removed one of the bottles. "Take this and fill it with water from among those dead fish." There was no way she was going to touch any of that rotting flesh. "I'll take another sample from the other side of the wire."

"And then?"

"And then we're going to follow this river upstream."

Chapter Thirty-Two

WHEN AMATI HAD BEEN laid to rest, the diggers, operating under Jade's instructions, cut one of the sacred trees and erected a *kuarup*. Raoni decorated it, using paints and brushes Osvaldo had brought from Cunha's store. Gilda guided his hand with the finer work.

When he had finished, the little boy lay down on his father's grave, embraced the earth as if he was embracing the man himself, and cried. Jade asked the others to join their hands, and bow their heads. No white men's words were used. Silva was surprised to see tears streaming down the cheeks of the digger with a wart next to his nostril.

No one spoke on the journey back to town.

THE VEGETATION was too thick for Maura and her guide to move upstream while keeping to the riverbank, but Fred Vaz had an unerring instinct for navigating the green wilderness, and he was often able to bring them close enough to take additional samples.

"You know what a GPS is?" she asked as she capped the fifth of her bottles.

"Yeah," Fred said with a smile. "I know. But I don't need one."

"Never?"

"Never. I've been in and out of this rainforest all of my life. In here, every place looks pretty much the same to most people, but not to me. You drop me down just about anywhere in here, and I can find my way home." And then, after a pause, "You hear that?"

She listened, shook her head.

"All I hear is flies."

"One of those flies isn't a fly."

Now Maura could hear it too, a deeper note, different from that of the buzzing closer to her ears.

"I don't like this," Fred said. "We're turning back."

"No," she said.

"The deal was to bring you to the place where there were dead fish. I did that. We're turning back." He passed her and continued walking in the direction from which they'd come.

"I'll pay you another two hundred Reais," she said.

He stopped short and turned to face her. "How much further do you want to go?"

"Until we get to the source of that sound."

He pursed his lips, then shook his head. "No telling how far away it is. We could be walking for hours, and believe me, you don't want to get stuck out here after dark."

"What if it's close?"

"That's possible, too."

"So let's set a time limit. Two hours?"

"No way."

"How about one?"

"Also too long. Thirty minutes."

"Forty-five."

"Okay. Forty-five minutes and then we turn back. But not for nine hundred Reais. You're going to have to make it an even thousand."

"Okay, a thousand."

Fred nodded curtly, passed her again and resumed leading them forward.

WHEN THEY reached the main road, the truck that had carried Amati's coffin turned left and vanished over a hill.

Arnaldo, now at the wheel of the lead jeep, turned right. He went first to the Grand, where Amanda was waiting with two bags of clothing. The next stop was Jade's home, where she packed bags for herself and the boy and sat down to write a note of farewell to her best friend.

Her first attempt was a failure. It wouldn't make Maura feel any better about being abandoned. Angry at not being able to find the right words, Jade crumpled the paper, threw it into the wastebasket, and started anew.

And this time, she wrote the one thing that would soften the blow of her departure. She broke her promise to Silva and confided everything she'd learned.

"I DON'T like this," Fred said. "You know what that sound is, don't you?"

They were closer now, and it was obvious.

"A gasoline-powered motor," Maura said.

"That's right. A power saw—or maybe a generator."

It was their first exchange in five minutes. Fred, talkative as hell up until he'd agreed to the time extension, had fallen into a worried silence.

"I don't think it's either one," Maura said.

She was thinking *gasoline-powered dredge*, but she was reluctant to tell him that.

"Whatever it is, it's in the Awana reservation, being run by white men and not supposed to be here. We're going back."

She glanced at her watch. "My forty-five minutes aren't up."

He turned to face her, came closer, and lowered his voice. "Senhorita Mandel, listen to me and listen good. The people who are making that racket are doing something illegal. I don't know what it is, but I guarantee you it's illegal, and they aren't going to look kindly on your finding out about it. This isn't São Paulo. You can't just stick your nose into another man's business and expect to get away with it, especially if it's illegal and in the middle of the rainforest."

"Our deal was forty-five minutes. You haven't earned that additional three hundred Reais we were talking about."

"Fuck the three hundred Reais. We're going back."

"Just a little bit further."

"You're not listening. It's dangerous, and it's Federal Police business, not ours."

"We're close now, Fred. Listen to how loud the motor is. Do you really want to turn back without a look? After coming all this way?"

"You bet I do."

"We'll be careful. We'll creep up on them, have a look, and sneak away again."

"No, we won't. Don't you feel it?"

"Feel what?"

"Like we're being watched?"

Maura sensed the hairs rising on the back of her neck. Now that he'd mentioned it, she *did* feel like they were being watched. But there was no way she was about to admit it.

"That's ridiculous. You're just trying to scare me."

"I'm not. I'm scared myself. And I want to get out of here. Now."

"Just—"

"Now. If they're watching, and we don't go any further, they might just let us go. But if we see what they're up to, and they catch us, they sure as hell won't. Believe me. They could put a bullet into both of us, bury us out here, and no one would be the wiser. Ever."

"I don't think—"

He cut her off. "What was that?"

She listened, shook her head. "I didn't hear anything."

"But I did, and you're not exactly Sheena, the Queen of the Jungle, are you? Let's get the hell out of here!"

His fear was contagious. Or maybe Maura herself had sensed something on a subliminal level. She felt the onset of panic, and this time she was unable to contain it. Suddenly, there was nothing she wanted to do more than get out of this suffocating green hell.

Chapter Thirty-Three

"THAT," SILVA SAID, AS the Cessna 182 lifted off the runway, "is a load off my mind."

The little aircraft eased into a turn, before leveling out on a course for Belem.

"You gonna call Irene?" Arnaldo said.

"Not until I have the details for the connecting flight. Let's see what we can learn from the kid."

They strolled over to the rude wooden shack that served as an office. The furnishings consisted of a desk, three chairs and a telephone. On the desk were a calculator, a ledger and a goose-necked lamp. A file cabinet stood in one corner. The walls were decorated with unframed photographs of various aircraft crudely cut out of aviation magazines. The kid was in one of his chairs, with his feet on the desk and his nose in a center spead showing a nude with a pout. He looked to be no more than seventeen.

"You're Max, right?" Silva asked.

"Sure am," the kid said.

"And your father is Felipe, the guy who just left for Belem?"

"Right again. What can I do for you?" Max dropped the magazine and put his feet on the floor.

"I'm Chief Inspector Silva. This is Agent Nunes. We're with the Federal Police."

"Yeah," Max said. "I know. I expect everybody in town does by this time."

"We've got a few questions for you."

"Fire away."

"Did you see the lynching?"

The kid looked pained. "I did," he said. "And you know what? I wish I hadn't. It wasn't at all like I thought it was going to be. I don't mind telling you, I'm starting to get nightmares about it."

"That's called having a conscience," Silva said.

"Doesn't everyone?"

"No, son, in my experience not everyone does. Did you recognize anyone pulling on the rope?"

"They were all wearing masks."

"I know that. It's not what I asked."

"I didn't recognize anyone," Max said.

"How would you feel if we were able to prove that some-one other than the Indian murdered Omar Torres?"

"What do you mean, how would I feel?"

"Just that. How would you feel?"

Max grimaced. "I'd feel like shit. But . . ."

"But what?"

"Those guys with the masks?"

"Yes?"

"They all live in this town. So do I. You don't."

"In other words even if you recognized someone, you wouldn't tell us."

Max licked his lips. "Maybe it's hard for you to understand—"

"No," Silva said. "It's not. So let's talk about something else." He took a piece of paper out of his pocket. "How about this? I give you some names. You say 'yes' to the ones that own aircraft, 'no' to the ones who don't, 'maybe' to the ones you don't know about either way. Got that?"

Max nodded.

"Omar Torres."

"Yes. It's a little—"

"I don't need details. Yes, no, or maybe will suffice. Hugo Toledo?"

"Yes."

"Roberto Lisboa?"

"Yes. Why do you—"

"Just answer the questions, please. Paulo Cunha?"

"Yes."

"Cesar Bonetti?"

"Yes."

"José Frade?"

"Him, too."

"That's a yes?"

"That's a yes."

"All of them then?"

"Uh-huh. Anybody around here with any money owns an airplane. You got a big ranch, you need one. You're an important businessman, like Cunha, you don't want to be left behind. You want to show you're as good as the next man, so you buy one, too."

"Any employ pilots?"

"Nope. They all fly themselves. My dad taught most of them. All of them, in fact, except for Lisboa. Where he learned, I don't know."

Silva put the paper back in his pocket. "I'd like you to show us those aircraft."

"I can't."

"Why not?"

"Because none of them are here. Why would anyone pay us to tie them down if they have their own airstrip? And all of them do."

"WELL, THAT wasn't much help," Silva said as they walked to their car. "Any one of them could have dropped the meat."

"And no felon would be stupid enough to put a flight on the day of the murders into a logbook," Arnaldo said.

"Probably not," Silva said. "But it won't hurt to check."

They were buckling their seatbelts when Silva's telephone rang. It was Lefkowitz, the chief crime scene technician in São Paulo.

"Wonder of wonders," Lefkowitz said. "I got through."

"Has it been a problem?"

"I've been trying Hector for the last hour."

"I'm not surprised. There's only one tower for mobile phones, and it's down about half the time. Arnaldo is here with me. I'm going to switch you over to speaker."

When he heard the change in the quality of the connection, Lefkowitz said, "Hi, Arnaldo. How's life in the jungle?"

"About like you might expect."

"I sympathize. I spent almost two years in Manaus, remember?"

"This place is worse."

"Nothing is worse than Manaus."

"I've been both places, and believe me, Lefkowitz, this is worse."

"Jesus. You've got my sympathy."

"What have you got for us?" Silva asked, cutting short the pleasantries.

"The blood on the Indian's clothing?"

"Yes?"

"It's not human. It's bovine."

"*Bovine?*"

"Yeah, Chief Inspector, you know, from a—"

"I know what bovine is, Lefkowitz. Are you sure?"

"One hundred percent."

"How about the knife?"

"Mostly human on the blade," Lefkowitz said. "Mostly bovine on the grip."

"And the prints?"

"All from the Indian, all on the grip, none on the blade. None at all. It was as if—"

Silva anticipated what he was going to say: "It had been wiped clean before someone pressed it into his hand."

"You took the words right out of my mouth."

"How about fingernail scrapings?"

"Nothing. There weren't any."

"Thanks, Lefkowitz. One more thing: Have you done anything to light a fire under Doctor Rodrigues?"

"I have. I used my powers of persuasion."

"In other words," Silva said, "you lied to her."

"Big time. I told her you'd sent samples to me as well, said I was beginning my analysis."

"And being the competitive person she is . . ."

"The race is on."

"Good thinking."

"Mind you, Chief Inspector, I have the greatest respect for Doctor Rodrigues's abilities in the field of—"

"Save your breath, Lefkowitz. I know that woman as well as you do. Anything else?"

"Not at the moment."

They hung up. Arnaldo started the jeep.

"Where to?"

"Back to the hotel. It's been a long day. I need a drink."

Chapter Thirty-Four

By the time Maura got to Jade's place, she'd managed to convince herself that her panic had been the product of an overactive imagination.

She counted out Fred's seven hundred Reais and told him he could earn a thousand by taking her back the following day.

He waved a finger in front of her nose. "Not for a thousand, not for two thousand, not for any amount." And then, exasperated: "You didn't listen to a word I said, did you?"

"I listened, but there is no way I'm going to let go of this story."

"That's your decision. As for me, I'm not going back there. Not tomorrow, not ever."

"If you don't, I'll find someone else."

"You do that. Thanks for your business. Goodbye."

Her response was to slam the door of his jeep.

The note she found on her bed was a revelation, and it did a great deal to cheer her up.

She went to the refrigerator and took out a beer. Her next step, she thought, should be to start interviewing the women. Can in hand, she went to Jade's desk and found the address book where her friend had told her it would be—in the top right-hand drawer. It was an old one, with a battered cloth cover, and pre-dated Jade's arrival in Azevedo by many years. There were even entries from their school days. Patricia Toledo's number was the last on a crowded page filled with Ts.

"And why do you want to talk to me?" Patricia said after Maura had explained who she was and whom she worked for.

"Not just you, Senhora Toledo. I'd like to talk to some of the other leading townswomen as well."

Calling her a leading townswoman struck a chord. "It's Patricia," she said, switching from cold to warm. "Let me rephrase the question, Senhorita Mandel—"

"Maura."

"Maura. What do you think I—we—might be able to tell you that you don't know already?"

Maura had anticipated the question and had her answer already prepared. "I came to cover the story of what happened to the tribe," she said. "And I got here to find there's been a lynching, but I've come to the conclusion that Azevedo has another story to tell, one that could be the basis for an entire series."

"Series?"

"Yes. I want to write about the women who are opening up Brazil's last frontiers. It's heroic, you know, doing what you're doing."

"It is?"

"Absolutely. There are precious few people in São Paulo and Rio who have any idea about the difficulties you've had to overcome, the privations you've had to put up with, the progress you've made. You're a shining example to women all over this country."

"We are?"

"You are indeed." She was laying it on thick, but she hadn't misjudged her audience. Patricia was lapping it up.

"I'm flattered."

Of course she was.

"So, if you could spare me some time? Perhaps tomorrow?"

"I'm pretty busy, but I suppose I could manage it."

"I'd like to buy you lunch at the Grand. And perhaps you could invite some others? The right kind of people? Women like you?"

"Did you have anyone particular in mind?"

There was a whiff of suspicion in the question. Maura sensed and countered it. "No, no one in particular. After all, you'd know better than I."

"Yes," Patricia said, satisfied, "I would. How many?"

"Three would be a comfortable number. I want to do the stories in depth, not spread the personalities too thin."

"Myself and two others?"

"Perfect!"

"I know just the people."

I'll bet you do. Gotcha!

After she hung up, Maura pawed through the other drawers in Jade's desk, looking for something to ship her samples in. She wanted to get them off before the airport closed for the night.

She settled on two padded envelopes, each big enough for three bottles. She tightened the caps and taped the envelopes together into one package. Then she went to the Grand to talk to Amanda.

"It's important that I get this stuff off before the airport closes," she said.

"I talked to the kid," Amanda said. "He and his old man are asking for sixteen hundred Reais."

"Wow! Pricey."

"He said it includes landing fees, gas, a night in a hotel, and meals, but I still think it's outrageous. Why don't you send it by truck? I could find you a driver going that way who would do it for two hundred."

"How long would it take?"

"With any luck, it would be there by tomorrow night."

"And without luck?"

"No way of telling."

"So I'd lose at least a day, maybe more?"

"Uh-huh. Sorry, but those are the two options."

"I'll bite the bullet then."

"Okay, but I'm right in the middle of preparing dinner, so there's no way I can go out there at the moment. And if I know that kid, you won't be able to count on him to make a pickup. Your best bet is to go to the airport and stand there, watching the oversexed little bastard until he takes off."

"Sounds like you don't like him."

"You think? His name's Max Gallo. You want to borrow my jeep?"

"MUST BE pretty important, huh?" Max said, taking the package and feeling it for some clue of what was inside. "To pay us all that money to take it, I mean."

"It *is* important," Maura said. "And it's fragile, so don't drop it. When can you leave?"

"Can it wait until tomorrow morning? My dad took a couple of people to Belem, and there's nobody else to mind the store."

"Negative," she said. "It has to go tonight. And you're charging me sixteen hundred Reais, remember?"

"Oh, I remember, all right. Okay, you've got a deal. I'll go tonight."

"So answer my question. When can you leave?"

"Well, first I gotta make a phone call, then I gotta file a flight plan—"

"I didn't ask you how to build a clock. I asked you what time you can leave."

"Hey," he said. "Touchy."

"You people want the money, or not?"

"We want it."

"Then get a move on."

"Okay, okay, just leave the package with me and—"

"I'm not going anywhere until I see you take off."

"Oh. Okay. Give me a credit card and take a seat."

The kid took the card she offered, turned his back on her, picked up the telephone, and carried out a conversation in a low voice. Then he hung up and started filling in some paperwork. Some fifteen minutes later, while he was still at it, the door opened, and a girl came in. She was petite, had long hair, was wearing a pink dress, and reminded Maura of a pixie she'd once seen in a cartoon. She was carrying a small overnight bag.

"We're going? We're really going to Belem?"

Max nodded. She squealed and started jumping up and down.

"We're going to Belem! We're going to Belem!"

Maura fled the display of youthful enthusiasm and went outside to wait in Amanda's jeep. She was still sitting there, twenty minutes later, when the young couple came out of the little terminal building.

Max waved at Maura, strolled to one of the Cessnas, and opened the door on the passenger side. The girl climbed in, and he made much of adjusting her seatbelt.

Copping a feel or two while he's at it, the little creep, Maura thought. Five minutes later, they were airborne. She glanced at her watch, reached for her cell phone, and called Nataniel Eder.

"Samples are on the way," she said and gave him the aircraft registration number and an approximate arrival time.

"I'll have someone meet him," the Belem bureau chief said. "I suppose this is a rush job."

"The rushest."

"Results noon tomorrow at the latest."

* * *

MAURA RETURNED Amanda's jeep and passed the few hours until dinner by interviewing people about the lynching.

There were new stories in circulation. Omar Torres was now being pointed to as the author of the genocide. *No Indians, no need for a reservation,* he was rumored to have said. And the Indian, people were saying, had become convinced that Omar was the man responsible for killing his people.

She had grave doubts about the veracity of both reports. And so, she soon discovered, did the federal cops.

"How about we go for a walk?" she said to Gonçalves after they'd finished dinner.

"Okay, but only if you don't repeat last night's performance."

"Deal."

"I mean it, Maura. It would be a waste of your time and mine. I have no intention of telling you anything."

"You don't have to, and I'm not going to ask you a thing. In fact, there are some things I intend to tell *you.*"

The weather was clear, and there was a full moon. They walked to the square where Amati had been lynched, picked out a bench, and sat down side by side.

"I know about the parachute," she said. "And the meat. And how you're waiting for an analysis of the poison."

"There's only one way you could have learned all of that," he said. "Jade told you."

"She did *not* tell me," Maura said.

It was true. Jade hadn't *told* her. She'd written it.

"Whatever," Gonçalves said, unconvinced but disinclined to argue. "Anyway, you promised we weren't going to talk about the case."

"No," she said. "I didn't. I promised I wasn't going to ask you any questions."

"So don't."

"I won't. In fact, as promised, I'm about to tell you something. All you have to do is to swear to keep it to yourself."

He crossed his arms and shook his head. "Negative. We play by different rules. As a cop, I can't hide behind journalistic ethics or client privilege. I'm obliged to come clean about what I learn."

"But if I don't tell you what I *could* tell you, and not telling you hampers your ability to solve this case, what then?"

"Is this the same information we were talking about last night?"

"No. Last night I had a suspicion. Now, I'm close to having proof. My information is more detailed and more complete. I have facts that will help you see this case in a whole different light. And to get me to tell you what I know, all I need is your word."

"Why tell me at all?"

"Because I want to see the guilty parties brought to justice."

"But that's not all of it, is it?"

"No. It's not all of it."

"Out with it then."

"I'm scared."

"You're *what?*"

"I had a scare today, out in the rainforest. I had a feeling I was being watched, watched by someone who has in all probability committed multiple murders, one of which you don't even know about yet."

"Jesus, Maura—"

"I want to tell you about it because if anything happens to me, you'll know where to start looking."

"If you have reason to believe—"

"I do."

"Then you should back off. Now. No story is worth getting killed for."

"I don't intend to get killed—"

"Nobody ever intends to get killed, but they do."

"I'm not going to back off on this, Haraldo. No way. So please stop beating around the bush. Are you willing to give me your word or not? Because if you don't, I'm not going to tell you a thing. It's my story, I unearthed it, and I intend to be the one to break it."

"I don't understand—"

"Of course you don't. You're not a journalist. Last chance, Haraldo. Your word. Yes or no."

"You're not giving me any choice."

"Is that a yes?"

"It's a yes."

"Hallelujah! Finally! Okay, listen . . . "

Chapter Thirty-Five

SILVA'S ALARM CLOCK AND telephone rang in quick succession. Switching off the first, he picked up the second.

"Did I wake you?" It was Lefkowitz.

"By a couple of seconds, no." Silva blinked his bleary eyes at the clock: 7:30 A.M. exactly. "Did you fall out of bed?"

"I got tired of sitting in São Paulo traffic for an hour and a half every morning. If I get up at five thirty, I miss the rush and get here in thirty-five minutes flat. Guess what I've got?"

"Insomnia?"

"Rodrigues's report."

"Already?"

"The time stamp on her email is five seventeen this morning. She must have pulled an all-nighter. You got email at that hotel of yours?"

"I'm not sure. And I don't need all the scientific gobbledygook. Just give me the bottom line. What was in that meat?"

"Batrachotoxin."

"Wait," Silva said. He grabbed his notebook and a pen. "Spell it."

Lefkowitz did.

"Got it," Silva said when he'd confirmed the spelling. "Now what, exactly, is it?"

"A steroidal alkaloid. A lethal dose for an oversized person like Arnaldo would be in the neighborhood of one hundred micrograms."

"Oversized person, eh? I'll tell him you said that. How much is one hundred micrograms?"

"Please do. That's why I said it. One hundred micrograms is roughly the weight of two grains of table salt."

"Whoa! Toxic is right."

"It's extracted from the skin glands of the *phyllobates terribilis.*"

"What the hell is a—"

"A frog, not much bigger than my thumb, but with enough poison in it to kill ten human beings. Some tribes tip the darts of their blowguns with the stuff; hence the little creature's other name: the poison dart frog. The poison blocks the transmission of nerve signals to the muscles."

"Stops hearts from pumping, lungs from breathing, that sort of thing?"

"That sort of thing. Fast-acting, too. Fast enough to drop monkeys and birds in their tracks. Administered orally, it takes a bit longer to kill, but it's just as lethal."

"Commercially available?"

"Yes. It has some uses I won't bore you with, but it's heavily controlled. Mara has already started checking sources, but I think it's more likely your killers extracted it themselves."

"And how would they have done that?"

"I don't know, but the Chocó tribe does it by impaling a frog on a piece of wood and holding it over a fire. Bubbles of poison form when the frog's skin begins to blister."

"How do you find out these things?"

"I have a secret. It's called the Internet."

"So ALL the poisoner—"

"Or poisoners," Gilda corrected.

"—or poisoners," Silva agreed, "would have to have done was to gather the little bubbles, get them into a syringe and inject the meat."

"But before that," Hector said, pouring himself more

coffee, "they would have had to have had specialized knowledge." He put down the pot. "Think about it. This is an obscure poison, right?"

"It certainly is," Silva said. "Anyone at this table ever heard of it before?"

They all shook their heads.

"So," Gilda went on, "they wouldn't only have to have known about it, but also how to extract it."

"And who the hell would have?" Arnaldo said, cutting into a piece of jackfruit.

"A pharmacist, or a biologist," Silva said.

"Or a doctor," Gilda said. "Not all of us are as ignorant of poisons as I am."

"Maybe somebody who knew the customs of Indians," Hector put in.

"Which means you could include almost any long-term resident of this area."

"Or someone who likes to read," Silva said, "because they could have taken their knowledge from a book."

"Or a priest who lived with one of the tribes," Arnaldo said.

"In short, knowing what the poison was doesn't bring us one iota closer to telling us who might have used it," Silva said. "Let's talk about who's going to interview whom."

HE CHOSE Paulo Cunha as the first subject for Arnaldo and himself. Cunha received them in the well-appointed office he kept above his pharmacy. Through the picture window behind his desk, the two cops could see his name in meter-high letters on the façade of the supermarket across the street.

"Do I think Torres rooted out that tribe?" Cunha echoed Silva's question. "I most certainly do."

"Why?"

"He hated to see those Indians sitting on all that land. Truth to tell, all of us did, but Omar was the only one who ever said he intended to do something about it."

"He said that, did he?"

"He did. I heard him myself, heard him say that if the government didn't solve the problem, he would. I thought he was bluffing, never thought he'd do it, but he proved me wrong. It just goes to show, you never can tell about people."

"Said he'd murder them?" Silva didn't try to keep the skepticism out of his voice.

Cunha backpedaled. "Well . . . no, not in so many words, but that's what he meant. And it wasn't just to me; he said it to a lot of people. Ask around. You'll see."

"All right. Let's assume he was guilty—"

"Assume it, Chief Inspector, because he was."

"—how could the Indian have learned that Torres was the one he should blame?"

"I can't tell you. But I know he did."

"How do you know?"

"Father Castori told me. And the Indian told *him* when that FUNAI woman took him there."

"If that's true, why didn't Father Castori also tell Senhorita Calmon?"

"Didn't he?"

"No. Doesn't that strike you as strange?"

"Not if you know Castori. The man has a drinking problem." Cunha glanced at his watch. "Can we speed this up? I've got another appointment in fifteen minutes."

"Okay," Arnaldo said, "how about we talk about that truckload of wood?"

"What truckload of wood?"

"The one you sent to Belem yesterday."

"Oh. *That* wood. What about it?"

"Where did you get it?

"I harvested it on my *fazenda*."

"How long have you had that *fazenda*?"

"What's that got to do with anything?"

"Just answer the question, please."

"Almost fifteen years."

"Fifteen years? And you still hadn't harvested all the wood on the property?"

"It was hardwood. Hardwood takes time to grow. I don't cut trees less than ten meters high."

"So that whole truckload was freshly cut?"

"I harvested it about a month ago."

"How about you show us the site?"

"You're suggesting I came by that wood illegally?"

"How about you show us the site?" Arnaldo repeated.

"I resent the implication. I have never, in all of my life, dealt in illegal wood."

"Then you should have no objection to showing us the site."

"I don't. Of course I don't. But it won't tell you a thing. I've already burned the boughs and leaves, unearthed the stumps. And yesterday, I plowed the land for planting."

"How convenient."

Cunha bristled. "You have no right to—"

"Where do you store wood before you have it loaded onto a truck?"

"In a covered area near my front gate. I suppose you want to see that, too."

"We do."

"It's empty at the moment."

"So you're not currently in possession of any wood at all?"

"None."

"We want to see your financial records."

"I've had enough of this! You want to see my *fazenda*? Get a search warrant. You want to see my records? Get legal permission."

"Just a few more questions. I'm told you own an airplane."

Cunha slammed a hand on his desk. "No, Agent Nunes, no more questions. I don't like your attitude. If either one of you has anything else to say to me, you can say it in the presence of my lawyer and with the paperwork that would obligate me to talk to you. Now if you'll excuse me, I have another appointment. My secretary will show you out."

Chapter Thirty-Six

THE MAYOR'S OFFICE WAS in the Toledo Building, the tallest in town, and the only one with an elevator. Beyond two glass doors and visible to anyone approaching from the street was a portrait, in oils, of a hunger-thin, fierce-looking man with a bristling moustache.

The mayor, in contrast, was clean-shaven, avuncular, and running to fat.

"Who's the guy in the painting?" Gonçalves asked when he and Hector were seated, drinking coffee.

"In the entrance hall downstairs?" Toledo said. "That's my old man, Hugo Senior."

"A good likeness?"

"Him to the life," Toledo said proudly, as if he'd painted it himself.

There was a distinct lack of similarity between the man in the portrait and the one seated in front them. Seeing a photo of Enrique Azevedo would have cleared up the mystery, but there was little chance of that. There *were* no photos of Enrique Azevedo, not a single one anywhere in the town. The elder Toledo had seen to that. In stark contrast to his wife, Hugo Senior had *hated* The Founder.

"Frankly, Delegado"—Toledo looked at the card Hector had given him—"Costa, I'd been expecting the courtesy of a visit from your boss. I am, after all, the mayor."

"Unfortunately," Hector said, ever the diplomat, "something urgent and unrelated to this case came up, so . . ." He opened his hands, palms upward.

"So here you are instead. Yes, I see. Well, let's get started then. First, let me say by way of introduction that the good people of this town, myself included, are horrified by recent events. Firstly, by what Omar Torres did to those Indians. There are those, of course, who—"

Hector held up a hand to interrupt him. "One moment, Senhor *Prefeito*. Are you telling me you're blaming Torres for the genocide of the Awana?"

The mayor blinked. A *little too innocently*, Hector thought.

"Of course. Why, otherwise, would the Indian have killed him?"

"We're not sure he did."

In the pause that followed, the door to Toledo's office opened and a shapely brunette walked in. Both the cops stood up.

"Hello, Hugo, I wonder if . . . oh, I'm sorry. You have guests."

"Ah," the mayor said. "What a pleasant surprise."

Toledo was a bad actor. This was no surprise. It was programmed. Hector was sure of it.

"I hope I'm not interrupting anything," she said.

"Not in the least." Toledo got up and shifted a chair from the nearby conference table to his side of the desk. "Please join us, my dear. Delegado Costa, Agent Gonçalves, this is my wife, Patricia."

She flashed them a smile and sat down. The cops resumed their seats.

"I came into town for lunch and had time for a cup of coffee," she said. "But I don't want to interrupt anything. If you're busy, I'll just stroll down to the Grand."

"Not at all," Toledo said. "You're welcome here. Isn't she, gentlemen?"

"By all means," Hector said. "We'd be grateful for your contribution."

"Then I'll have that coffee," she said.

"Coming right up." Toledo filled a cup from the thermos flask on his desk. She took it, reached for the sugar and served herself two spoonfuls.

"I suppose Hugo has told you," she said, "about how horrified we are by what's happened."

Same word her husband used, Hector thought. *Horrified.* "Yes," he said. "He has."

She took a sip, studying the two cops over the rim of her cup. "Omar hated having those Indians there," she said.

"Not that he was alone," Toledo said. "Truth to tell, that reservation has always been a thorn in our sides. We're productive people. We grow crops. We raise cattle. We contribute to the wealth of the nation. The more land we've got, the more the nation benefits. More food means lower prices. Our success generates tax income, makes the wheels of commerce go around. Commerce generates jobs. Now, you take the Indians. What do they produce? Nothing! They were sitting on land we could have turned productive. And worse, it was costing taxpayer money to keep them there. After all, who do you think pays the salaries of people like Jade Calmon? People like us, that's who."

It was a politician's speech, obviously prepared in advance. Toledo was warming to his theme. His face was getting red. But Patricia was no wallflower. As soon as he paused for breath, she stepped in.

"The Awana were going to have to join the twenty-first century sooner or later. That's all we ever wanted them to do: join the twenty-first century. Rooting them out never crossed our minds. And when Omar brought it up, we laughed at him. We never expected him to go out and do it."

"How come you're so sure he did?" Gonçalves asked.

"He kept going on and on about it. Not just to us. To everyone."

"Who's everyone?"

"Everyone. Frade, Lisboa, Cunha, Bonetti, Doctor Pinto. Ask them, they'll tell you."

"What makes you sure the Indian knew who to blame?" Hector asked.

She turned to her husband. "You didn't tell them?"

"I was about to when you arrived." She turned back to the cops. "We had it from Father Castori," she said. "And *he* had it from the Indian's own mouth."

"When was this?"

"Just after that FUNAI agent brought him to town," Hugo said.

"Jade doesn't speak the Indian's language," Patricia said. "She had to use the padre to translate for her."

Hugo Toledo leaned forward in his chair and stared directly into Hector's eyes, the very picture of sincerity. "Look, Delegado Costa, do you want my advice about all of this?"

"Please."

"It's this: We're public servants, you and I. We have to think about what's best for the town, we can't get caught up in the details, we have to look at the larger picture." The mayor was a hand-waver. He illustrated what he was saying by pointing first at Hector, then at himself and then extending his arms and as if to embrace *the larger picture*. "The man who poisoned the tribe has been punished. The man who murdered him has been punished. The people who lynched the Indian are good citizens. They might have gone overboard by taking the law into their own hands, but they did what they thought was right. Public sympathy is on their side. You won't find anyone who'll be willing to identify them or to testify against them. Attempting to do so will be a complete waste of energy. And even if you could find out who they are, which you won't, to punish them would be a travesty of justice."

"What if the Indian didn't do it?"

The mayor expelled an exasperated sigh. "I've told you what Father Castori said. Go and speak to him, if you don't believe me."

"I didn't say I didn't believe you."

"No, but you seem to harbor serious doubts. I've told you why we think the Indian was guilty. Now, please, tell me why you think he wasn't. Do you have some kind of forensic proof?"

"We think we do."

"The Indian was found, drunk, next to a corpse. He was covered in blood. The murder weapon, they tell me, was pried from his hand. You think you can explain all of that away?"

Hector stood up. Gonçalves took his cue and did the same.

"It would be premature," Hector said, "to go into details about that at the moment. Thank you, Senhor *Prefeito*, for your time. And for yours, Senhora. You've both been most helpful."

They hadn't, of course. But it served his purpose to let them believe they had.

Chapter Thirty-Seven

MAURA VEILED MOUNTING DISTASTE for her luncheon companions with a smile and pushed the remaining fish on her plate under a leaf of lettuce. Amanda's menu had billed it as *pacu*, but it looked suspiciously like piranha. Or maybe *pacu* and piranha were the same thing. She didn't know and didn't want to ask.

All her questions up to now had been about the vicissitudes of living on one of Brazil's last frontiers and how the women coped with them. They coped, in fact, extremely well. They were rich. They had servants. They traveled. They had spacious houses and air conditioning, drank imported beverages, and ate imported foods. Theirs was anything but a hardscrabble existence. And it was boring as hell. It wouldn't make for a decent story.

She was about to ask her first important question of the afternoon, and had just turned to Patricia Toledo to do it, when she felt the vibration of her phone.

She excused herself and took it from the hip pocket of her jeans. It was Nataniel, calling from Belem.

"We got the results," the bureau chief said. "Congratulations."

"I'm on to something?"

"You sure as hell are. There's enough mercury in just one of those little bottles to kill a whale. You should get the IBAMA onto it right away."

"I don't think that would be a good idea."

"Oh? Why not?"

"I'm having lunch with some ladies. I'm afraid I can't get into it right now."

"You think he's taking bribes?"

"Yes."

"Happens all the time. Want some advice from an old warhorse?"

"Always."

"Talk to him anyway."

"You're suggesting I go to the fox—"

She stopped before she gave the game away. The women were staring at her, paying close attention to every word she said. Nataniel, sharp as a tack, picked up on it straightaway.

"And complain about somebody stealing the chickens? I am indeed."

"Why?"

"Politics. The IBAMA big shots in Brasilia are jealous of their turf. An issue like this? It's theirs. You've got to play it through channels. Any other way is going to get their noses out of joint."

"That's ridiculous!"

"It is. But that's the way it works. First you complain to him, then you complain to his superiors. That way, if he fails to solve the problem, they get a chance to distance themselves from whatever he might have been up to, and they can be seen to have taken corrective measures as soon as they learned about it. Believe me, if you do it any other way, they're going to be pissed off. And getting them pissed off will get a certain publisher pissed off and . . ."

"He'll fall on me from a great height."

"He will."

"All right, Nataniel. I'll take your advice."

"You'll find I'm right. I'm looking forward to reading your stuff."

She thanked him, hung up, and turned back to Patricia. "I'm sorry about that," she said. "So, Patricia, you were saying that you ladies were all appalled by what Omar Torres did to that tribe, but . . ."

"But what?" Patricia asked.

"Are you sure he did it?"

"Everyone in this town is," Patricia said. "Everyone who *is* anyone heard him threatening to do it at one time or another. Isn't that so, ladies?"

The other two women nodded.

"I heard him say it myself," Rita said.

"Me, too," Maria said. "Many times. And the Indian knew it, too."

"The Indian knew who was responsible?"

"That's right. He told Father Castori that Torres did it."

"And how did the Indian discover that?"

"He didn't say. But it doesn't matter, does it? I mean, the important thing is that he knew, and he revenged himself upon Torres because of it."

"Last night," Maura said, "I had a chat with one of the federal cops. They seem to think the Indian was innocent."

"I heard that not two hours ago from one of those same federal cops," Patricia said. "And it's a ridiculous assertion. The savage was lying right next to Omar's body, dead drunk. He had a knife in his hand. He was covered with Omar's blood. Who else could it have been?"

"It's not as complicated as those Federal Policemen are trying to make it out," Rita chimed in. "It's all simple and straightforward. Omar poisoned the tribe, and the Indian killed him in revenge. That's it. End of story."

"There's also the lynching," Maura said.

"That," Patricia said, "was unfortunate."

"Very," Maria agreed.

"And so unnecessary," Rita said. "The sort of thing that could give this town a bad name. I hope that when you write up that part of the story, you won't tar the whole town with the same brush, go blaming all of us for the actions of a few."

"Of course not," Maura said. "By the way, were any of you there when it happened?"

All three women shook their heads.

"But I heard that our delegado, Fernando Borges, tried to stop it," Patricia said. "Unfortunately, he was overwhelmed."

"And *I'm* told that Osvaldo, the owner of this hotel, also tried to stop it," Maura said.

"I heard that as well," Maria said. "But you have to take into account that he gets carried away about Indians. I think his mother was one. Or his grandmother. Or both. Can we please talk about something else? Some of your past stories, for example. Anything that was syndicated? Anything I might have read? Cesar and I get all the papers from Belem."

There was nothing Maura liked to talk about more than her past successes. But this time, she resisted the temptation. First she wanted to drop her bombshell.

"Just one more question," she said. "Fish are dying in the Sapoqui River. Did any of you hear anything about that?"

The ladies shook their heads.

"How did *you* hear about it?" Maria asked.

"A fishing guide told me."

"Lots of fish?" Patricia asked.

"Thousands."

"Probably an exaggeration."

"No," Maura said. "It isn't. I went there to have a look."

"What in the world could be causing that?" Rita said.

"I asked myself the same question, so I took some samples of the water and sent them to Belem to be analyzed."

A silence fell, but whether it was caused by guilt, surprise, or a lack of knowledge, Maura couldn't tell. There was nothing to be read in their faces.

"I suspect," she went on, in the hope of provoking response, "that it might be mercury."

The faces continued to be blank.

A few more seconds went by before Maria said, "Why mercury?"

"It's used to extract gold," Maura said. "It shouldn't be, but it is."

"There's no gold mining around here," Maria said with conviction.

"There is if those samples come back positive."

"And when is that likely to be?"

"I'm not sure. A couple of days, perhaps." Maura could lie like a trooper if she had to.

Chapter Thirty-Eight

HECTOR AND GONÇALVES HAD crossed paths with IBAMA representatives before. As a rule, they'd found them to be crusaders: men and women deeply concerned with Brazil's flora and fauna. Their mission often led to them being grouped together with their non-governmental counterparts—organizations like Greenpeace. But unlike those other "tree huggers" and "greenies," the IBAMA had real power behind it, not just the power to move public opinion, but the power to engage the forces of law enforcement within Brazil's federal government.

Raul Nonato, however, didn't fit the mold. He wore no beard, no shorts, no sandals; his skin was pale, not browned by exposure to the sun. His linen trousers were freshly pressed, there wasn't a scratch on his polished boots, his wristwatch was a stainless steel Rolex, and he was using cologne Hector had previously smelled exclusively on politicians—a sure sign it was expensive.

He received them in his living room, the home of the much-vaunted sixty-inch television set. "My office is in back," he said. "But we'll be more comfortable here. Make yourselves at home." He pointed to a couple of plush armchairs.

"Never thought of taking an office in town?" Hector asked, sinking into the soft fabric.

"I prefer working from home," Nonato said, taking a seat on the couch. "Besides, it saves the agency money."

"Nice TV," Gonçalves said.

Nonato smiled, gratified by the admiration. "A gift from one of my rich uncles. A kinder person never lived. How about that Indian, eh? Slaughtering a white man like that? And then the lynching. This town hasn't seen that kind of excitement since I got here."

"How long ago was that?"

"A little over two years."

"Like it?"

"Oh, it's not so bad once you get used to it. So what can I do for you?"

"You're an outsider," Hector said, drawing him in, "and not involved in any of the recent events, so we thought you might see them from a different angle."

"Well," Nonato said, "I don't know about that. I mean, it's pretty straightforward, isn't it? From what I hear, Omar Torres was running around town, telling folks that the Indians had to go and—"

"Who told you that?"

"José Frade," Nonato said promptly.

"How come you remember so well?"

"Because it was only this morning. Frade was in town to stock up on a few things. We met on the street and got to talking. The whole story came out."

"What whole story?"

"Same one you must have heard."

"We've heard *a* story. But we'd like to hear it the way Frade told it to you."

"He said Torres was always going on and on and on about what he called 'the Indian problem,' and if the government didn't do something about it soon, he would."

"And by 'the Indian problem' he meant?"

"Getting them off the reservation. Opening up the land to more productive uses. And you know what? I can't say I disagree with him. As long as it could have been done legally, of course, and without the Indians getting hurt."

"I'm a bit surprised to hear you say that," Hector said.

"You are? Why?"

"Doesn't it conflict with the IBAMA's brief?"

Nonato waved a finger. "Not at all! Don't confuse us with the FUNAI. *They're* the ones who are supposed to be looking out for the Indians. We don't do people; we do environment, and if you think we stand in the way of progress, you're laboring under a misconception. The IBAMA is all for development, it just has to be *sustainable* development. But don't get me started on that. I'll talk your ears off."

"Okay. So you were saying . . ."

"Torres poisoned the Awana, and the last man standing, the one they lynched, found out about it—"

"How?"

"I don't know, but he told Father C that he did."

"Castori?"

"Yeah, Castori."

"And how do you know that?"

"Same source. José Frade. And then you heard about where they found them, right? Torres's neck all slashed to hell with a machete? The state the Indian was in? The bloody knife right next to him?"

"Yes, we heard all of that."

"So that's it. You know what I know."

"Okay then," Hector said. "Thanks. I think that about covers it. By the way, just out of curiosity, what keeps you busy around here?"

"What do you mean?"

"Your duties. What does an IBAMA agent do all day?"

"We patrol. We make sure nobody's breaking any environmental laws."

"Ever catch anybody?"

Nonato grinned. "Not yet. My predecessor did a damned good job of cleaning up the place, got rid of the illegal loggers and all, didn't leave me hardly anything to do."

"Do you know Paulo Cunha?"

"Sure. Everybody knows Paulo Cunha. Why?"

"We're told he sends a lot of hardwood to Belem."

"He does."

"And you issue him transport permits."

"I do. Why wouldn't I? It's all legal."

"Where does he get the wood?"

Nonato shrugged. "Some he buys from his neighbors; some he cuts on his own land." He glanced at the clock on top of his monster TV set. "Hey, you guys want to see São Paulo play Palmeiras? It's starting in about five minutes, and the picture on this thing puts you right there on the field."

Chapter Thirty-Nine

AFTER STRIKING OUT WHEN she mentioned the gold, Maura made a final attempt to elicit a useful response by bringing up the name of Welinton Mendes.

But there, too, her luncheon companions disappointed her. No one, they told her, gave credence to anything old Welinton ever said. (Maria: *one nugget, querida, hardly constitutes a strike*). They also dismissed the disappearance of the prospector, preferring to believe he'd suffered some accident (Rita, taking a stab at humor: *the old drunk probably fell into the Jagunami and drifted out to sea*).

The luncheon ended with kisses and hugs all around—and the three interviewees all got up and left at the same time.

"Why the frown?" Amanda said when she came to clear the dishes from the table. "From over there, it looked like you all got along."

"We did," Maura said. "They all invited me to tea."

"So I repeat, why the frown?"

"Because I didn't learn a damned thing. And I shudder at the thought of having tea. They're not my kind of people."

"I agree they're not your kind of people. But what were you hoping to learn?"

Maura liked Amanda—and instinctively trusted her. With Jade gone, she needed at least one ally. "If you've got a minute," she said, "I'll tell you."

"I'm off to the supermarket. I need some stuff to prepare dinner. But if you want to tag along . . ."

"Sure."

They were almost there by the time Maura finished her story. She concluded it by sharing the test results.

"But nobody knows about that except for you," she said, "so I'd appreciate it if you'd keep it to yourself."

"I will," Amanda said. "I promise. So the old coot was right after all?"

"He was."

Maura paused on the wooden sidewalk under the supermarket's awning. The street, at that time of day, was virtually deserted, but she didn't expect that to be the case inside. Better to finish their conversation out there in the heat, with only stray dogs and flies as witnesses.

"You think someone killed him?" Amanda asked. "To take over his strike for themselves?"

"That would be my guess. Ana's, too."

Amanda brushed away a stray fly. "Isn't it about time you clued in the cops?

"Not yet," Maura said. She explained her reasons, told her she'd already confessed her suspicions to Gonçalves.

"Not good enough," Amanda insisted. "You've got to speak to the Chief Inspector himself."

"And I will. But not yet. Let's go inside, shall we? Get out of this heat?"

Before she could turn around and go through the door, Amanda put a hand on her arm. "It could change the focus of their whole investigation. You know that, don't you?"

"Well, duh! Of course, I do."

"And if Welinton's strike is on the reservation—"

"Which it probably is, it could well have been the reason for murdering the tribe. Yes, I know that too. So I'm not going to let any grass grow under my feet. As soon as I get some photographs—"

Maura stopped talking when a young woman carrying a baby on one arm and lugging a shopping bag with the other exited the supermarket's front door. She greeted Amanda, and acknowledged Maura with a little smile, but was too heavily-laden to stop and chat.

Amanda lowered her voice and said, "Photographs? You're not planning on going back there?"

"I am."

"That's crazy! If those people, whoever they are, killed Welinton, what's to prevent them from killing you?"

"I'll be careful. Besides, I'm not going alone. I'm going to bring Nonato, the IBAMA agent."

Amanda raised her eyes to heaven and snorted. "Nonato? That guy is useless. He knows no more about the rainforest than you do. No, Maura, my advice is to tell the federal cops and to tell them now."

"Stop insisting, Amanda. I *can't*. Don't you see? If I do, Silva will freeze me out."

"You don't know that."

"He did it before. If he does it again, that would be the end of my scoop. I'm not going to take that chance."

Amanda heaved a sigh. "I can see your point, but—"

"It's not going to take long. I'm going to talk to Nonato this afternoon."

"I wouldn't do that if I were you."

"Why?"

"Because I heard the feds discussing their plans. Nonato was on their list to be interviewed. You might run into them there. And if they haven't gone yet, it will be worse. He's a blabbermouth, that one. He'd tell them straight off what you're up to."

Two scruffy kids with similar features, the eldest about nine and clutching a five-Real note, the other perhaps a year younger, passed them and went inside. They were talking about something their mother had said. Both women ignored them.

"Tomorrow, then. And when he and I get back, and I've got my pictures, I'll talk to Silva. Can you help me find a new guide?"

"What's wrong with Fred?"

"He got skittish. He doesn't want to go back, thinks it's too dangerous."

"He's right. If someone really is mining gold—"

"As a fishing guide, he's right. As a journalist, I see it from another angle."

Amanda sighed. "And there isn't a damned thing I can say that's going to change your mind, is there?"

"Not a thing."

"Then I'll think about the problem of the guide, but first let's get out of this heat."

Ten steps beyond the front door, Amanda stopped short. "Sonia Frade," she said.

"What?"

"Sonia Frade. That's her, over there."

She lifted her chin, indicating a slim woman in a shapeless dress. Sonia was pushing a shopping cart, putting one foot in front of another like an automaton. Maura was struck by her eyes. They were brown, downcast and sad.

"Introduce me?" she said.

"Sure. Come on."

Just then, a tall man came around the far corner of the aisle and approached Sonia from behind. Again, Amanda stopped short.

"Her husband," she said. "He's pissed off about something."

Maura studied the scowl on José Frade's face and shrugged. "So what? Should we care?"

"You wouldn't ask if you knew the man. When he's like that, folks around here stay out of his way."

Frade reached out, grabbed his wife's arm and squeezed it—hard. Sonia's face contorted. She took in a breath. Maura opened her mouth to say something.

"Don't," Amanda said in a low voice. "You'll make it worse."

"What's the *matter* with him?"

"He's a sick bastard, that's what! He treats her like that all the time."

Frade spotted them whispering to each other. He moved toward them without loosening his grip. His wife, still pushing the cart, was forced to stumble along beside him. She didn't once look up.

"Come on," Amanda said.

She turned her back and beat a hasty retreat. After a moment's hesitation, Maura followed her around the corner into another aisle.

"Was he coming to talk to us?"

"He never has anything to say to me, and I doubt he even knows who you are. I think they're just on their way out."

"He wasn't even embarrassed," Maura said, fuming.

"He never is," Amanda said.

"I'm going to tell the federal cops about that guy."

Amanda put a hand on her arm. "Seems to me," she said, "that we already had that conversation. Your telling them isn't likely to do any good—and it could do Sonia a lot of harm. If they come after him, sooner or later, he's going to go after her."

"He can't just be allowed to go on like that!"

Inadvertently, Maura had raised her voice. Amanda made a placating gesture and put a finger to her lips. "Keep it down," she said. "He'll hear you."

"Maybe he should."

Amanda shook her head. "He definitely shouldn't. I used to feel the same way, but I kept turning it over and over in my head, and I came to the conclusion that it's best to just stay out of it."

"If it was me," Maura said, "I'd kill him."

"If it was you," Amanda said, "you probably would. But it's Sonia—and there's no way she's going to do that."

Chapter Forty

WHEN THEY DROPPED BY to speak to the lawyer, Renato Kassab, Gonçalves and Hector were told he was "in conference" at the *delegacia.*

"Two birds with one stone?" Gonçalves suggested.

The next person on their list was the delegado, Fernando Borges.

"Why not?" Hector said.

Some conference. They found the delegado and the lawyer drinking coffee and smoking cigars.

"Drop in to say goodbye?" Borges asked, taking his feet off his desk and pushing himself to his feet.

"We're not going anywhere," Gonçalves said. "Not yet. Not until we get some answers about what really happened around here."

"What really happened, young man," the lawyer said, "is that Torres rooted out the tribe, and the one man he didn't kill killed him. That's it. End of story. No one in this town will tell you any different."

"You're right about that," Hector said. "No one in this town will."

"But?"

"Despite all the stories we're being told, there are a number of things that don't add up."

The lawyer removed his glasses and started polishing them on his necktie. He was probably the only man in town who consistently wore a suit. "Such as?" he said.

"Such as," Hector replied, "when we got here, nobody

was talking about Omar Torres threatening the Indians or Amati being aware of it. Now, all of a sudden, it appears as if everyone is."

"Perhaps you were talking to the wrong people," Kassab said.

Hector turned to Borges. "How about you, Delegado? Did Torres say anything of that nature to you?"

"Well, er, no, not to me personally."

"And you, *Doutor* Kassab?"

"No. But I have no reason to disbelieve what I've been told." The lawyer didn't say, *Why should you?* But that's what his tone-of-voice implied.

"What about the case against the Indian?" Gonçalves asked.

Kassab returned his glasses to his nose and looked at him. "What about it?"

"You realize, don't you, that the only person who claims to have heard him threaten Torres was Father Castori?"

"It's my understanding, Agent, uhh . . ."

"Gonçalves."

"Agent Gonçalves, that the FUNAI woman was there as well."

"She was," Gonçalves said, "and she didn't hear the Indian say any such thing."

Kassab looked at him as he might look at a hostile witness—and phrased his next question accordingly: "Ah, but isn't it true, Agent Gonçalves, that her knowledge of the language is imperfect?"

"Yes, it is." Gonçalves admitted.

"So there you have it. I submit to you that the Indian said it, but she didn't understand it, and the priest failed to translate it."

"And why, *Doutor* Kassab, would he have, as you say, *failed* to do that?"

Most men would have taken offense at Gonçalves's tone, but the seasoned lawyer, veteran of many a courtroom battle, did not. He merely shrugged.

Gonçalves persisted: "I really would like an answer to that question, *Doutor* Kassab."

The lawyer thought about it for a moment, chose his words carefully. "Out of delicacy, perhaps? Or out of reluctance to spread an unsubstantiated rumor?"

"Are those your opinions? Or merely speculation?"

"Merely speculation."

"So what's your opinion?"

"Knowing Father Castori as I do, I think it's far more likely to have had to do with his consumption of alcohol."

"In other words, the priest is a drunk? And he simply forgot to translate that part of the conversation?"

"If you want to put it that baldly, yes."

"And you don't think there's any chance that Father Castori might have altered his story after the fact."

"Nah!" Borges said, rejecting the suggestion out of hand. "Why would he? He's got nothing to gain. He's got no motivation."

"I agree with the Delegado," the lawyer said.

Hector tried another tack: "Look, aside from Osvaldo Neto, you two are the only men in this town we're sure had nothing to do with the lynching of the Indian. You"—he pointed at Kassab—"were in your office with Jade when it happened, and you"—he pointed at Borges—"made an attempt to stop it."

"That's true," Borges said. "I did. And I wish that Chief Inspector of yours would give me more credit for it. He acts like I just stood back and let it happen."

"Which is patently untrue," the lawyer said. "The delegado and I both had a stake in preventing that lynching. We have our livings to make, and people who take the law into their own hands don't need policemen—or lawyers."

"No," Hector said, "they don't. So how about giving us a helping hand? Think about it. Who might have had a motive to kill Omar Torres and pin the crime on the Indian to cover it up?"

Kassab shook his head, as if he was tired of trying to explain something to a child unwilling, or unable, to understand it. "You truly believe that's what happened?"

"I think it's a real possibility."

"Well, I don't."

"Me neither," Borges said.

Silva and Arnaldo found the priest sitting on his front porch. A florid-faced man with a clerical collar, he was leaning back in a chair and staring blankly into the upper branches of a tree. Until Silva spoke, he seemed entirely unaware of their approach.

"Father Castori?"

The priest looked down, blinked, and brought his visitors into focus. "That's me," he said. "Who are you?"

"Chief Inspector Silva, Federal Police. This is Agent Nunes. Might we have a word?"

"By all means. Come on up." He waved them forward with the hand he wasn't using to hold his glass.

The two cops mounted the steps.

"How about a drink?" Castori said. He looked drunker than he sounded. There was hardly a slur in his speech.

Silva and Arnaldo exchanged a glance. "We wouldn't mind," Silva said.

"Good. Cachaça or beer?"

"Beer," Silva said.

Castori stood up, went into the house and came back with

a tray. On it were two cans of beer, two glasses, and a bottle. He put the tray on the table, handed each of the cops a can and a glass and used the bottle to top off his drink.

"Fire away," he said, when he'd resumed his seat.

Silva leaned forward, popped the can and concentrated on pouring a glassful of beer. Arnaldo took the lead.

"Amati told you Omar Torres murdered his entire tribe, correct?"

"Correct," the priest said.

"How did he reach that conclusion?"

"I have no idea."

"How come you never translated that part of the conversation to Jade?"

The priest's mouth rounded in an O of surprise. "Didn't I? My goodness, I thought I did."

"Not according to her."

Castori avoided their eyes by looking at the little church next door. A low mudbrick wall divided the two buildings.

"She . . . she caught me at a bad time. I wasn't expecting visitors."

"What does expecting visitors have to do with it?"

Castori took a deep breath and met Arnaldo's eyes. "My burdens occasionally get me down." A sigh and a shrug. "That was . . . one of those days. I'd had a bit too much of this." He waved his glass at the bottle. "I'm afraid I don't have total recall of the incident."

"We'd be grateful," Silva said, "if you could tell us what you remember."

The priest scratched the crown of his head, drawing attention to how bald he was at the top, and took another sip of cachaça.

"I recall the Indian telling me how he and his son came back to their village to find the entire tribe dead. I recall him saying they were poisoned, and that Torres was responsible. I remember him telling me about Jade's arrival, and how he agreed to come back here to get justice for his tribe."

"Those were his words? *Justice for his tribe.*"

Castori rubbed his chin. "No. I think they were Jade's. I've got it all mixed up you see. I don't even remember them leaving. I woke up in bed, the next morning, with a god-awful headache."

"Did you, personally, ever hear Omar Torres make any remarks about doing away with the Indians?"

"Several times. But I never expected him to do it. I thought he was letting off steam. Now, of course, after everything that's happened, I think otherwise."

"In other words, you agree with the Indian. You think Torres murdered his tribe?"

"Yes." The priest lifted his glass. This time it was more than a sip that he took. It was closer to a gulp.

"And, after what the Indian told you, don't you think it would have been a good idea to warn Torres? Tell him his life might be in danger?"

Castori waved his glass in denial. "The Indian never actually made any threats. I thought the intention was to attempt to prosecute Torres in a court of law. I never, ever, expected the Indian to do what he did. I know . . . knew . . . the Awana. They were, in the main, a peaceful people. This particular savage turned out to be an exception."

"We've been told," Arnaldo said, "that you were present at the lynching."

"I was. It was a terrible thing. I'll never forget it. It haunts me even now."

"You tried to stop it?"

"I did. But the crowd was out for blood. There was nothing I could do. Nothing. Once they'd overpowered the delegado, and the Indian was in the hands of the mob, his death was inevitable."

"Inevitable?"

"Inevitable. At that point, all I could do for him was to make his passing easier. And it would have been, if he'd embraced Jesus. But he spit in my face and went to his death an unbeliever. The fact that he's going to be damned for all eternity is his fault, not mine. I gave him his chance. He chose not to take it."

Arnaldo flushed. Silva intervened before the exchange could turn acrimonious. "We know now," he said, "that the tribe was poisoned by a piece of meat dropped by parachute from a small plane."

The priest sat back in his chair. "Well, that explains it then," he said. "Omar was a pilot. He owned his own aircraft. He must have flown low over the village, low enough for the Indian to have recognized him when he dropped it. Perhaps he told me that. But, as I said, there are whole parts of our conversation of which I have no memory. No memory at all. How's it going with that beer? Can I offer either of you gentlemen another?"

Chapter Forty-One

RANCHES AND FARMS IN Brazil tend to be larger than those of almost any other country in the world—and in the country's north and northeast, they're the largest of all.

"Three hours, more or less," Osvaldo said when Hector asked him, after dinner that evening, how long the drive to Nelson Lisboa's place was likely to take.

"*Three hours?*" Gonçalves exclaimed. "Hell, you can get from São Paulo to Rio in four and a half, and that's almost four hundred and fifty kilometers."

"It's a big spread," Osvaldo said, "and the house is a number of kilometers from the border of the property, but it's also the road. You're going from São Paulo to Rio, you're driving on asphalt. From here to Lisboa's place, you'll be driving on mud. You'd better get an early start."

THEY GOT up at seven. By nine, they'd learned, first hand, why the hotelkeeper had suggested they get an early start. In the low-lying areas, where water had collected from the recent rains, there were vast pools of mud. On the higher ground, where it was drier, the surface of the road was rutted and uneven. Vegetation hemmed them in on both sides for much of the distance, and the shoulders looked dangerously soft. There was no signage to prevent them from making false turns. Twice, they had to be set right by *vaqueiros* caring for Senhor Lisboa's cattle, and that cost them at least another hour.

It was past noon when they topped a rise and came in sight of an elegant mansion. The land around it had been deep rainforest not twenty years before, but not a single tree remained. Between the cops and the *casa grande*, there was nothing but pasture.

"You can work wonders with matches," Hector said.

Slash and burn, the ecologist's nightmare, was the method used to clear land in Pará. The few trees left standing after such an exercise tended to be sturdy hardwoods, the kind most resistant to fire. They were promptly harvested. Lisboa met them on his spacious veranda. He was accompanied by a man he introduced as his foreman, Toni Pandolfo.

Pandolfo had tattoos on his arms, the grip of a pistol protruding from his waistband, and the eyes of guard dog. And, like a guard dog, he followed them into the house. The cops were waved into two chairs. A maid brought coffee, served it, and left them alone.

Lisboa's earlobes were pierced and adorned with gold studs. A massive bracelet of the yellow metal encircled one wrist. A golden cross dangling from a necklace of nuggets glittered on his chest.

Gonçalves, mindful of what Maura had told him, let his eyes flick from Lisboa's chest, to his wrist, to his earlobes and back again, before directing his attention to the other man on the couch. He was more than a little surprised to find Pandolfo staring at him with jealous hatred. He must have misunderstood the scrutiny, taken it for sexual appraisal.

One of the many things women found endearing about Gonçalves was that he blushed easily. He did it now, which made the situation worse.

Hector missed the silent exchange. He was already asking the usual questions.

"I can't recall his exact words," Lisboa said.

"Try," Hector said.

"The boss already told you," Pandolfo growled, making

it clear that he hadn't been entirely distracted. "He don't remember."

"How about you then," Hector said. "You ever hear Omar Torres talk about killing Indians?"

"All the time," Pandolfo said.

"And what, exactly, did you hear him say?"

"I'm like the boss. I don't do exact."

Hector looked from one to the other. "So, in summary, neither of you has any reason to doubt it was Torres who poisoned the Awana?"

Pandolfo shook his head.

"No," Lisboa said.

"Do you own an airplane, Senhor Lisboa?"

"If you run cattle around here, they're a necessity. The herds graze freely, you see. With a large spread, and little fencing, you have to—"

"I don't need a justification. I merely asked if you had one."

"I do. A Cessna One Seventy-Two."

"Where is it?"

"In the barn next to the landing strip."

"Where do you keep your logbook?"

"In the aircraft."

"May I see it?"

"Why would you want to—"

"I'd just like to see it. Please."

Lisboa shrugged and turned to his foreman. "Toni," he said, "go get the logbook out of the plane. It's in a pocket, in the door."

Pandolfo didn't move.

"Toni," Lisboa repeated.

"I'm going," Pandolfo said. But he waited another beat before he got up.

When the door closed behind him, Hector said, "Other than the Indian, who else might have had a reason to kill Torres?"

Lisboa waved a dismissive hand. "The Indian was found lying in the alley next to Omar's corpse. The murder weapon was in his hand. He was covered in blood. Why would you look any further? Isn't that proof enough for you?"

"If it was, Senhor Lisboa, I wouldn't have asked you the question. And I'm still waiting for an answer."

"Anybody else? No, nobody else."

"Isn't it true that you owed Torres money?"

Lisboa leaned back and crossed his arms over his chest. "I owed him some money, yes. Who told you?"

It had been Osvaldo, but Hector wasn't about to tell him that.

"It doesn't matter," he said. "The way I heard it, *some* is an understatement. The way I heard it, you owed him a lot."

"Okay, so it was a lot. And before you ask, yes, it's convenient for me that he's dead, but I wasn't anywhere near that alley on the night he was murdered."

"No? Where were you?"

"On my way back here. We'd all been playing cards. I got up about five minutes after he did. One of my *vaqueiros* is getting married the day after tomorrow. We had the party to organize."

"So you're Pandolfo's alibi, and he's yours?"

"That's correct. We were together all the time, all night at the card table, all the way back home."

And maybe even all night in bed, Hector thought.

"Any questions, Haraldo?" he asked.

Gonçalves was still impressed by the quantity of gold Lisboa was wearing. He would have liked to ask him if he knew the prospector, Welinton Mendes. But he couldn't think of how to broach the subject without breaking his agreement with Maura.

He shook his head.

"In that case, I think we're done," Hector said. "I just want to have a glance at that logbook before we go."

Chapter Forty-Two

Silva was a great believer in dropping in on potential suspects unannounced. Cesar Bonetti lived within an hour's drive of the town, so he decided to chance a visit in the hope of finding him at home.

He wasn't.

"Cesar usually keeps track of our cattle with the airplane," his wife said. "But it's got some kind of mechanical problem, so he's doing it the old-fashioned way—on horseback."

"How long has your aircraft been out of service?"

"Almost three weeks. The idiots sent us the wrong part twice. I can't tell you how annoyed Cesar is. He hates sleeping rough."

"So he's likely to be away overnight?"

"Hard to tell. It depends on how long it takes him to find the herd he's looking for. It's a big property."

"Is he carrying a phone? Can you call him?"

Maria shook her head. "He'll be too far from the tower. But why don't you come in? We'll have coffee. Maybe I can help."

She led them into a study lined with bookshelves. While she was fetching the coffee, Silva studied the spines of the books in her library.

"I see you have an interest in biology," he said when she returned with a tray.

"More than an interest, Chief Inspector. I studied it at university, worked at it, too, before Cesar and I were married. Sugar?"

"Black, thank you. Ever heard of a creature called a poison dart frog?"

"The *phyllobates terribilis*? Cute little thing. Deadly though. Why do you ask?"

"Its venom was used to poison the Awana."

"You don't say." She handed Arnaldo a cup. "Sugar?"

"Please." He took two heaping spoonfuls from the bowl.

"So are you telling me it wasn't Torres after all?" she said. "That it was other Indians?"

"Oh, no, Senhora Bonetti. A white man did it all right. We're sure of that."

"Are you? Mind if I ask how you discovered that?"

Silva made a snap decision. He decided to tell her so he could judge her reaction. "The poison was injected into a piece of pork. Indians don't keep pigs, and there are no wild ones in the forest. It's white men's meat—exclusively."

She frowned. "Sounds pretty conclusive."

"There's more. It had been attached to a parachute and dropped from an airplane."

She pondered what he told her and nodded. "Well, that seems to prove it, doesn't it. It was Torres after all."

"Did you hear him threaten to kill those people?"

"Not personally, no. He wasn't the kind of person I'd choose to spend time with. He was vulgar. Stupid. Some women might have found him an attractive animal, but he was an animal all the same."

"Other than the Indian, can you think of anyone who might have had a reason to kill him?"

"Surely, you don't think the Indian was innocent?"

"Suppose he was. What then?"

"Some jealous husband, perhaps, or one of the wives Torres seduced and abandoned."

"Yes, we've been told he was a womanizer. Can you share the names of some of the ladies with whom . . ."

Silva's voice trailed off. She had begun shaking her head before he was halfway through the question. "I'm sorry, Chief Inspector," she said. "It's all gossip. It wouldn't be right to spread it."

"You wouldn't be spreading it. We'd keep the names confidential."

Again, she shook her head. "I really wouldn't feel right about it. I hope you understand."

"Something else then. You'll pardon me for asking, but . . ."

"Where was I on the night he was killed?"

"Yes."

"Right here. With two friends. Do you want their names?"

"I don't believe that will be necessary. And your husband? Where was he?"

"Playing cards at the Grand."

"With Torres?"

"And some others. Torres left first. My husband was still at the table when his body was discovered."

"Were you present at the lynching?"

"No."

"Was your husband?"

"No."

"Would you be kind enough to ask your husband to call us when he gets home?"

"Of course."

Silva stood up. "Thank you, Senhora Bonetti. We won't take up any more of your time."

She remained seated. "They're all doomed, you know," she said.

The non sequitur took Silva by surprise. He sat down again. "I beg your pardon?"

She took in a deep breath and let out a long sigh, as if the subject saddened her. "The Indians. Doomed. The lot of them, not just the Awana. Oh, we still have our uncontacted tribes—more than sixty, according to the most recent estimates, and more here, in Brazil, than anywhere else on earth. But their numbers are shrinking from year to year, and their demise is inevitable. The people who try to stop it are swimming against the tide. They're wasting their time and our money. And they're not helping the Indians. Instead of trying to preserve their culture, they should be putting their energies into helping them adapt to ours."

"So you don't agree they have a right to live as they've always lived? That they have as much right to the land as we do?"

"Simply because they were here first? Of course not. Think about it. Who was first in the United States? And how many are left? And what kind of a country would it be if they ruled it now? And look at Britain at the height of its empire. Could those little islands have ruled the world if they'd continued to have been populated by a bunch of people who painted themselves blue and worshipped rocks? No, they became the most powerful nation of their time because they'd been invaded successively by Vikings, Romans, and Normans, all of whom took the land from their predecessors. We, the Brazilians of European extraction, are the ones who've raised this country to the sixth economy of the twenty-first century. The Indians haven't made any contribution to what we've become. In fact, it's the other way around. They drain our resources."

Her little speech surprised him. Silva wasn't expecting that degree of erudition, not from a rancher's wife in a backwater in Pará.

"I'm not quite sure I understand what you're saying, Senhora Bonetti," he said. "Surely you don't agree—"

"With genocide? Of course not! I'm no Nazi. No, Chief Inspector, *assimilation* is the solution to our Indian problem, not genocide. May I offer you another cup of coffee before you go?"

"SMART," ARNALDO said when they were getting into their jeep.

"Yes," Silva said.

"Want me to look into that spare part?"

Silva shook his head. "As you said, she's smart, too smart to lie about anything that easy to check. They ordered one all right. But who's to say their aircraft really was out of service? We only have her word for that."

"True."

"And yet . . ."

"What?"

"She was too glib, too sure of herself. There was something about the way she was looking at me. I think the woman is an accomplished liar. And she's used to getting away with it."

"So what do we do?"

"Do?" Silva smiled. "For now, my friend, we let her think she's done just that—gotten away with it."

"SENHOR FRADE? José Frade?"

"That's me."

Frade was a big man, running to fat, prematurely bald. His frame filled the entrance to his home like another door.

"I'm Delegado Costa," Hector said. "Federal Police. This is Agent Gonçalves. We have a few questions we'd like to ask. Can we come in?"

"Yeah. Sure." Frade stepped aside. "Drink?"

"A beer would be nice."

When they were seated and drinking, Hector said, "How about we invite your wife to join us?"

Frade swigged some of his beer before he shook his head. "Waste of time. She doesn't know shit. Hardly ever goes out, hardly ever talks to anybody."

"We're going to have to touch base with her sooner or later. It will save us time if we do it now."

Frade made a sound somewhere between a sigh and a snort, got up from the couch and left the room. Two minutes later he came back, trailed at a distance of three paces by a woman in a shapeless housedress. The first thing Hector noticed about her was a black eye. The second was her nervousness. She couldn't seem to stop wringing her hands.

Frade saw Hector staring at the eye. "Walked into a door," he said. "She's clumsy as hell. Aren't you, Sonia?"

"Yes," she said.

"Say it!"

"I'm clumsy."

"This is Delegado Costa, and this is Agent Gonçalves. This is my wife, Sonia. Say hello, Sonia."

"Hello."

"I already told them," Frade said, "that you don't have shit to say. That's right, isn't it? You don't have shit to say?"

"No, José."

"But they wanted to talk to you anyway. So sit down and answer their questions."

"Yes, José."

The two cops asked their questions. Sonia didn't offer a single reply. It was her husband who gave all the answers.

Poison dart frogs? He'd never heard of poison dart frogs. Log book for his airplane? He didn't keep one. Not necessary. There was a clock that kept a running total of engine hours. He'd memorized the requirements for maintenance. That was all he needed. The genocide? Torres, of course. Torres's character? He was a lying, arrogant, two-faced *filho da puta* nobody liked.

At that point, Sonia shot him a look, half-fear, half-disagreement. Hector saw it and pounced.

"And you, Senhora, do you agree?"

Frade glanced at her. The look was gone, her features composed. She nodded, first with just a small inclination of her head, then more emphatically.

"But how well did you know him?" Hector said.

Her hands writhed in her lap. "Not well," she said. "But . . . people said he wasn't a nice man." It was her longest speech.

"*Not nice?*" Frade said. "Well there's a stupid, half-assed remark if ever I heard one." He glared at Sonia. "The fucker wasn't nice at all."

"No, José. I'm sure you're right."

"Right? Of course, I'm right." He looked back at Hector. "But not being nice wasn't a reason to kill him. Only the Indian had a reason for that."

"So there's no one else you can think of? No white man who might have had it in for him?"

"Enough to want to kill him? Nobody."

"It's our understanding there were some husbands whose wives were—"

"Nobody."

"How about you, Senhora? Were you aware that Torres was reputed to be somewhat of a ladies' man?"

"*Reputed?*" Frade exploded in laughter. "*Somewhat?* That's rich. Talk about understatement! The truth of the matter, Delegado, is that Torres didn't give a shit who he fucked. He woulda stuck his dick in a sheep if it stood still long enough. Isn't that right, Sonia?"

She bit her lip.

"I asked you a question, Sonia. Would Torres have stuck his dick in a sheep if it stood still long enough?"

"Yes, José," she said.

Chapter Forty-Three

CESAR BONETTI SPENT THE night in the little shack he'd constructed at the dig. He didn't get home until nine the following morning.

Their bedroom was the one place in the house where Maria was sure they wouldn't be overheard by their servants. He hadn't been in the house for more than thirty seconds before she hustled him there and told him about her lunch with Maura.

He ran a nervous hand through his hair. "Jesus Christ. So she knows."

Maria shook her head. "She *suspects*. She doesn't *know*. She won't *know* until she gets the test results."

"You think she told the cops?"

Maria shook her head. "If they'd known, they would have let something slip. That was the other thing I had to tell you. They were here looking for you."

He repeated the gesture with his hair. "Looking for me? Why?"

"A routine visit. They're asking the same questions of everyone. Don't worry. I took care of it. They don't have a clue about what we're up to."

"Why would she keep it to herself? It doesn't make sense."

Maria shook her head. "It makes total sense. She's a journalist. She wants a scoop."

"So why did she tell you?"

"She was digging for more information. We've got to stop

her before she gets it. Clean up the dig, kill her, and we'll be home free."

"Cleaning up the dig is easy. I can do it in an hour. Killing her is something else. Old Welinton was easy. Nobody misses him. Hell, there are even people who think he's still out there, prospecting away like he always did. But if a reporter from a big-time São Paulo newspaper disappears—"

He stopped talking when she put a hand on his arm. "I've had plenty of time to think about this," she said, "and I've got it all figured out. She's going to have an accident."

"What kind of an accident?"

"A fatal snakebite."

"You think people will believe that?"

"Why not? She's a city girl. What does she know about snakes? She wouldn't be careful about where she steps like we are. Who's to say she didn't put her foot on one?"

He smiled. "Clever girl."

"We just have to make sure she doesn't show any other wounds."

"How are we going to do that?"

"I've got her phone number. I'm going to call and tell her I've learned something about a gold mine from one of our *vaqueiros*. I'll invite her to tea."

"And then?"

"Lock her in that empty storeroom—the one with the steel door—until you get back with the snake. Then we throw it in there so they can get acquainted."

"IT'S THIS way," Raul Nonato said, taking Maura's arm and guiding her down the hall. "There," he said proudly, stopping at the door of his living room. "Isn't she a beauty?"

"Nice," Maura said.

"Nice?" He was crestfallen. "Is that all you've got to say? Nice?"

"I've seen televisions that size before, Senhor Nonato."

"You have? In someone's home? Someone who actually *owned* one?"

"They're pretty common, these days."

"Common?"

"In São Paulo. That's where I come from, São Paulo."

"So it's not what you came to see? When you said you were a friend of Jade's I thought—"

"I'm a journalist," she said. "I'm here about something more serious."

"More serious?" He pointed. "What's more serious than that? That's a seriously big television set!"

"Have you ever heard of a prospector by the name of Welinton Mendes?"

"What about him?"

"He claimed to have struck gold. And then he disappeared."

His enthusiasm gone, Nonato flopped down into one of his comfortable armchairs and waved her to another one. "I remember. So what?"

Gingerly, Maura sank into the soft leather. "I did a story a while back on Serra Pelada, how mercury used to extract gold poisoned the soil and water around the site of the old mine. I figured that if someone killed old Welinton for what he knew, the same thing might be happening around here. I contacted a fishing guide and asked him if he knew a river where fish were dying. He did, and he took me there. I found thousands."

"Thousands of dead fish?"

She nodded.

"Lots of things kill fish."

"I'm not finished."

"Oh. Okay. Finish."

"I sampled the water and sent it to Belem for analysis. I just got the results: high concentrations of mercury."

"Jesus Christ!"

"Yeah. Jesus Christ."

"Who else knows about this?"

"My bureau chief in Belem, the guy who did the analysis, me—and now you."

"How about the guide? Who's he?"

"Fred Vaz. He knows something's killing the fish, but he doesn't know what it is."

"How about those federal cops? Did you tell them?"

"No. And I'm not going to. Not until we get more proof. If we do this on our own, I get a scoop, and you get a pat on the back from your superiors. But if we hand it to those federal cops, they get all the credit. And you, Senhor Nonato, are going to look like an idiot for not having discovered it before they did."

He nodded vigorously. "You're absolutely right. And I gotta thank you, Senhorita Mandel, for coming to me first. So what do you suggest we do? How are we going to tackle it?"

"I suggest we go there and take photos of the operation."

He sat back in his chair, suddenly cautious. "Wouldn't that be dangerous?"

"Not if we're careful. I've got a camera with a telephoto lens. We don't have to get too close."

"Where's the river?"

"On the Awana reservation."

"Wait."

He went out, came back with a topographical map, unrolled it, and anchored it with three books and an ashtray. "Show me."

She ran a finger along the Jagunami until she came to the Sapoqui. "Here," she said, tapping the map.

He leaned closer to look. "That's all thick jungle, that is," he said.

"Yes, it surely is. And we can't just follow the Sapoqui upstream along the banks. The vegetation is too thick. We need a guide."

"Vaz again?"

"Not Vaz. He's frightened. He won't go back."

"Okay, you leave the guide to me."

"I don't have to. I already asked Amanda—"

"No. We need someone who knows how to keep his mouth shut. You leave finding the guide to me."

Maura didn't think the choice made any difference. She didn't intend to tell a guide what they were looking for before they went. And they'd already have the evidence when they got back. She considered telling Nonato about her confessions to Gonçalves and Amanda, but he seemed anxious to keep everything confidential, so she decided not to. On the other hand, what if he was in on it?

If he is, she thought, *too late now. I'll just have to be bloody careful.*

He was a little man, smaller than she was. And she had plenty of chemical mace back at Jade's place. Two whole cans. They could put down four people his size.

"All right," she said. "Finding the guide is with you. I'll tell Amanda I no longer need one."

"And you won't tell her what we're up to?"

"No."

He looked relieved. "Good," he said. "I suggest we leave first thing tomorrow morning."

"Why not today?"

"Too suspicious, contracting a guide on the spur of the

moment and asking him to leave right away. Besides, it's already getting late."

She looked at her watch. It wasn't yet one in the afternoon.

"Late?" she said. "It's not late."

"But you don't really know how far we have to go, do you? We should leave at first light. That way, we'll have all day to do the job. We leave now, and there's always a chance the sun will go down before we find what we're looking for. And we sure as hell don't want to get stuck out there in the dark, do we?"

"No. I suppose not."

"You were right to come to me," he said.

Cesar Bonetti put the telephone in his pocket and went back into the house.

"Forget something?" Maria asked.

"No. I got a call from Nonato. That bitch of a journalist just left his house. She told him she already has her results. She knows there's mercury in the water."

"Damn! Does he know if she told the federal cops?"

"That's the good news. She didn't. Not them, nor anyone else."

"Thank God. Then we're still okay. What was she doing talking to Nonato?"

"She wants to follow the Sapoqui upstream, wants him to go with her, wants to take pictures."

"When?"

"Tomorrow morning."

"So we've got to get to her today."

"Yeah. Today."

"Let's stick to the plan, just move the schedule up a bit. You get out there, clean up the site and find the snake. I'll call the snoop."

* * *

Maura had been surprised to get a phone call from Maria Bonetti and even more surprised when she heard what the woman had to say. According to her, one of her *vaqueiros* had been out hunting. He'd crossed over into the reservation and seen something there that Maura simply *must* hear about. It was linked to the conversation they'd had at lunch. The journalist tried to extract details on the telephone, but Maria kept insisting she hear the story firsthand.

"I don't want to spoil it," she said. "It's got to be directly from him, and it's going to knock your socks off."

Maura didn't like the idea of going out to the Bonetti place on her own, but the temptation of the scoop was strong.

"I don't have a car," she said. "Couldn't you bring that *vaqueiro* to me?"

"Cesar is away, the truck has gone to town, and the battery on my jeep is flat. I hear your friend Jade left town with the Indian kid. How about you use her jeep?"

"Good idea. But I can't remember where I put the keys. I'll ring you back when I find them."

A little later, Maura called back to confirm that she was on her way. Maria gave her detailed instructions to reach the house.

An hour and a half later, with a dry mouth, a perspiration-soaked shirt, and both cans of chemical mace tucked into her shoulder bag, Maura pulled up in front of the Bonetti's veranda.

Maria answered the door herself. "It's the servants' day off," she explained.

It hadn't been, but they'd all been delighted to have it declared as one. And they hadn't questioned her sudden generosity when she'd shipped them all off to town in the truck.

"And the *vaqueiro?*" Maura asked, putting aside her anxiety in her eagerness to hear his story.

"I've sent him a message. He should be here anytime now. Tea or coffee?"

"Coffee."

"Coffee it is."

"But if you don't mind, I'd like to freshen up first."

"I thought you might," Maria said. "Put your purse over there. Towels, soap, everything you'll need is in the bathroom. It's this way."

Going to the Bonetti's home had been Maura's first mistake. Her second was to set down the bag and follow Maria into an unlit hallway.

"In there," her hostess said, pointing to a doorway with nothing but blackness beyond. "The light switch is on the left."

But it wasn't, and Maura was still trying to locate one when the door slammed shut behind her.

Chapter Forty-Four

IT HAD BEEN DARK for over an hour when a frowning Haraldo Gonçalves entered the bar. "Anybody seen Maura?"

Hector and Arnaldo shook their heads.

Silva didn't react. He was on a slow burn. Earlier in the evening, Hector had told him about their visit to José Frade's place and how he'd treated his wife. Subsequently, Silva had gone to Osvaldo for more information about the couple, and Amanda had told him about the chance encounter in the supermarket. Now he'd fallen silent, trying to think of a way to help the woman without prejudicing her more. It was a small issue in comparison to everything else on his plate, but little issues of injustice sometimes bothered him as much as the larger ones. It was an aspect of his character.

"No chance she's with Gilda?" Gonçalves persisted.

"Gilda had a headache," Hector said. "She's gone to bed."

"Wasn't Maura supposed to be with you?" Arnaldo asked.

"She was, but she didn't show up."

"Show up where?"

"Amanda's place. We, uh . . . had plans."

"Plans, huh? No note?"

"No, nothing. The place is locked up. The lights are off. I've been sitting on the back porch since dinner."

"It's not like there's anything else to do in this town," Hector said. "You either stay home or you come here."

"Exactly," Gonçalves said. "I'm worried."

Silva had been listening to the conversation with one ear. "Why should you be worried?" he asked.

Gonçalves wouldn't meet his eyes. It immediately put the Chief Inspector on the alert.

"Look at me, Haraldo."

Gonçalves did. And as quickly looked away again.

"You know something we don't," Silva said, his musings about Sonia Frade suddenly forgotten. "And I want to know what it is. *Right now.*"

Concealing something was one thing, telling a lie was another; Gonçalves couldn't do it. He confessed.

Silva's voice, when he found it, was cold. "So you, Agent Gonçalves, have been aware all the damned time that there was an additional motive for what's been happening around here?"

"Not all the time, Chief Inspector. She only—"

"Why the *hell* didn't she come clean with us?"

"She was angry with you for freezing her out of the investigation. She felt she was onto a good story, and she didn't want it to happen again. She was going to tell you, but, well . . . later."

"Later, eh?" Silva said.

Gonçalves blushed, the redness of it creeping up from his collar to cover his entire face.

Silva's face was red too—but from anger. "I allow my men one mistake," he said. "One. This has been yours."

"Consider yourself lucky the Chief Inspector was here," Hector said. "If he wasn't, Haraldo, I swear to God I would have had your badge. And don't think you've heard the end of this, because you haven't."

"Hector, you . . . you don't understand."

"You're goddamned right I don't."

"Enough!" Silva said. "We haven't time to bicker." He pointed to the table where Doctor Pinto, José Frade, Delegado Borges, Renato Kassab, Father Castori, and Paulo Cunha were drinking together.

"Go over there," he said to Gonçalves, "and ask each of those gentlemen about the last time they saw Maura."

Arnaldo stood up. "Let me do that," he said.

"Sit down, Arnaldo. I want Gonçalves to do it."

When he was gone, Silva continued, "Those people were here before dinner. My hunch is we can exclude their involvement."

"So why did you send Gonçalves over there?"

"To give both of you a couple of minutes to cool down. I think the kid's in love. People do crazy things when they're in love."

"Babyface Gonçalves?" Arnaldo said. "Our Don Juan? In love? How about that!"

"You like him, don't you?" Hector said. "Otherwise you wouldn't be cutting him so much slack."

"Oh, I like him all right," Silva said, "and I like her. I think she's an admirable young woman, even if she is a journalist. But I have every intention of making him damned sorry he cut us out of the loop."

"How about we transfer him to Belem, to work with Barbosa?"

"That would be way over the top," Arnaldo said.

"Leave the disciplinary measures to me," Silva said. "Let's concentrate on finding Maura."

Gonçalves came back shaking his head. "Nobody knows anything. It was the lawyer who saw her last. That was about three o'clock this afternoon. They didn't speak, just nodded to each other on the street."

"That's it, then," Silva said, standing up. "Let's go."

"Go where?" Gonçalves asked.

"LOOK," BORGES said, "They're leaving,"

Kassab and Pinto turned around and glanced at the backs of the retreating cops. Cunha took another sip from his glass of whiskey.

"Fuck them," he said, slurring his speech.

"How about we have another round?" Father Castori said.

"Not for me," Frade said, steadying himself in his chair. He was even drunker than Cunha.

"Where do you suppose they're off to at this time of night?" Doctor Pinto said.

"Fuck them," Cunha repeated.

"A round for everyone except José?" Father Castori asked, holding up a hand to capture Osvaldo's attention.

"I've had enough," the doctor said.

"What I've had enough of are our visitors from São Paulo and Brasilia," Borges said. "They don't treat me like a colleague. They don't tell me a damned thing about what they're doing. They don't share their conclusions. I wish they'd all pack up and go home."

"Patience, Fernando," Kassab said. "Nobody's telling them anything. It won't be long before they wise up and realize they've hit a brick wall."

"I don't give a shit if they go or stay," Frade said. He looked at Cunha. "I got nothing to fear from those fuckers—unlike some other people."

"What do you mean by that?" Cunha said.

"Gentlemen, gentlemen," Kassab said, "that will be enough of that."

"Enough is what I've had of him." Cunha pointed at Frade. He got to his feet and, somewhat unsteadily, walked out.

Osvaldo appeared at their table. Castori ordered fresh drinks for himself and Borges. The doctor tossed a banknote on the table and stood up.

"That will cover my share," he said.

Frade stood with him. "I gotta get some air," he said and followed the doctor out the door.

The doctor turned right toward his home. Frade turned left and, like Omar Torres before him, stumbled into the alleyway.

Chapter Forty-Five

No lights were showing at Raul Nonato's place, but from afar they could hear a voice: *Zezinho to the Artist, the Artist shoots . . . Goooall!*

A crowd erupted into raucous cheers. Silva pounded on the door. The audio went mute. A few seconds went by and then, "Who's that?"

"Federal Police, Nonato. Open up!"

They heard him slip the bolt. The IBAMA agent was in pajamas, blue ones with black trim. He'd been drinking. They could smell the scotch. "What do you people want at this time of night? What's so important it can't wait until morning?"

This was a different Raul Nonato from the one Hector and Gonçalves had met on their first visit. The alcohol had turned him belligerent.

"We need to talk," Silva said.

"I'm busy. Come back tomorrow."

"Now. Step out of the doorway."

He put up an arm to block their access. "You got a search warrant?"

"No. Now, step out of the doorway."

Nonato, filled to the brim with liquid courage, stood his ground. "We can talk right here," he said. "State your business."

"We're looking for the journalist, Maura Mandel. We have reason to believe she's been kidnapped."

"Really? What's that got to do with me?"

"We believe that the people who kidnapped her are extracting gold illegally."

"And?"

"And we think you know who they are."

"I got no idea what you're talking about. Fuck off and let me get back to my game."

"May I?" Gonçalves said.

"You may," Silva said.

He and Arnaldo stepped aside.

"Senhor Nonato, I'm Agent Haraldo Gonçalves—"

"I don't give a fuck who you are."

Gonçalves drew his Glock and put the muzzle against the IBAMA agent's left temple.

"—and if you tell us one more lie, I'm going to kill you."

Nonato ducked his head, weaved, and tried to move away. Gonçalves grabbed him by the collar and pushed the muzzle more firmly into his head. Nonato lost control of his bladder. A stench of urine overpowered the odor of the scotch.

"Stop struggling," Gonçalves said. "I don't want this thing to go off by mistake."

Nonato froze.

"Now, let's start again. Where's Maura Mandel?"

"Maybe . . . maybe at the Bonetti's place. I don't know for sure, but she could be there."

"Thank you," Gonçalves said, and pulled the trigger.

CESAR'S TRUCK needed a new muffler. Maria had heard him coming and was standing on the veranda to greet him

"What took you so long?"

"I wanted to be thorough, didn't I?" he said. "And don't think it was easy getting back here in the dark."

"You could have called."

"I tried. Fucking tower must be down again."

"Everything taken care of?"

"The dredge is at the bottom of the river. The rest, I burned."

"So that's it then. There's nothing to tie us to the place?"

"Nothing. And I even brought a present." He went around to the back of the truck and retrieved a jute sack, the mouth of it tied together with a piece of rope. When he shook it, an angry rattle emanated from the inside.

"A *cascavel?*" she said.

"You know anything else that makes a sound like that? He's a huge bastard. And mean. Have we got her?"

"We've got her."

"How did she get here?"

"Driving her friend's jeep. I suggested it."

"Good thinking. That way, she didn't have to tell anybody where she was going, right?"

"Right. And I didn't have to pick her up, so no one saw us together."

He looked around. "So where is it?"

"Where's what?"

"The jeep."

"I hid it in the barn. We'll take it halfway to town and leave it near her corpse. That way, it'll look like she was far, far away from here when the accident happened. Bring the sack. I'm itching to introduce the nosy little bitch to her new friend."

THE SLAMMING of the door had left Maura in total blackness. She'd spun around, grabbed for the doorknob and found it locked. She'd switched her attention to the door itself and pounded on the hardwood. The only result had been to hurt her hand. Next, she'd tried screaming at the top of her lungs.

"Senhora Bonetti! Maria! What the *hell* are you doing? Let me out of here!"

There'd been no response. None at all.

She began to explore the space.

Setting off to the left of the door, she felt her way along the walls in hope of finding a switch.

And did. She tried it, but the room remained as black as ever. They'd either removed the bulb or the fuse, or there hadn't been one or the other in the first place.

She kept going: a corner, another, a third, a fourth—and she was back at the door. Nothing along the way had impeded her progress. There were no fixtures, there was no plumbing, there were no shelves. Whatever the space was, it wasn't—and never had been—a bathroom.

She took a step away from one of the corners and crossed to the opposite wall. And again. And again, until she'd cross-hatched the room in its entirety. Five paces, and a little more in each direction. The same on the other axis.

Square. Completely empty. And no way out except for the door. There was nothing else she could do. She leaned against one wall, sank down upon her haunches, and waited.

AN HOUR passed. Or maybe it was two. Without her cell phone, and unable to see her watch, Maura had no way of telling.

Suddenly, she heard a key turning in the lock. She started scrambling to her feet, but the adrenaline in her system had dissipated and she wasn't fully erect when the door was flung open.

A silhouette appeared, deeper black against the blackness of corridor. An arm was raised. Something was flung at her head. When Maura attempted to fend it off, her fingers touched rough fabric. She clenched her fists, caught the object and had just enough time to see what she was holding—some kind of bag, or sack—before the door slammed shut. Still dazed, and with the image of what she'd seen persisting on her retina, she stood there for a moment, clutching the cloth.

And then it moved. There was something inside, something alive. She released her grip. The bag hit the floor with a soft *plop*, followed by an angry rattle. A second later, something slithered over her foot.

Chapter Forty-Six

Nonato wasn't dead. There'd been no bullet in the chamber.

Gonçalves holstered his pistol, took out his handcuffs, and none too gently shackled the man's hands behind his back.

"Tell us the rest of it and be quick about it," Silva said.

Nonato was still trembling. He was opening and closing his mouth like a fish starved for oxygen.

Gonçalves grabbed him by the collar of his pajamas and shook him. "Talk, you *filho da puta*."

It all came out in a rush: "She came here, told me she took water samples from the Sapoqui, told me she found traces of mercury. She wanted my help to discover who was behind it, go out there to make photos of the site, shut them down."

"So she didn't know it was Bonetti?" Silva said.

"No."

"And you didn't tell her?"

"No."

"Did you call him after she was gone? Warn him?"

"That's all. That's all I did."

"And what did you expect him to do?"

"Talk to her. Offer her money."

"That? Or kill her?"

Nonato looked at his feet. If he'd said even a single word, handcuffed or not, Gonçalves would have hit him.

Cesar and Maria were unwinding with a drink when they heard a knock.

"Cesar, it's me, Raul. Let me in."

Bonetti looked at his watch. "Fucking Nonato," he whispered. "What does he want at this time of night?"

"Reassurance," she whispered back. "He's a nervous little bastard."

"I'm getting nervous myself."

"Calm down, Cesar. It's all over now."

"I don't like having her body back there. The hell with waiting until tomorrow morning. As soon as he's gone, we'll take her out and dump her."

"Get Nonato to help. It'll remind him that he's in as deep as we are."

The knock came again, more urgently this time.

"Cesar? Maria? You guys in there?"

Bonetti held a finger to his lips to cut their conversation short. He went to the door, slid back the bolt and opened it. "Cops!" he shouted when he saw Nonato wasn't alone.

Maria scuttled toward the back of the house, fumbled with the lock, and flung open the door only to find Hector waiting on the other side. He handcuffed her and brought her back to the living room where her husband, wearing cuffs of his own, was spewing abuse at Nonato.

"You weak, stupid little bastard! I'll kill you for this!"

"Shut up," Silva said. "Your killing days are over. Where's Maura Mandel?"

"I got no idea."

"We're going to search the place," Silva said. "If you're lying, this gentleman here"—he hooked a thumb at Gonçalves—"will give you a severe beating."

"That's crap! You can't do that. You're cops."

Gonçalves hit him in the stomach—hard.

"Think again," he said as Bonetti fought for breath.

"Leave him alone," Maria said. "You're too late. She's dead."

When he heard that, Gonçalves turned to Maria. She saw the look on his face and recoiled in fear.

"If you're not wrong," he said, "you're dead."

Silva put a hand on his arm. "Take us," he said to Maria.

She led them to a door in an unlit hallway. By the time they got there, her hands were trembling too much to insert the key. Gonçalves, cursing, grabbed her wrist and took over the task.

Inside in a pool of light cast by Silva's flashlight, they found Maura facedown on the floor. And from somewhere in the dark they heard an ominous rattle.

Chapter Forty-Seven

IT WAS FOUR IN the morning. Maura, now out of danger, was resting comfortably, Gonçalves at her side. The other three cops, Gilda, and Doctor Pinto had adjourned to Jade's living room.

"That snake was a mess," Gilda was saying. "You shot it, right?"

"Babyface shot it," Arnaldo said. "Six times. I was standing right next to him when he did it. The room was tiny. I don't think my ears are ever going to be the same."

"Whose idea was it to bring us the remains?" Doctor Pinto asked.

Arnaldo pointed at Silva.

The doctor turned to face him. "Quick thinking, Chief Inspector. Without that, she'd be dead."

"It was a close call," Gilda explained. "There wouldn't have been time to run tests for the proper antivenin."

"And speaking of dead," Doctor Pinto said, "I'm sure it will interest you to hear that we've had another murder."

"Another one?" Silva said.

Pinto nodded. "Just a few hours ago. I don't recall ever having—"

"Who was the victim?"

"José Frade," the doctor said shortly. His expression showed he didn't take kindly to being interrupted.

"Where?"

"In the same alleyway where the Indian murdered Omar

Torres. And with a machete to the neck, while urinating. The two killings were similar in every way."

"But not," Silva said, "committed by the same person."

"Of course not," Pinto said. "How could they have been? The Indian's dead, isn't he?"

Gilda shook her head from side-to-side. "The Indian wasn't the murderer of Omar Torres."

"He was. And that's what my report is going to reflect."

"You're wrong."

Silva intervened. "So you're in agreement about one thing, at least: Torres and Frade were killed by two different people?"

"On that," Gilda said, "we agree."

"Yes," Doctor Pinto said.

Silva addressed Gilda. "You saw Frade's corpse *in situ?*"

She nodded. "It happened just below my window. A crowd gathered when they found him. The noise woke me up. I was just getting out of bed when Amanda knocked on my door."

"Interfering woman," Doctor Pinto grumbled. "It was none of her damned business."

"Doctor Pinto feels," Gilda said, "that I invaded his territory—"

"*And* interfered with my work. I'm the medical examiner in this town, not you."

Gilda ignored him. "But I really don't give a damn what Doctor Pinto thinks, because I totally disrespect him as a professional—"

"Why you little—"

"That's enough, Doctor," Silva said, "Get a handle on your temper, or I'll expel you from the room. Go on, Gilda."

"—so I borrowed a flashlight, went down to the alley, made a cursory examination, and found significant differences between the two murders."

"Tell me."

"The killer took the murder weapon."

"But you have reason to believe it was the same kind of knife?"

"Very similar, I'd say."

"Okay, go on."

"The first blow to Frade's neck, as with Torres, was administered from behind, but delivered by a shorter, and weaker, individual. The wound was slanted upwards and nowhere near as deep. I think, but this is just a guess, that it might have been delivered with some hesitation."

"Why do you say that?"

"The full force of the killer's arm wasn't behind it."

"And then?"

"Frade turned around, exposing the other side of his neck."

"So he looked into the face of his killer?"

"He did."

"How can you be sure which blow was delivered first?"

"He was facing the wall, urinating. The murderer wouldn't have been able to sneak up on him otherwise."

"Makes sense. What else?"

"The first killer was right-handed. The second was left-handed. The second blow to Frade's neck was delivered with more conviction that the first. It was deeper and much deadlier. I don't think a two-time killer would have held back when he first struck. That's speculation on my part, but—"

"It's all speculation on your part!" Pinto sputtered. "I can refute everything you said."

Silva held up a hand to silence him. "And you must feel free to do so, Doctor, *when* she's finished. Go on, Gilda."

"The first wound would have frightened him more. A little liquid goes a long way. If you have any doubts about that, try throwing a bottle of ink against a wall."

"Yes, but why the fright?"

"A nick creates a small aperture, and a small aperture would have caused the blood to exit the body with more pressure behind it. It would have spurted much further. Scary, if you're on the receiving end. The second wound, the one that severed the artery on the other side, wouldn't have been as spectacular to watch, but it would have released his blood in a gush rather than a spurt. It would have drained him of a hundred milliliters of blood with every heartbeat. He would have lapsed into unconsciousness in less than twenty seconds, probably more like fifteen. Until he did, though, he tried to defend himself. There are slashes on his forearms. He held them up for protection."

"Tell me this, Gilda, when you examined Torres's body, you told me the wounds were deep, that they would have to have been inflicted by a man, or a very strong woman."

"Yes."

"And in this case? Could it have been a woman?"

She thought about it for a few seconds, then said, "I think so, yes."

"I don't," the doctor said. "No woman in this town would have taken on José Frade. He was—"

"Thank you, Doctor," Silva said, cutting him off. His next question was also directed to Gilda.

"You think he was able to inflict a scratch or two on his killer?"

"I think he might have, she said.

"You bag his hands?"

"I got Amanda to bring me some plastic bags from her kitchen. Makeshift, but they'll do."

"No scrapings as yet?"

"I was waiting for you to tell a certain party"—she shot her eyes in Pinto's direction—"that I was authorized to take them."

Silva turned to the certain party—and told him.

Chapter Forty-Eight

EARLY THE FOLLOWING MORNING, Max Gallo, the teen-
aged Casanova of the skies, took off for the State capitol.
Accompanying him on the aircraft were a willing and enthusiastic blonde and two plastic envelopes containing scrapings
Gilda had taken from under the fingernails of José Frade's
corpse.

An hour after his departure, Hector spoke to Alex Sanches,
the young federal agent who worked with Barbosa—or as
Arnaldo put it, worked *instead* of Barbosa. Sanches promised to
meet the kid upon arrival and forward the samples to São Paulo.

Lefkowitz, in the course of another phone call, promised
to subject them to DNA analysis and phone back the results
in record time.

After Hector reported his telephone conversations to his
uncle, the two senior men set out on a short walk to the
delegacia.

"I'm beginning to think," Arnaldo said, "that you have a
pretty good idea about who killed Frade."

"Don't you?"

"Uh-huh. Pretty damned obvious when you think about it,"
Arnaldo said. "I guess there's no particular hurry about making
an arrest."

"No," Silva said. "We'll go after we've finished with the
Bonettis."

"I'M KEEPING them as far apart as I can," Borges said when
they got there.

"Which isn't far, is it? Silva said.

"No. They've been shouting at each other all night. I don't think either one got any sleep. I sure as hell didn't."

"Recriminations?"

"Big time. Can I go home now? My wife is about ready to kill me."

"Not yet, I'm afraid," Silva said. "Do you have a video camera?"

"Yeah. Why?"

"We'll question her first. I want you to record it. After which, we'll question him, and I want you to record that. *Then* you can go home."

"How long is this gonna take?"

"Based upon what you've just told me," Silva said, "I don't think it's going to take long at all."

THE DELEGACIA was small, and there was no space given over to a room for interviewing suspects. It had to be done either in a cell or in the delegado's office. Since Silva didn't want either suspect to hear what the other one was going to tell him, he elected to use the delegado's office.

They took Maria first. She was perfectly willing to talk, anxious to shift the blame onto her husband.

"It was all Cesar's idea," were her opening words on the videotape.

"Was it?" Silva said.

She nodded emphatically. "When he showed up with that old coot, it was a total surprise to me."

From down the hall, they could hear Cesar Bonetti scream out the single word, "Bitch!" The timing was perfect, as if he could hear what she'd just said. He couldn't, of course. It was just another addendum to the thoughts he'd been voicing throughout the night.

"And that was on the night Welinton sold his nugget and treated everyone to drinks at the Grand?" Silva asked, ignoring the outburst.

"Yes," she said, casting a nervous glance in the direction of the cells. "No one's going to let him out of there, are they?"

"No, Senhora, they're not. And at about what time was this, your husband's arrival with Welinton?"

"Late. Past midnight."

"So your servants were all in bed?"

"Long since."

"Do any sleep in the house?"

"No. We've got an *edicula*. It keeps them out of our hair."

"Bitch!" Cesar Bonetti screamed again.

"That guy's got one hell of a set of lungs," Borges said, without taking his eye from the viewfinder. "It's amazing he isn't hoarse by now."

"Please go on, Senhora," Silva said.

"Cesar always told me he *just happened* to run into Welinton when he was leaving Crazy Ana's."

Silva raised an eyebrow.

"But I never believed him," she went on hurriedly. "Never! He was waiting to waylay him. I'm surprised nobody else was, what with the old fool shooting off his mouth like that."

"Yeah," Arnaldo said, "in a town like this, I guess you gotta expect things like that."

She missed the irony. "Exactly," she said.

"All right," Silva said, getting her back on track, "so there you were at home, and your husband showed up with Welinton. What happened next?"

"He made me fetch them drinks."

"And by that time, do you think he'd already made up his mind to kill him?"

She paused. "Probably," she admitted. And then, quickly,

"But Welinton didn't know that. He thought he was there to negotiate terms for a partnership. Cesar started by agreeing to take half the profits in return for buying the equipment and working the site. That's what Welinton kept calling it. The site. Not the claim. He said we couldn't claim it, because it was inside the reservation."

"Uh-huh. So that's why Cesar decided to kill the Indians? So the reservation would be dissolved and he could turn it into a real claim?"

She opened her eyes wide. "The Indians? Kill the Indians?"

"I think you heard me, Senhora."

"I did. I was surprised, that's all."

"Because?"

"Because he had nothing to do with that."

Silva frowned. He thought he'd solved that case as well. Now, it appeared that he hadn't. Before he could say anything she plunged on. "I have no idea who killed those Indians. Neither one of us do. Cesar was furious when he found out. He said it would draw attention to what we'd—to what *he'd* done. And for once, the stupid shit was right. If some idiot hadn't rooted out that goddamned tribe——"

Silva brought her up short. "Please finish the story, Senhora Bonetti."

"Where was I?"

"Cesar agreed to take half the profits—"

"And Welinton said he wanted a contract before they went any further. So Cesar got paper and a pen, and they wrote it all out. Meanwhile I served them more drinks. It was all cordial up to that point. Or at least the old coot thought it was."

"And then?"

"Then Cesar said, since they now had an agreement, all signed and proper, that he wanted Welinton to tell him where he'd made the strike. And Welinton said he'd only do that after he'd put the paper somewhere safe. He said he trusted Cesar and all, but he'd been at Serra Pelada, and he'd seen what gold could do to some people, so he'd always been cautious after that. Up to that point, Cesar thought it was going to be easy to get the old man to talk, but now he saw it wasn't."

"He lost his temper?"

"Not really. He just got up, knocked Welinton out of his chair, and sat on his chest. Then he made me get a rope."

Silva was tempted to ask how her husband could have *made* her do anything if he was sitting on the old man's chest but didn't.

"And then he tied Welinton to a chair," she went on. "I objected. I told him he was crazy. But he said that he didn't want any paper floating around with evidence of what they'd discussed. I think that's maybe when Welinton realized that something bad was going to happen to him."

"What did he do?"

"He got all pale, and he said that Cesar could have it all, that there was always more gold to find out there someplace, and if Cesar would just let him go, he'd sign over the whole thing."

"And what did Cesar say to that?"

"That the paper wouldn't have any value, since the strike was on Indian land, and it wasn't Welinton's to sign away."

"What happened next?"

"He made Welinton tell him where he'd found the gold. And I mean exactly where. Somehow, the old man had learned to use a GPS. He'd written down the coordinates, latitude and longitude, right to the second, and put them on a paper he was keeping in his wallet. When Cesar saw that paper, he figured Welinton wasn't lying about the location, so—"

"Wait. How did he get Welinton to talk? By torturing him?"

She nodded.

"How?"

She hesitated. It wasn't for long, not even as much as a second, but it was enough to tell Silva that what was coming next was going to be a lie.

"I don't know. I couldn't stand to watch. I left the room."

"At which point you could have called the police."

"It wouldn't have done any good. You know how far we live from town. It would have taken them an age to get there. Cesar would have killed the old coot by the time they did. And, anyway—"

Silva knew what was coming. He said it before she could. "You feared for your life."

"I did. I truly did. If I hadn't gone along, Cesar would have killed me for sure."

"Uh-huh," Silva said.

She studied his face. "You sound like you don't believe me."

"I didn't say that, Senhora."

"No, but you implied it. It was they way you said *uh-huh*."

Silva didn't respond to that. Instead, he asked, "Do you know where the prospector's body is buried?"

"Yes."

"You'll take us there?"

"Yes, and I'll testify against my husband in court, tell the whole story to a judge and jury. That's what I can do for you. What are you prepared to do for me?"

"We'll discuss that," Silva said, "after we've spoken to your husband."

"She's full of crap," Cesar Bonetti said when they related his wife's account of the murder. "It was her idea from the get-go. I wouldn't have done a damn thing if it wasn't for her. Let me tell you what really happened."

"Please," Silva said.

"You getting all this?" Cesar said to Borges.

"I'm getting it," Borges said from behind the camera. He was propping his elbows on the table to steady the image.

"Well, then, it was like this. I was in the bar at the Grand when Welinton came in and started shooting his mouth off. That much is true. But then I went home, and I told the whole story to Maria, and what does Maria say?"

"You tell us. What did she say?"

"She said this was our chance of a lifetime and asked me where Welinton went. I told her he went to Crazy Ana's, and she told me to go there, wait until he left, and bring him back with me. I asked her what she had in mind. She said we were going to strike a deal with him. So I did what she said, and I even negotiated something along the way. Fifty percent each. That was our deal, and I was happy with it."

"But she wasn't?"

"No, the greedy bitch wanted it all. Once Welinton was in the house, she pulled a gun and told him to sit down. Then she made me tie him up."

"*Made* you tie him up."

"She was holding a gun, Chief Inspector. I know her. Nobody better. She would have used it."

"On you?"

"On both of us. Why else would I go along?"

"Why else indeed?" Silva said, drily. "And then?"

"And then it was like she said. Except *she* tortured Welinton, not me. And *she* killed him, not me."

"How did she torture him?"

"With a blowtorch."

"What?"

"A blowtorch. The kind you screw onto the top of a little canister of gas. She burned him when he wouldn't answer, burning him even when he *did* answer. He was a hairy guy, and she burned that hair off his whole body. His armpits, his eyebrows, his chest, even his balls. The smell was awful—stank up the whole room."

"Jesus!" Arnaldo said and ran a hand over his face.

Bonetti looked at him and bobbed his head up and down. "Honest to God. And she enjoyed it. She enjoyed every god-damned minute of it. She even got hot on it. After he was dead, and even before we buried him, she dragged me to the bedroom and made me fuck her, so hot she was."

"Who killed him?"

"She did."

"How?"

"She cut his throat."

"With what?"

"A knife we use to kill pigs. But you know what?"

"What?"

"The calculating bitch made me put a *lona preta* on the floor first. You know what a *lona preta* is?"

"No."

"We use them to cover compost and for some other things. Every *fazendeiro* has them."

"A plastic sheet?"

"Yeah. Basically. But thick plastic. And then she made me grab one side of his chair, and she grabbed the other side, and we moved him onto it."

"So his blood wouldn't stain the floor?"

"That's right. He figured out what we were up to, and he started to scream. She enjoyed that, too, but I didn't, so I gagged him."

"And then you killed him and buried him."

"*She* killed him. *I* buried him."

"And you'll show us where?"

"I will! You believe me, don't you?"

"Yes, Senhor Bonetti, I'm inclined to believe you. Just one more question, did you have anything to do with the poisoning of the Awana tribe?"

"Not a goddamned thing," Cesar Bonetti said.

Chapter Forty-Nine

When Sonia Frade saw them approaching her veranda, she put down her teacup and wrapped both arms around the child in her lap. The little girl looked to be about two years old.

"And who have we here?" Silva asked, mounting the steps, his eyes on the little one.

"Lucinda," her mother said. "Her name is Lucinda."

The little girl clutched a doll in one hand and kept the thumb of the other firmly planted in her mouth. Silva knelt down and stroked the doll's blonde hair with a forefinger.

"And what's this one's name?"

Lucinda held the toy tighter, as if she feared he'd take it away.

"Jaqueline," she said, removing her thumb just long enough to say the word.

"That's a beautiful name. And so is Lucinda. And so is Sonia. You all have beautiful names."

"I knew you'd come eventually," Sonia said, "but I didn't expect you quite this soon." She raised her voice—but only slightly—and called out, "Geralda."

A chocolate-colored woman appeared in the doorway. She looked anxious. "Senhora?"

"Would you please give Lucinda and Laura some cake?"

"Cake! Oba!" the little girl said.

She clambered from her mother's lap. The maid opened the screen door, ushered her in, and followed her.

Sonia picked up her teacup—and, as Silva had expected,

did it with her left hand. She hadn't bothered to conceal the scratches. They stood out on her pale arms, damning witnesses to her husband's last struggle.

"I'm Chief Inspector Silva. This is Agent Nunes."

"Would you like to sit down?"

"Yes, thank you."

Each man took a chair.

"Tea? Coffee?"

"Nothing, thanks," Silva said. "We won't be here long."

"No," she said, "I suppose not." She let her eyes drift, staring, without seeing, at a herd of Tabapuã grazing on the border of the rainforest. "I suppose you want me to tell you about it. Well, there's not much to tell, not really. I waited for him outside the Grand. I'd waited for him the night before, and the night before that, but he hadn't been drunk enough."

"You didn't think you could kill your husband unless he was falling-down drunk?"

"Maybe. But I wasn't sure, and I wanted to be sure. And I didn't want to run the risk of doing it here because of the children. I'd planned to take him when he reached his jeep, but when he stepped into the alley I saw my chance, and I followed him."

"So there was nothing symbolic in it? That you killed him in the same place he'd killed Torres?"

"No. Nothing symbolic."

"And the weapon you used?"

"That was deliberate. I wanted him to suffer the way Omar suffered."

"Where is it?"

"Buried behind the milk barn. Do you want me to take you there?"

Silva didn't respond to the offer, said instead, "Your husband told you, didn't he? Told you he'd murdered Torres?"

She nodded.

"And Torres was your lover?"

She nodded again. "It was wrong," she said. "I know it was wrong. And God knows Omar wasn't much of a man. He was fickle, and coarse, and he drank too much, but I loved him. I loved him because he took me out of my daily misery and gave me something, other than my daughters, to look forward to when I got up in the morning. And I have to admit, there was a malicious side to it as well. I knew José would hate it if he ever found out. But I didn't expect him to find out, and I certainly didn't expect him to do what he did."

"How *did* he find out? Any idea?"

"I know *exactly* how he found out."

"Tell us."

"Patricia Toledo. She wasn't willing to accept that Omar was finished with her. She suspected he'd taken another woman into his life. She wanted to know who it was, so she started following him. One night, she saw us going into the back door at the Grand. Omar's arm was around me, so there wasn't much doubt about what we were up to. The next day she called him, and told him that if he didn't leave me and go back to her, she'd tell my husband."

"How did Torres react to that?"

"He laughed. Said that if she told José about me, he'd tell Hugo about her."

"But she told your husband anyway."

"She did. I denied it, said that Patricia was only saying that because she'd slept with Omar herself. He didn't believe it. He beat me and asked me again. I denied it again, and he beat me again and he said he was going to go on beating me until I confessed. And I was in pain, and I wanted to hurt him back, so I told him. And do you know what he did then?"

Silva shook his head. "No, Senhora, what did he do?"

"He started to laugh."

"Laugh?"

"And while he was laughing, he asked me again about Patricia, asked if it was true Omar had been sleeping with her before me."

"And you confirmed it?"

"I did, and he said that was good to know because he could use it to get into her pants."

"Blackmail her into having sex with him?"

"Yes. And he did."

Her face contorted with a revulsion too strong to have been caused by the illicit sex alone. There was more, but she was reluctant to talk about it. She avoided his eyes.

Silva gave her a gentle prod: "And then?"

She still refused to look him in the face, but it came out in a rush. "He came home, dropped his pants, and forced my nose into his crotch. He made me smell her on him. And then he put himself in me without washing off."

Now, she *did* look at him, looked straight into his eyes, the revulsion replaced by anger. "I was his wife, Chief Inspector, his *wife*, but he made me feel like a whore. And that's what he kept telling me I was. 'Whore! Whore!' Saying it over and over again while he . . . while he was . . . fucking me."

The obscenity seemed out of place coming from her mouth.

Silva rubbed his chin. "After which he went out and vindicated his honor by killing Torres?"

She nodded. "He locked me up first and took away my telephone, so I couldn't call and warn him."

"And Amati? Where did he come into it?"

"Amati? Was that the name of that poor Indian?"

"Yes, Senhora, that was his name."

"José bragged to me about that."

"Please explain."

"He had a machete waiting in his jeep. They were all playing cards at the Grand, and he was waiting for Omar to get drunk enough so he could follow him outside and kill him, when one of the other men at the table started speculating that the Indian might be sleeping in the hotel."

"And that gave him the idea?"

"Yes."

"Simply because the man was close by, and because people in this town would be all-too-willing to believe that an Indian was guilty?"

"Yes."

"Jade told us she and Osvaldo brought Amati up to his room by way of a back stairway. They were keeping his presence in the hotel a secret. How did your husband know where to find him? Do you know?"

She took a deep breath and leaned back in her chair. "Oh, yes," she said. "I know. I know everything. He was so proud of himself, thought he'd been so clever, couldn't wait to tell me how brilliant he'd been."

"Please tell us."

Off in the distance, one of the cows starting lowing. It was a mournful sound, one that Sonia must have heard many times before. She paid it no mind.

"While they were talking about the possibility of the Indian staying there," she said, "someone suggested they ask Osvaldo about it. And someone else said he'd never tell. And then Omar suggested that a chambermaid by the name of Rita would know, and he turned out to be right. She'd been one of Omar's conquests, but she'd been one of my husband's as well, and she was always hoping to get him back. That night, she was on duty cleaning the toilets. My husband got up from the table to use one and ran into her. She told him straightaway. Ironic, isn't it? That Omar himself should be the one to suggest the scapegoat?"

"Yes, Senhora, it is. What did your husband do next?"

"He did what he'd been planning to do all along. He followed Omar outside and killed him. Then he took Omar's key to the back stairwell out of his pocket—"

"He knew about the key?"

"Everybody did. Omar used to brag about it. He didn't tell people *who* he was . . . entertaining, but he liked to let people know what a success he was with women. So José took the key, went up the back stairway to the Indian's room, and knocked him senseless. He carried him downstairs, put him next to Omar's body, wiped off the knife, pressed it into the Indian's hand, and forced cachaça down his throat."

"And then?"

"He left."

"Did he tell you anything about blood?"

"Oh, yes, I forgot. He'd done some shopping earlier in the day. He'd bought a big bag of meat—kilos of it. We stock up once a month, and he brings it home from the butcher in big plastic sacks. That was the day. He didn't think the Indian looked bloody enough, so he poured blood all over him. He was proud of that. Thought it was the perfect finishing touch."

"You don't slaughter your own cattle?"

"They're milk cows. The meat we get from the butcher is better. I think *he* gets it from Lisboa." She changed tack: "Do you know what makes me saddest about this?"

"No, Senhora. What's that?"

"It wasn't Omar who suffered the most, and it wasn't my husband, and it won't even be me. The true victims are my little girls. Last night, I thought about killing myself. And I would have, if I could have kept it from them. But it would have all come out in the end, the whole sordid story, and then they would have hated me all the more. I don't much care about what the law does to me, but if I'd thought more about the consequences for them, for Lucinda and Laura . . ."

"You wouldn't have done it?"

"No, Chief Inspector, I wouldn't have done it." She reached out and put a hand on Silva's arm, a touch as light as a feather. She looked into his eyes, anxious for him to understand. "I was crazy mad with hate. I started thinking rationally again when I saw he was dead. But by then, of course, it was too late. I'm not looking for pity, Chief Inspector, and this is by no means an excuse, because I don't think there can be any excuse for murder, but that man made me suffer. Oh, how he made me suffer! I'd just turned eighteen when I met him. It was in Porto Alegre, where it gets cold in the winter, and where we sometimes have snow up in the mountains. God, I miss that cold weather! José was there to buy cattle, and he had dealings with the lawyer who'd probated my parent's estate, what little of it there was. They'd both been killed in a car crash the month he arrived. I never had brothers or sisters. My best friend, just about my only friend, had just gotten married, and I didn't like her husband. Rightly, it turned out. He cheated on her within a year. They're divorced now. I'm getting off the track, aren't I?"

"Just tell it your way, Senhora."

"Cristina, that was my friend's name, Cristina Melo. She didn't like José any more than I liked the man she married. She told me so, and that led to a split. So there I was, eighteen years old, an orphan, just divested of my closest friend and feeling sorry for myself. José proposed, and I accepted. He was fifteen years my senior. I'd known him for less than a week."

"How old are you now, Senhora?"

"Twenty-four. I look older, don't I?"

"I wouldn't say that, Senhora."

"You would if you were being honest. Why am I telling you all of this?"

"Because I asked you to. Please go on."

"We got here, and he changed—just like *that*." She snapped her fingers. "He didn't want a wife, or a companion, or even a friend. He wanted someone to keep house for him. He treated his servants badly, you see. They kept leaving him. He wanted a drudge he could train to do things his way. He beat me. He beat me all the time."

"You could have left him."

"You think so? I was eighteen years old, Chief Inspector. I was naïve, and innocent, and during the first few months of our marriage, I blamed myself, not him. I kept trying to change, kept trying to please him. It didn't work, but by the time I'd come to the conclusion that the fault wasn't on my side, I was pregnant."

"Even then, you could have left him."

"I intended to, and I told him so. He said that if I did, he'd hire lawyers and get custody of Laura. I'd never see my own baby, ever again! He was rich. I was poor. He could have done it."

"Yes, Senhora, you're right. He could have done it. Money buys justice in this part of the world."

"Yes, Chief Inspector, it does. And I couldn't bear the thought of leaving my child alone with him."

"I see."

"And then I got pregnant again, and when Lucinda was born, things got worse. He didn't want another girl. He'd never wanted the one he already had. Girls for him, were lesser creatures, just like me. Both of our girls are afraid of him. Or were."

"So they're glad he's gone?"

"They are. But how would you feel if you knew your mother murdered your father? No matter what kind of monster he was?"

"Yes, I see your point." Silva thought for a moment, slapped his knee to signify he'd made a decision, and stood up. "Good."

"Will you give me time to pack a few things? There are some pills I take—"

"You have no need to pack anything, Senhora. You're not going anywhere."

She opened her mouth in surprise. "What?"

"Justice wouldn't be served by taking you away from your daughters. You're no danger to society. The man you married deserved everything he got. This conversation never took place. Do you understand? It never took place. And you mustn't tell anyone what you've told us, ever. Goodbye, Senhora Frade, I wish you joy in your new life."

"And I, also, Senhora," Arnaldo said. "As far as I'm concerned, you did this world a service."

It left her speechless. She recovered her voice when they were halfway down the steps. "Wait," she said. "We're not done."

Both men turned around.

"Please, come back and sit down. There's more to tell— and some papers you have to see."

Silva preceded Arnaldo up the steps.

Sonia went into the house, then returned with an envelope.

Chapter Fifty

"What I'm about to tell you now is in the strictest confidence," Silva said.

They were, once again, crowded into his room at the Grand. Hector and Gilda were seated side by side on the bed. Arnaldo occupied the room's only chair. Gonçalves sat in another, brought from his room down the hall. The Chief Inspector had elected to remain on his feet. He was addressing the entire crew, but when he said the words *strictest confidence* he locked eyes with Gonçalves.

"Which means you don't shoot your mouth off to Maura," Arnaldo said, driving the point home.

Gonçalves blushed. "Understood," he said.

Silva waited a beat, as if to emphasize what his partner had said. Then he told them about Sonia's confession—and what he intended to do about it.

"Nothing?" Gilda said when he was done. "You're not going to do *anything at all?*"

"Correct."

"So how can you ever prove to the people in this town that Amati was innocent?"

"We can't. For them, he's always going to be a murdering savage and lynching him was the right thing to do."

"That's *so* wrong," Gilda said.

Silva nodded. "But it would be an even greater travesty of justice to deprive those little girls of their mother."

The eyes of the others moved back and forth between Gilda and Silva, following the exchange like it was a tennis match. And like a tennis match, the spectators had their favorite. Gilda was getting no support, not even from her fiancé, but she persisted:

"You talk about injustice, but what about Raoni? Don't you think *he's* entitled to justice? Do you intend to let him go through life believing his father was a murderer?"

"I'll tell him I'm convinced his father was innocent."

"But never tell him who was guilty?"

"Perhaps, someday. Look, Gilda, it's not a perfect solution, far from it, but the alternative is worse."

The others looked at her while she gave it some thought. Finally, she nodded.

"You agree?" Silva insisted.

"I don't like it," she said, "but I agree."

"Good," Silva said. "Now, let's talk about this." He showed them the envelope Sonia Frade had given him.

"What's in it?" Hector said.

"Love letters. Omar Torres gave them to Sonia Frade, Sonia gave them to us, and I intend to use them to entrap the people who murdered the Awana."

"You know?" Gilda said. "You know who did it?"

"We do," Silva said.

"But we still have to prove it," Arnaldo said. "How about you guys back up and tell us the story from the beginning?" Hector said.

Somewhere, just outside, two dogs started barking. The Chief Inspector walked to the window and shut it. The dogs kept on barking, but it was no longer so loud that he couldn't be heard.

"It all begins with Omar Torres," he said.

"So he really did do it," Gilda said, "killed the entire tribe, just like everyone has been telling us?"

"No, Gilda, he did not."

"Then?"

"Omar, as we've learned by now, was a philanderer. He had relationships with many of the women in this town. One of them was Patricia Toledo."

"The mayor's wife?" Gilda asked.

"The mayor's wife," Silva confirmed. "For him, Patricia was no more than a milepost on the road, but she saw their relationship as something far more serious. She was crazy about him."

"Crazy enough to write him the letters in that envelope?" Hector asked.

"Yes."

"Can I have a look?"

Silva handed them over. "Those are photocopies," he said. "The originals are in the hotel's safe. They haven't, as yet, been fingerprinted—but we're going to tell our subjects that they have been."

Hector started shuffling through the papers and gave a whistle of surprise. "Hot stuff," he said. Gilda leaned in to read over his shoulder.

Silva kept on talking: "When Torres turned his back on her, Patricia was furious, but she managed to convince herself he did it out of fear of her husband, and also because, as long as Hugo was around, there couldn't be any future to their relationship."

Gonçalves scratched his head. "So?"

"So she hatched a plot to get rid of him."

"Get rid of her husband?"

Silva nodded. "Yes. Her husband."

"Wait a minute," Gilda said, looking up from her reading. "First you're talking about the genocide of the Awana, and then you're talking about some plan that Patricia Toledo had to get rid of her husband. What's the connection?"

"They're one in the same."

"Whoa!" Gonçalves said.

"Juicy story, eh?" Arnaldo said. "But you . . ." He pointed at Gonçalves.

"Yeah, yeah, I know. I'm to keep my mouth shut about it. Go on, Chief Inspector. Like Hector said, this is hot stuff."

"Hugo Toledo," Silva went on, "had long coveted the Indians' land—and owned the only *fazenda* with easy access to it."

"By way of the old Azevedo place," Arnaldo clarified.

"Moreover," Silva said, "he had the political power to get the reservation declassified—as long as he could get rid of the Indians. So, first, he tried getting the entire tribe transported to the big reservation in the Xingu."

"But that didn't work," Arnaldo said. "He couldn't drum up enough support in Brasilia."

Gilda broke their back-and-forth rhythm with a question: "So the bastard made up his mind to kill them?" She snapped her fingers. "Just like that?"

"No," Silva said, "not just like that. It hadn't occurred to him to take such a drastic step. It had gotten to the point where he'd decided to accept the status quo and give up on the project."

"What made him change his mind?" Hector asked.

"Not what," Silva said. "Who. *Patricia* got him to change his mind. She fed him the idea of the genocide, overrode his objections, convinced him he should do it and even told him how to go about it. She was a close friend of Maria Bonetti, a biologist. One time, when they were having a chat, Maria mentioned a curious little creature, and showed her a picture of one in a biology book."

"The *phyllobates terribilis*?" Gilda said.

"Exactly," Silva said, "each one containing enough poison

to kill ten adults. Hugo's motive for the murders was greed, pure and simple. Patricia's was entirely different."

"Wait," Gilda said. "You're telling me that she arranged to kill forty human beings just so she could get her hooks into a man?"

"That's exactly what I'm telling you," Silva said. "Her scheme was to convince Hugo to kill the Indians, which he did, and then to turn on him, claim she had nothing to do with it, denounce him to the FUNAI and to Barbosa in Belem. He'd be arrested and taken out of the picture. Then, while he was sitting in prison for the next forty years or so, she'd have all the land and could go off into a golden future with Torres. Putting their holdings together would have created the biggest *fazenda* in the whole state. It would be a snap to get him elected as mayor. She could go on being the First Lady."

"And she told Torres that?" Hector said.

"She did," Arnaldo said, "but she didn't consult him ahead of time. She just did it. And then, after the genocide had taken place, she called him up, 'crowing' was the way Torres described it."

"Described it to Sonia, that is?" Hector asked.

"Uh-huh," Arnaldo said. "To Sonia."

"According to his account," Silva said, "and there's no reason to disbelieve it, he told Patricia he had enough land, told her he didn't want to be mayor, told her that he had no intention of coming back to her."

"Must have been a big disappointment to the dear lady," Gilda said sarcastically.

"With an even bigger disappointment to follow," Silva said.

"Which was?" Gonçalves asked.

"He told her he was sick of her."

"Ouch!"

"Ouch is right," Arnaldo said. "Patricia went ballistic. Her reaction was so strong it scared the hell out of him."

"She threatened him?"

"She did. And Sonia too."

"Sonia?" Hector wanted to know. "How did she know about Sonia?"

"She knew Torres's habits. When he broke up with her, she expected that another woman was involved, and she wanted to know who it was. Her husband spent a lot of time drinking at the Grand, so she started accompanying him into town and keeping an eye on the alley in the back of the building. One night she saw Torres going upstairs with Sonia. Later, when she and her ex-boyfriend had their conversation, she told him she was willing to forgive him for what she called his *infidelity*, but only if he came back to her. Otherwise, she said, and this is a direct quote, *he and that bitch had better watch their asses.*"

"And what you're telling us now," Hector asked, "is all based on what Torres told Sonia and what she told you?"

Silva nodded. "All of it. The whole story. And I should add here that both Arnaldo and I have bought into it. If someone was lying, it wasn't her. And I don't think it was Torres either."

"I think we all trust your judgment, Chief Inspector," Gilda said. "Yours, too, Arnaldo. What happened next?"

"What happened next," Silva said, "was Patricia's big mistake. The one that's going to help us to convict her. She was so hungry for vengeance that she went straight to Sonia's husband and told him what his wife was up to."

"In the hope that he'd revenge himself on both Torres and Sonia?"

"Just so. But what she hadn't anticipated was that Torres

had already briefed Sonia—and suggested something they might do to defend themselves."

"Which was?"

"Use Patricia's letters to blackmail her into keeping her mouth shut," Silva said.

"But," Arnaldo said, "by the time they had their plan in place, it was too late. Frade acted first. He killed Torres, set Amati up for it, forced Patricia to have sex with him and went home and told Sonia all about it."

"Run that by me one more time," Hector said.

Silva did. Slowly, with all the details that Sonia had given them.

Hector ran a hand through his hair. "Why didn't Sonia tell us any of this before? We could have solved her problem for her, arrested her husband for the murder, taken him out of her life."

Silva shook his head. "She didn't want us to take him out of her life. She wanted to do it herself. José Frade killed the only thing in life that mattered to her except her children. She decided to pay him back in kind. And she did. Anything else, she thought, would be too good for him."

"Okay," Hector said, "I've got it now. But, if we're to use those letters to nail those people, there's one crucial question you've left unanswered."

Silva anticipated it. "You want to know if there's an admission of the genocide in one or more of Patricia's letters? Answer: no. There isn't. Not a word. And no threats either."

"Meaning that, as far as the genocide is concerned, all we've got, at the moment, is the testimony of a dead man, about a telephone conversation that Patricia will deny ever took place."

Silva shook his head. "We've got more," he said. "We've got the pride of a jealous husband, and a wife who knows what he'd be capable of if he were free to get at her."

"Jealousy and fear. You think that's going to be enough?"

"That," Silva said, "and a little gentle massaging of the truth. Enough talk. Gilda, please go to the Grand and tell Osvaldo we'll need a room on the second floor with a good, strong door. Hector, you and Babyface"—Gonçalves winced, but didn't object when Silva used his hated nickname—"go to the Toledo's home, arrest Patricia, bring her to the hotel and lock her in that room."

"And meanwhile?" Hector said.

"Arnaldo and I will arrest Hugo at his office. We'll be bringing him to the *delegacia*."

"So we're going to keep them apart?"

"Yes, and if either team happens to encounter them together, separate them immediately. I intend to begin with her husband before you get back, but don't worry, you won't be missing anything. He's not going to crack, not right away. *She's* the one who's going to crack. We'll meet you at the hotel just as soon as we've completed our first session with his honor, the mayor."

Hugo Toledo's initial reaction, when they told him about his wife's affair with Torres, was disbelief. "Patricia? With Torres? Impossible! She couldn't stand him."

"She lied," Silva said. "Have a look at these."

He offered the stack of photocopies.

Toldedo snatched them out of his hand. "It looks like her handwriting," he admitted, after reading the first three, "but I still don't believe it. These are forgeries."

"And if I were to tell you that her fingerprints are on the originals?"

"Is that true?"

"Yes, Senhor Toledo, it is."

The mayor tossed the stack on the table. "That bitch!" he

said, his eyes narrowing. And then added, suspiciously, "Why are you telling me this?"

"I'm hoping you'll get angry enough to tell us your side of the story."

"My side of the story? There is no *my* side to the story. Those are letters from my wife to Torres. What's that got to do with me?"

"Your wife was planning to get rid of you so she could take over your *fazenda* and marry Torres."

"Torres wasn't the marrying kind. And, as far as getting rid of me, how do you think she was going to do that? Have me killed? Get serious!"

"I *am* being serious Senhor Toledo. Deadly serious. She wasn't going to have you killed. She was simply going to denounce you for mass murder."

"Mass murder?"

"Of thirty-nine people. I'm talking about the poisoning of the Awana tribe."

Toledo slammed a fist on the table. "She's full of shit."

"We think not. We think she's telling the truth."

"The hell she is!" He stood up. "Get her in here. I want to talk to her."

"Sit down, Senhor Toledo. She's not here. She's at the hotel. She asked us to keep her there."

The mayor sat down again. "Why? Why the hotel?"

"Isn't it obvious? Because she doesn't want to be anywhere near you. Now that she's confessed, she's afraid of what you might do to her."

"She should be, lying about me like that. It's her word against mine. That's all you've got? It's not enough! I know my rights. I demand you let me go."

"We're entitled to hold you, without charge, for twenty-four hours."

330 Leighton Gage

"And that's what you intend to do?"

"It is."

"I don't believe a word of what you're telling me. About the Torres part, okay, I have to accept that. But, as far as the Indians are concerned, hell, why would she start spreading lies?"

"Lies, are they?"

"You're damned right they are. Torres is dead. Torres isn't going to fuck my wife, or anybody else, ever again. So why would Patricia start shooting her mouth off now? It doesn't make sense."

"My guess is that she wants to punish you for killing him."

Toledo's face turned red with pure rage. "Punish me for . . . That's absolute crap! I didn't kill Omar Torres."

"Didn't you?"

"No, damn it, I didn't. I might have done, if I'd known he was fucking my wife. But I didn't know, so I had no reason to do him in."

"And we're supposed to accept that?" Silva had a vague hope that he might be able to drive him over the edge, but he didn't really expect it—and it didn't happen.

Toledo took a deep breath, then another. And then he said, "My lawyer's Renato Kassab. I'm not going to say another word until he gets here."

"As you wish. Arnaldo?"

"Mario?"

"Call Borges's deputy in here. Senhor Toledo is to be allowed one telephone call. Then he's to be shown to a cell."

Two hours later, in a room at the Grand, Patricia Toledo was staring at the photocopies in disbelief. "He told me he'd destroyed them," she said.

"So you don't deny you wrote them?" Silva said.

She put the letters down on the table in front of her. "Would you believe me if I did? My fingerprints must be all over them."

"Quite," Silva said.

"So what? So what if I did write them? Since when is it against the law to be in love with someone?"

"We're not here to talk about love, Senhora Toledo. We're here to talk about murder."

"You think Hugo killed Omar?"

"Do you?"

"He would have—if he'd known, but he didn't."

"Correct," Silva said. "He didn't know. Not until we told him—and showed him your letters."

She put her hand on the stack. "You showed him these?"

Silva nodded. "That's what I just told you."

"How . . . how did he react?"

"He was very angry—and anxious to talk to you."

She sat up straight in her chair and stared him down. "Your indiscretion is despicable. You had no reason to destroy my relationship with my husband. And for what? You've already admitted he knew nothing about the affair, so there would be no reason for him to have killed Omar Torres. He's innocent, and so am I."

"No, Senhora, you're not innocent. Neither is your husband. And it's not what happened to Omar Torres that concerns us at the moment. It's other murders."

"What other murders?"

"The genocide of the Awana tribe."

"Oh."

"That's all you have to say? Oh?"

"What else do you expect me to say? I know nothing about it."

"Don't you?"

"No."

"What if I were to tell you, Senhora, that Omar Torres made a recording of your conversation?"

"What conversation?"

"The one in which you proposed denouncing your husband."

The color drained from her face.

"And in which he told you he wouldn't come back, even if you got rid of Hugo."

"He didn't record that conversation. He wouldn't!"

"He was a cautious man. He kept your letters. Why should you think he wouldn't record your voice?"

"That bastard! I'm not going to say another word! I want my lawyer."

Hector looked at Silva. This seemed to be ending the same way that the interview with her husband had ended.

But Silva was prepared for it—and had other ideas.

"You'd be better advised," he said, "to stick to your original plan."

"What original plan?"

"The plan you had to denounce your husband."

"Why should I? What would be the point?"

"The *point*, Senhora Toledo, would be to obtain a lighter sentence. If you don't take advantage of this opportunity, and start talking to us right now, you and your husband will go down together. And, if you do, I estimate you'll both get between thirty-five and forty years." Silva fell silent, let her mull it over. She was quiet for some time. And then she started to talk.

"It was Hugo's idea," she said. "All of it. I had no inkling of this until he'd gone and done it. And once those poor Indians were dead, the reason I didn't tell anyone is because he threatened me."

"Your husband threatened you?"

"Yes. He swore he'd kill me. I feared for my life."

It was like Maria Bonetti all over again: the same shifting of blame, the same defense, exactly the reaction Silva had been hoping for. If she'd been able to monitor his heart, she would have heard it kick up a few beats, but not a muscle on his face moved.

"Do you have anything to back up your allegation?" he said. "Anything in the way of evidence?"

"There's a trader he bought the frogs from. Across the border in Peru. They're more common there. The Indians trap them. I can give you his name, tell you where to find him."

"Good. Anything else?"

"I know where Hugo put the syringe. It will contain residue from the poison, have his fingerprints are all over it. And I'll tell you where he got the parachute. You think that's enough?"

"Yes, Senhora, I think that's enough."

By nine that evening, the cops had everything wrapped up.

While the rest of their party celebrated in the bar of the Grand, Maura and Gonçalves seized an opportunity to spend a final evening together. They commandeered Jade's jeep, drove to the old Azevedo place, and began a companionable stroll toward the river.

"So then," Gonçalves was saying, "we went back to Hugo and confronted him with everything."

"And you taped that, too?" Maura said.

"We did."

"Can I get a peek?"

"You can. The Chief Inspector authorized it."

"How come he's my new best friend?"

"He feels bad about not having been able to protect you better."

"That's ridiculous. It wasn't his fault."

"Maybe not. But that's the way he is."

"So what's going to happen to the land? Who's going to get their hooks into it?"

"Hopefully no one. The Chief Inspector says it's Raoni's birthright. He's going to do everything he can to convince the powers-that-be, in Brasilia, to keep it on the list of reservations."

"All those thousands of hectares held in keeping for a single child? You think they'll buy that?"

"This is a huge country. There's a lot of land. The Chief Inspector is owed a lot of favors by a lot of people."

"And the boy? You think he'll ever want to live there again?"

"After a few years in Brasilia? Probably not. But it's where his people are buried. Gravesites are sacred to the Awana. And the alternative to maintaining the reservation is to see those gravesites plowed under. The Chief Inspector doesn't think that would be right."

"I agree with him. I hope he can pull it off. And dropping the meat by parachute? Whose idea was that?"

"Patricia's. They went up together, but she was the one who actually tossed the parachute out of the plane."

"What a bitch that woman is!"

"I couldn't agree more."

"It's probably . . . no, it's *definitely* the most selfish thing I've ever heard of, causing the death of all of those people just to get your hooks into a man."

They kept strolling, quiet for a while, then she said, "So nobody else had anything to do with the genocide? For a while, it was beginning to look like half the town was in on it, but in the end, it was just those two?"

"Just those two. Lisboa and that *pistoleiro* of his are completely in the clear. Cunha is into wood, and that's all he cares about. He was getting some of that wood out of the reservation, taking it through Toledo's land, and Toledo knew it, but he was willing to keep his mouth shut for a cut of the action. Cunha and that IBAMA guy are sure to go down for illegal logging."

"And this whole story of Torres threatening to root out the Indians?"

"All lies. All made up."

"By the Toledos?"

"By Patricia. She was the brains of the operation, but it was Hugo who called a meeting of the Big Five, invited the doctor and the priest, and got all of them to spread the story around. *For the general good*, he said."

"General good," Maura snorted. "Forty Awana dead and the last survivor of the tribe an orphan. And that story about Amati threatening to kill Torres? That was fabrication as well?"

"Mm-hm. Suggested by Hugo, who got the padre to lie about it."

"Can I print that?"

"The Chief Inspector wishes you would. He's hoping the Church hierarchy will take action against Castori."

"So it was José Frade who killed Torres?"

"Uh-huh. And, if he hadn't, I don't know if we'd ever have gotten to the bottom of this. It was that murder, in a way, that was crucial to helping us to solve the case."

"How so?"

"I can't tell you that."

"Who killed Frade?"

"I can't tell you that either."

"Why not?"

"I just can't."

"Here we go. It's the Chief Inspector all over again, isn't it? Forcing you to keep secrets?"

He took her arm, brought her to a stop and faced her. "It is and it isn't. But, in this case, I agree with him one hundred percent." She brushed his hand away, but gently, as if reluctant to do it. "Not ninety-nine, Maura. One hundred. There's a damned good reason for me not telling you. You have to believe that."

"Oh, I do, and it makes me all the more curious. But you know what, Haraldo, I'm going to get it out of you eventually."

"Never!"

"Never? Not even if we were to get married?"

He gaped. "I can't believe you just said that."

She smiled. "I can't either."

He extended his hand, she took it, and they crossed the bridge together.

Author's Notes

BRAZIL'S INDIGENOUS TRIBES HAVE been victims of genocide for over five hundred years.

These days, the federal government is attempting to put a stop to it, but it isn't easy. Success is hampered by deep jungle, vast distances, the attitudes of the people who prey on the tribes—settlers, illegal loggers and gold miners—and even the difficulty of identifying which of the many accounts of abuse are true and therefore require an investment of the very limited resources available to investigate them.

It is believed, for example, that an eight-year-old Awá girl was tied to a tree and burned alive in January of 2012 in a remote area of Maranhão State. The perpetrators were said to be illegal loggers, trying to frighten the tribe off land where they intended to cut timber.

The Indigenous Missionary Council, a Catholic group, believes the death occurred. They claim the loggers laughed while they did it and that a video of the child's charred remains exists.

The Brazilian government, however, will neither confirm nor deny the report—but they concede that illegal loggers are, indeed, active in the area.

A better-documented case is the genocide of the Akuntsu, in Rondônia, reduced at this writing to a total of just five individuals, the last known survivors of their people.

For more information on threats to indigenous peoples

throughout the world—and what you might be able to do to help them—please visit this web site: survivalinternational. org/tribes

In addition to the clearing of land for agriculture and cattle ranching, major threats to the Indians include mineral extraction and illegal logging.

Here's an example of what can happen: as recounted in this book, a six gram nugget found at Serra Pelada, in the State of Pará, kicked off the last great gold rush in history. In a few short years, between 1980 and 1986, an estimated 360 tons of gold were wrested from the ground, but the cost in human lives, and to the environment, was immense.

A number of Sebastião Salgado's brilliant black and white photographs of the great open pit during its heyday are to be found on the Internet. If you've never seen one, I suggest you do a search. I think you'll be amazed. It's like looking into Hell.

Small scale gold-mining in Brazil is often carried out with the use of mercury. Part of the process involves reducing it to a gas that can travel thousands of miles in the atmosphere. It often settles in river beds in North America and Europe, and, from there, moves up the food chain to fish—and thence to humans.

Illegal logging, too, can have a direct and deleterious effect on North Americans and Europeans.

The trees in that rainforest produce more than twenty percent of the world's oxygen.

And the world can't afford to lose it.

Santana do Parnaiba, SP
Brazil
February, 2013